## A Rare and Powerful Magic

THE MAKING of these glass beads is a dying art. But without their magical protection, the hunter can have no power over his prey and worse still, the monstrous Lame Ones are free to ravage human villages.

Now the Lame Ones are rising, and the ancient Vigen of Darst must pass on his powers of glassmaking to a young apprentice. Sixteen-year-old Kyala of Darst has the rare glassmakers' talent, but how can a female practice the Vigen's art? Even if she is strong and quick-witted, with an eye for color and a steady hand—can the power of Ormek the creator still speak through her?

The Old Masters of Glass are dead. The pigments are scarce. The days of the legends are past. But perhaps it is a time for new legends...

# MASTERS OF GLASS

## M. Coleman Easton

**POPULAR LIBRARY**

An Imprint of Warner Books, Inc.

A Warner Communications Company

*Cover art by Victoria Poyser*

Popular Library books are published by
Warner Books, Inc.
666 Fifth Avenue
New York, N.Y. 10103

 A Warner Communications Company

Printed in the United States of America

First Printing: July, 1985
10   9   8   7   6   5   4   3   2   1

# The Vigen of the Mountains

There was a village of the mountains so remote that few outsiders had ever heard of it. And in this village there lived, as would be needed in such an isolated place, a *Vigen:* a skillful shaper of glass. More essential to the villagers than any crafter of knives or fletcher of arrows was the Vigen, because his talismans protected people against creatures that feared no weapons.

This glassmaker, Kolpern by name, was devoted to his craft, and so fretted constantly over the difficulties of obtaining his materials. Sand and chalk and ash he possessed in abundance, from these he cast clear glass in his kiln. He produced vials and bottles and even small panes of translucent window glass, all of which delighted the villagers. But this was not the essence of his art. A Vigen must have mineral pigments to color his glass, and such pigments had always been scarce. Kolpern had busied himself for many summers, traveling to the highest passes, following the receding snows, so that he could dig the old workings where the minerals were found. Each year he would return with fewer and fewer vials of the precious earths; his sources were becoming exhausted, and new ones were increasingly difficult to find.

The Vigen would labor all winter, firing his kiln to turn raw powders into the colored glass that formed the basis of his craft. Each batch he cast possessed its own unique hue, and each he would carefully grind for later use. By mixing these he created talismans, fusing the powders in the kiln to get a precisely chosen effect.

To aid the hunters he shaped glossy orbs of browns and oranges and golds, varying the shading in each piece to match the eyes of different creatures. With such a bead, if the match was good, one could influence the will of an animal, drawing prey closer to the spear or driving away an attacking beast. Most valued of the Vigen's beads were those tinted with dark *astablak*, for only these talismans controlled the fearsome Lame Ones. Everyone in the village wanted such protection.

Now Kolpern might have lived out his years quietly. But Dyelo, the most clever of the Lame Ones, was active in the land at that time. While the creature's brothers were content to spring on lone travelers or to smash in doors of isolated cottages, Dyelo used his wits to obtain his food. This two-footed beast had learned a trick that no other Lame One ever mastered: he could wear clothing and speak like a man. Despite his repulsive appearance, he had succeeded in mingling with guests at a wedding feast, quietly leading off the merrymakers until the last few ran screaming into the night. Once he had even set himself up as an innkeeper, devouring the entrails of his guests and then hurling their remains into the snow behind his inn.

It was late one evening when Kolpern still labored at his kiln. His apprentice had long since gone to bed, but the Vigen was still shaking out fragments of his colored glasses onto the little squares of his mixing board. He had much to finish, for spring would arrive soon and he would abandon his workshop to trek once more toward his diggings in the mountains. In the midst of his concentration, Kolpern was startled to hear the knocker clattering against his oaken door.

"I hunter wandering," said a coarse, unfamiliar voice outside. "I trade meat for beads."

Kolpern stiffened at once. The vial fell from his hand and rolled to the edge of the mixing board. The voice carried a strange quality, a deep resonance that touched him in a way he could not explain.

"Trade meat for beads," the visitor repeated. His request was not unusual; Kolpern often dealt with hunters. As for his peculiar manner of speech, he might have been a traveler from the eastern lands. Though Kolpern was suspicious, he felt a compulsion to admit the stranger at once. "What sorts of meat do you carry, hunter?" he demanded, turning his attention toward the planks of the door.

The voice hesitated. "Bear . . . deer . . . weasel."

"Ha," said Kolpern. "You are doing well enough without my beads."

"But I raccoon need. Wife sick and raccoon tail meat the cure."

"Raccoon tail!"

"Wife sick . . . Need bead for raccoon so that I catch one."

The Vigen had some knowledge of healing, but had never heard of such medicine. Surely this was a ruse; the man was not what he claimed to be. But Kolpern's thoughts became muddled as the voice spoke again.

"Door open," the hunter said in grating tones, and Kolpern found himself moving to obey. In his mind the act was justified. Could he let the man's wife suffer because of his ignorance of the ways of foreign healers? If raccoon-eye beads were needed, then Kolpern was obliged to provide them. He lifted the heavy bar and admitted the visitor to the workshop.

The Vigen's misgivings returned when the hunter stepped into the light of his lamps. The man, if he was a man, was huge. Stooping to clear the lintel, he entered, covering his face with his enormous gloved hand. Such concealment by itself was not odd. To Kolpern's chagrin, the villagers still shielded their faces from him, fearing that to show a glass-maker the color of one's eyes was to offer him the mastery of one's will. So it was not the action but the hand itself that fed the Vigen's suspicions; no man possessed a hand of such breadth as the stranger's.

Of the visitor's head, he could see nothing but the top of his hood and the wiry black hairs at the bottom of his beard. The hunter, contrary to his offer, carried no meat. He walked awkwardly, as if one leg was wounded. His boots hit the floor of the workshop with a strange dead sound as if they were partly hollow.

"Need beads . . . many beads," said the hunter as he pushed closer to Kolpern's workbench. Through splayed fingers he inspected the unstopped vials, then turned his attention to the cabinets above the bench. "You making," he said. "Blue beads. Gray. Green. All shades."

"You said . . . you said you wanted to hunt raccoon." Now the Vigen's fingers were shaking, for the stranger was certainly no man. With the door closed, the kiln quickly heated the air that had blown in during the stranger's entrance. Kolpern stood bare chested, and yet the visitor did not even throw back his fur-covered hood.

"Hunter, make yourself comfortable," the Vigen said uneasily. "You must know that beads, like all things, require time."

"I stand here. Watching." The odor of the stranger was not that of the skins he wore. It was foul, with a rank undertone like none Kolpern had ever breathed.

"Then tell me what you need," said the Vigen in a hoarse voice, aware now that he would not likely survive this night. From where could he summon help? The apprentice in the adjoining room had always been a heavy sleeper. Kolpern's wife was in the house some distance up the path; she would not know what was happening here. No, he could not expect that someone would sound an alarm.

"Making all colors. All blue. All gray."

The voice carried with it a compulsion to obey. But for a moment the Vigen broke free and his tone became defiant. "It is not enough to take us one at a time. With my beads, you'll take us all and force us to do your will. I know you, *Dyelo!*" The stranger was startled for an instant by the sound of his name. Quickly Kolpern pulled open a drawer on the bench and snatched out a handful of talismans. The stranger, forgetting his need for concealment, swiped at Kolpern's hand with his huge glove and thus allowed him a momentary glimpse of his face. Half the beads fell to the floor, and when Kolpern saw the visitor's eyes he dropped the others in despair. The stranger was indeed a Lame One; in the beast's eyes, fire flickered over the deepest blackness he had ever seen. But the drawer, as he now recalled, held no astablak talismans. Kolpern, in his eagerness to please the villagers, had traded the shop's last astablak talisman that morning; he had with him no defense against the creature.

"Making *now!*" shouted Dyelo, his glove raised again to his face.

Kolpern rubbed at his arm where the blow had struck. He could find no hope for himself. "I . . . I have only these pigments," he said, pointing to the bottles of colored fragments on his shelves. All the minerals he had gathered had been consumed in their preparation. "The mountains grow barren."

"Making *all*," insisted the Lame One.

On the bench lay the mixing board where the hunters' glass, the browns and golds, had been poured out. The Vigen made a brief attempt to scrape up the colorings. Impatient Dyelo, this time using his free hand, knocked the mixing board off the bench so that the precious powders scattered about the floor. "Blues," he insisted. "Grays." He removed one glove with his teeth so that Kolpern could see the enormous talons of his paw. Then the beast rested the sharp points against the huge muscles in Kolpern's arms. A single motion, the Vigen knew, would strip the flesh from his bones. But it was not the threat that kept him from refusing. The voice, the cursed voice...

"Give me room to work," Kolpern said, biting off his words. "I cannot move with your daggers in my flesh."

The creature backed off one step and the glassmaker began to take down his treasured vials. He knew what the Lame One wanted, and there was no use pretending otherwise. The colors of men's eyes—the human shades of the rainbow—were the ones the Lame One needed. With a broad selection of such beads, Dyelo would capture the wills of many men.

Kolpern retrieved his fallen mixing board and set it on the bench. He began to shake out powders into the small squares. Moving slowly, he ordered the hues from sky blue to midnight. Then he took out a long clay mold and began to fill its thumbnail-sized depressions. From one end of the board to the other the Vigen worked, taking a pinch from one square and a pinch from the next square over, mixing the colorings slightly differently in each pit of the mold so that a spectrum would result. Mold after mold he prepared in this way. When the blues were exhausted he laid out the greens, then the grays.

At one point he hesitated, his hand in midair. If these fragments were fused, and the beads taken by Dyelo, then many of his friends and kinsmen and neighbors would be lost. Whoever by chance matched a talisman would fall under Dyelo's control. Kolpern could not say which of them would be destroyed. But what of his wife, the person he most cared for of all he had known? He was certain of her eye color, and the next bead in sequence would be her perfect match.

"Making *all*," said Dyelo, leaning closer. As if of its own accord, his hand continued the interrupted motion. Kolpern could not break his pattern and omit her shade.

At last the mixing was complete. In the center of each bead, he dropped a dark speck to serve as pupil. Now all that remained was the firing. *There must be a stop to this*, he thought. *If only I can be free for a moment*. He made a show of counting the logs that lay beside the kiln. "I haven't enough wood here," he said suddenly. "The firing takes time. I'll need to get more." The last words he spoke in overly eager tones. He moved quickly toward the doorway.

"Not!" The Lame One turned to block the way. "*I* getting wood," said Dyelo. "You staying here."

The woodpile lay just outside the door. The creature was gone briefly, leaving the glassmaker a few moments in which to work with his vials. Then Dyelo reentered, walking with his eyes averted from the Vigen, and carrying an enormous load of logs across his arms. The logs fell with such a rumble and clatter that Kolpern thought surely his apprentice would waken, run out, and blow the alarm horn. But there was no stirring from behind the heavy curtain. Under his breath, Kolpern berated the slumbering youth, but he knew that if he were to cry out and waken the lad that Dyelo would kill the Vigen at once and then force the boy to complete the firing. So he kept his fears to himself and began to slide the long molds into the shelves of the kiln. He pushed fresh logs in over the coals, closed up the stones, and began to work the bellows.

The Lame One shut the door of the workshop and shuffled closer to Kolpern. "Quicker!" Dyelo said. "Needing beads before dawn."

Kolpern turned toward the creature, but all he could see was the bulky cloaked body, the gloved paw that shielded the face, and the ungloved talons that were raised in threat. "By dawn they'll be ready," he answered softly. Then he kept silent for a long while, working the bellows and stopping only to feed the fire. The Lame One became restless, striding back and forth, his strange boots thumping at the floorboards. From time to time he would peer out through the door and then Kolpern would feel a rush of cold air at his back.

"Light coming!" shouted the Lame One at last. "Having those beads."

So Kolpern left his bellows and took up a poker to knock away the door stones from the front of the kiln. Within the fire still burned. A great wave of heat spilled into the room, and perspiration poured down his chest and from under his arms. Behind him he could hear the panting of the Lame One as the creature tried in his own way to cool himself.

"Making done?" Dyelo demanded, pushing the Vigen aside, then crouching to peer into the glowing interior of the kiln. "Making done!" he declared with satisfaction.

"The beads must cool slowly," Kolpern warned as Dyelo reached toward the molds, then drew back as the hairs on his forearm began to singe.

"No time," said Dyelo. "Needing beads now."

"Then bring me snow. Buckets of snow."

The Lame One, still crouching, swung his arm at an empty bucket by the Vigen's feet. "You get," he said. "I watch here."

Kolpern, his heart racing, picked up the wooden bucket and stepped out into the frigid air. Did he dare run? He looked up at the roof of his cottage, its outline barely visible against the dawn sky. He could warn his wife, send her to hide in the forest. Perhaps he would have time to warn some of the other villagers. And then? The beads would cool. The creature would have the means to capture many men, and could use the talismans many times over. How many villages would suffer?

The Vigen shook his head. Then he dipped his bucket, packed down the freshly fallen powder, and scooped up more snow. Dyelo had allowed him outside, but had given him no freedom at all.

"Make room," said the glassmaker when he found the Lame One still crouching before the kiln. With his metal tongs he reached in for the one bead that the creature would not want cooled, the one that Kolpern had prepared while Dyelo was picking up the wood. The tongs shook in his hand, and for a moment he was not sure he could pick up the soft gobbet. He put one hand atop the other to control the trembling. Then, with a last effort of will, he plucked out the dark glass and dropped it into the snow. The water sizzled and steamed as he shook the bucket.

"Show here!" said Dyelo, and Kolpern dipped his fingers into the icy water to retrieve the talisman, which was hard on the outside but still pulpy beneath the skin. This one in particular, he knew, must cool slowly to show its proper color—cavernous darkness with an overlay of flame. Yet Kolpern saw that despite his haste the glass had taken a fiery sheen. The creature groaned when he saw the talisman and tried to knock it from Kolpern's hand, but the Vigen jumped back out of reach.

"Dyelo, you take the others from the kiln," said the Vigen. For a moment the creature did not move, and Kolpern feared that the red glimmer was too weak. "Dyelo, take out the molds," the glassmaker repeated, wondering still if his work had succeeded. The surface of the dark bead flickered as if rimmed with fire; he could see that the match to the beast's eyes was true. "Take out the molds," he said again. Then slowly, as if fighting with every sinew the compulsion of the bead, the Lame One reached his unsheathed paw toward the heat. His coarse hair began to smoke, and he bellowed with pain as he clawed at the clay molds.

"Crawl closer, Dyelo," said the Vigen, and when the creature began to shuffle on his huge knees, Kolpern picked up a log from the woodpile, swung a heavy blow, and smashed Dyelo's head into the opening of the kiln. The head held fast, resealing the opening. The Lame One cried out, but his words were muffled by the stones. Quickly the Vigen returned to the bellows, while the beast's enormous legs kicked against the floor and his free paw scraped helplessly at the outside of the kiln.

Kolpern worked the bellows as no man had ever done. He pumped until his arms screamed from pain and then he pumped some more. All he could think of was the dear face of his wife, for she alone amongst the villagers had revealed her eyes to him, trusting him not to make a bead that would steal her will. It was for her that he worked the fire to such a fury that the roar of the flames was like the roar of the storming wind.

When the beast stopped struggling at last, and his huge body fell away from the kiln, the Vigen looked inside to see that all the molds had been upset. The talismans—the grays and blues and greens—had all fused into a puddle the color of lake water. And the beast's face and paw had turned to ash and vanished amongst the coals of the fire.

Now that the danger was over, the apprentice came forth yawning from his bed and complaining about frightful dreams in the night. "I'll give you a frightful *day*," said the Vigen, "if you don't clean up this workshop at once." And so saying, Kolpern stepped over the beast's body and strode from the workshop to the house, where his wife was preparing breakfast.

When the villagers learned that Dyelo was dead, they dragged the remains of the creature to their market square and began a celebration. The Vigen joined them as they stripped the clothing from the body. The boots came off and Kolpern marveled at the huge claws of the feet—larger on the left side than on the right—the cause of the beast's awkward gait. The villagers crowded around the glassmaker with their thanks and good wishes, and for the first time since he took up his craft they did not hide their eyes from him. He was astonished and gratified by this offer of trust.

All began to dance, and Kolpern joined in the merriment. Around and around the body they whirled, the Vigen and his wife dancing as lightly as the youngsters of the village. But as the pipers and strummers filled the air with sweet tunes, Kolpern began to fret. Because of Dyelo almost his entire store of colored glass had been consumed. Many of the reds and golds, scattered to the workroom floor, had been lost. All his blues and browns and grays had been ruined in the kiln. How could he now serve the people of the village? Spring was coming, and he would go off as ever to seek new supplies of minerals. And every spring thereafter he would follow the melting snows, so that he might replenish his store of pigments.

"Dyelo is dead!" shouted someone. Others took up the cry; the music quickened and the dancers circled the body, turning and laughing. This was a moment for joy, not reflection. But Kolpern could not put aside his concerns. True, he had won his battle, and for a time the people would be safe. For the rest of his lifetime, he could hope, they would not be troubled by such creatures. But there were other Lame Ones, deep in the forest. Long after Kolpern was dead there would be Lame Ones. . . .

# Chapter 1

It was Watnojat's habit, when the afternoon shadows lay across the snow, to climb the knoll behind the houses of the town and gaze out over the Western Sea. While Ormek the Sun dropped into His evening bed, Watnojat would stare toward his own final destination. More and more often the old Vigen would think of that place. His hair was gone now, and his unruly white beard spread in all directions about his burn-scarred nose. He walked bent over, no longer able to straighten his stocky frame. Now he felt himself brother to a certain aged oak, an oak that had long awaited the wood-cutters. Watnojat had chosen his pyre tree; he and the oak would burn together. What a fine blaze it would make to speed him toward Ormek's heart.

On this day Watnojat's struggle up the path was fiercer than usual. His legs felt so heavy that he could barely lift one foot ahead of the other, and his joints ached severely despite the promises of the herb-healer. *A fine price I paid for his new cure*, Watnojat thought ruefully. The Vigen shook his head as he struggled up the slope. He had concerns just then that troubled him more than aching limbs.

His apprentice, Torged, had not returned. At dawn the young man had gone off to cut wood. He had not since been seen. Torged would not be late of his own accord. There was no resemblance between this burly and energetic youth and the lazy apprentices of the folk tales. The Vigen's assistant could split oak for hours without tiring, and afterward spend half the night pleasing a young lady of the town. Moreover, he had already mastered the secrets of the Vigen's art. Watnojat could scarcely distinguish the young man's works from his own creations, and several travelers already owed their lives to protection from Torged's beads.

The Vigen shuddered as a gust of wind blasted his face. He reached the top of the knoll and stared out to sea. *Clouds coming. Snow clouds.* The cold reached him despite his thick parka with its extended hood. Turning to the inland hills, he glimpsed the zigzag track that frequent trips had cut into the snow and followed it as far as he could in the direction of the hardwood forest. He squinted, trying to sharpen his view. Where was Torged? Still facing the hills, Watnojat eased himself down onto the stone that so often served as his seat. Below him the snow-covered fields spread eastward. Stands of pine and fir were the only nearby landmarks not obscured by the white blanket. To the north, he glimpsed in the distance the broken ice on Asep River. But nowhere in that vast landscape could he find signs of the missing apprentice.

He considered the possibilities. Torged might have had trouble with a pony. But if one animal went lame, he could easily reharness the other three to pull the sledge. Perhaps the sledge had broken a runner. If so, then Torged would have left his load and ridden a pony home. Certainly that was the sensible course. But Torged might have tried, with his simple tools, to make repairs.

Watnojat was certain that if he called for a search party they would wait until morning before starting. Only Pelask, Torged's father, might be willing to trek to the forest in darkness. But Watnojat had never been on the best of terms with the fisherman. He would not go to Pelask for aid until he was certain that Torged was lost. For now he would watch and hope. The light was fading; nonetheless he resolved to stay on. Torged would carry a lantern. Watnojat might see the flame moving along the path.

The wind shifted and caught the Vigen's face, but he scarcely felt the chill. Deep in his mind were possibilities he dared not explore. *The pigments, the accursed pigments,* he thought. Perhaps they had failed him after all.

"Uncle!" He heard Kyala's voice behind him, then felt something strike his back. She had thrown a stick at him— such disrespect! This was her way of calling him to dinner at her mother's house. Watnojat glanced up at a smiling, narrow face. "Uncle, we'll leave nothing for you," she taunted. Strands of chestnut hair, uncommon in shade amongst the fair-haired people of the region, blew about her uncovered head. "By the time you get home, everything will be eaten," she added. Then the tall girl turned and ran gaily down the slope.

For the sake of her mother, Balin, Watnojat had long tolerated Kyala's teasing. There were times, in fact, when he felt great fondness for the young woman. Despite her manner of addressing him, Watnojat was kin to neither mother nor daughter. In exchange for staples that the glassmaker received in payment for his works, Balin supplied him with meals and a bed. This was more than a business arrangement. In effect, ever since the passing of Watnojat's wife, the Vigen had been treated as a member of Balin's household.

"I am coming, little demon," he replied to the vanished Kyala. But he did not rise at once, hoping at this last moment to see a light spring up in the darkening snow. But there was no trace of the missing apprentice.

The Vigen, feeling little hunger but craving company, roused his stiff frame from the stone and began his trek to

Balin's house. Night was upon him; already he could see lamplight cast against windowpanes of the nearby cottages. Partly melted snow slumped on the peaked roofs of the blocky stone houses. In the gloom he barely discerned the carved disks, images of Ormek, that hung from the eaves of every roof.

He did not think much about the growing chill or about his aches as he descended the grade. His mind drifted to thoughts of the young Torged as he had appeared on the day his father first brought him to the Vigen's workshop: a frightened boy with his blond hair cut short and with the beard not yet showing on his face. *Is this the one I must train?* Watnojat had wondered. The stripling looked so frightened that the glassmaker expected him to bolt out the door and hide until a new apprentice was chosen. But Torged stood firm and within an hour was confidently working the bellows. So matters had progressed.

Torged's youthful face faded from Watnojat's mind as he found himself standing before the forest scene that was carved into Balin's front door. He rapped softly. "It's only the old sheep," came Kyala's voice, loud enough for the Vigen to hear clearly. This remark, which she had spoken more than once, was followed by a sharp slap of discipline. Then the door opened slowly, and Kyala's reddened face ducked away into the dimly lit interior. He closed the door behind him, then turned to see that the others of the household were already seated about the long plank table. The odor of boiled fish filled the room.

The glassmaker removed his parka and hung it on a peg. The hide shirt and breeches beneath were all the clothing he required while inside the well-sealed cottage.

"Good evening, Tem Watnojat," said Balin, as the Vigen seated himself beside Balin's red-bearded son Ilak. The woman's broad countenance was cheerful as usual, in contrast to Kyala's scowl and the indifferent expressions of the others. Balin was a stocky woman of middle years, with a tiny chin set beneath fleshy cheeks. A circular mark on her forehead, barely visible in the lamplight, attested to her service long ago at Ormek's Temple.

"Good evening, Lady-of-the-House," the Vigen replied. Behind Balin, the hearth's flames danced. Above her head hung the *sene,* the traditional glass dish suspended by three stiff cords attached to the rafters. As the sene already contained its samplings of the meal before them, Watnojat muttered his Appreciation alone, then spooned out a small helping of cream-colored fish chowder into his wooden bowl. He did not eat at once, but lost himself again in thoughts of his missing apprentice.

"Tem Watnojat, you have no appetite," said Ilak, as he reached for the large chowder pot.

Ilak's wife, Mara, slapped playfully at her young husband's arm. "Don't you see that the Vigen is preoccupied?" she said. "You would do well to have thoughts in your own head besides food and . . ." She left the sentence unfinished, but Ilak laughed into his soup and slopped some onto the table. He rose and made a grand show of lifting the bread knife and cutting a piece from the loaf. "What is there besides food?" he said, grinning. Then he applied his chunk of bread to mopping up the spill.

"Indeed, I'm troubled, as you observed, Mara," said Watnojat. He picked up his spoon and made an effort to swallow a bit of the salty broth. "Torged's missing." He waved the empty spoon at her. "Gone since dawn to the hardwood forest."

"I hate that old forest," said Kyala.

"The forest is Ormek's gift to us," Balin retorted, her smile gone. "Sometimes I think you have nothing but feathers between your ears. Would you rather freeze?"

"Patra's brothers were there yesterday and they saw Lame—"

"Enough!"

But Watnojat's heart had already turned to ice. He stared at the impudent daughter and wondered how to finish her sentence. Saw Lame Ones' *spoor* perhaps? Prints in the snow? The news, if it held any truth, had passed through two mouths he considered untrustworthy. But he could not dismiss the report.

In the past, when Darst Town was little more than a cluster of rude cottages, Lame Ones would come down from the hills and terrorize the inhabitants, killing or maiming any they could catch. Watnojat remembered hiding with his sisters and brothers under the floor while the shuffling and scratching of the beasts sounded all about the walls of the house. The children had not dared to move and lay there numb from cold until their parents pulled them out.

Old Reslunin, the previous Vigen, had finally put an end to the fear. His beads of astablak, the one pigment that colored glass to match a Lame One's eye, had saved the town and permitted it to grow. The beasts now feared the power of the talismans; they avoided towns entirely. They also kept away from humans in the forests, though they were known to attack ponies when their masters were absent. *Ponies.* Now there was a thought. "Were your friends' animals harmed?" Watnojat asked suddenly of Kyala.

A mischievous look came over the girl. "Gobbled up," she said, spreading her arms. "Eaten hooves and all." Her wrist collided with her younger brother's shoulder and her spoon dropped from her fingers and landed with a splash in his bowl.

"You sit here," said the boy angrily when he saw the mess. He stood up, pushed his sister along the bench to his place at the table, and seated himself at hers. He lifted her bowl to his mouth and continued to eat.

Watnojat, aware that Kyala was having fun at his expense, abandoned his questioning. After dinner he would trudge over to talk to Patra's brothers and perhaps from them he'd learn the truth. But he wondered if Lame Ones might have destroyed all four of Torged's ponies in his absence, and if so, how long it might take him to walk back to town.

The meal soon ended. Mara began to clear the table with

scant assistance from Kyala. The Vigen did not rise with the others.

"Tem Watnojat?"

For a moment he did not know what Mara wanted. "Oh, the bowl. Yes. Take it." Then, as she removed his spoon, a loud rapping sounded at the door.

"Vigen, are you there?" came a deep voice he knew well. Watnojat left the table and went reluctantly toward the entrance; he knew why Torged's father had come.

"Pelask." The glassmaker opened the door to see the burly fisherman standing with a lantern in one hand. Snow had begun falling. A dusting of white showed on the man's hood and on his shoulders. The shadow from the flame added size to the fisherman's lumpy nose.

"Torged didn't come home," Pelask said. "He's not in your workshop, and no one has seen him."

"He went to cut wood this morning."

"Then we'd better go look for him. If we wait, the new snow will cover the tracks."

Watnojat looked wistfully toward the warm interior of the cottage. The air from the doorway was chilling him through his goatskins. Yet he was glad the fisherman had come; he could not bear to wait until daybreak. "As you say, Pelask. As you say. We should go now." He retrieved his parka from the peg and then explained briefly his plans to Balin. "I'll bed with Torged's kin," he said, "if I sleep at all tonight. I'll not trouble you before morning."

"But Vigen," she protested, and began to lecture him about his health. Nonetheless, he resolved to follow the fisherman.

"At least take these," she insisted as she reached for a shovel. She scooped some hot bedstones from the pile at the edge of the hearth and poured them into one of her heavy hide warming bags. Watnojat nodded and stuffed the packet up under his parka. Then he followed Pelask out into the darkness.

The fisherman stalked ahead of him. By the time Watnojat

reached Pelask's cottage, the gray ponies were already outside, stamping their broad hooves on the newly fallen snow. While Torged's younger brothers were hitching the animals to the sledge, Pelask brought out a sack of provisions and several spears. The Vigen climbed aboard, and shortly they were sliding through the streets of Darst.

They began the gentle climb across the fields, guided only by a small lantern hung above the sledge. The powdery snowfall stung Watnojat's cheeks; tiny flakes melted on his skin or clung to the hairs of his beard. The fisherman held the reins slack, trusting the grays to find their own way up the track. Watnojat, seated beside him, could see nothing beyond the animals. Nor could he guess what beasts lay waiting in the darkness.

"String your bows," Pelask called to his sons, who rode the second bench. They were approaching high and possibly dangerous ground. Watnojat felt the rising of the grade as the ponies veered left and continued to ascend. The Vigen braced his feet against the kickboard, then crossed his arms, clutching tighter the warming pouch within his parka. The heat from the stones was comforting, but he knew he soon would lose this warmth to the storm's chill.

They rode on in silence, the sledge creaking as the grays made the turns of their own accord. The Vigen lost all sense of location. He only knew that they were climbing ever higher and that the snow never ceased blowing. Then at last the path leveled out. White-coated branches hung directly overhead. Pelask shouted, "Soso!" and the animals halted.

"Torch!" said the fisherman. One of the boys brought out a heavy stave with a winding of oily cloth about its end. Pelask opened the lantern and ignited the brand.

"Shall I walk ahead, Father?" asked one boy.

The light showed little more than the width of the path. Watnojat heard tiny sizzles as snowflakes expired in the flames.

"Mount it," said the fisherman, and so the torch was placed in the socket that hung from a leather band stretched between the lead ponies. The animals glanced at the blaze nervously and bobbed their stout necks, though Watnojat was certain that they were accustomed to carrying a light. Was something troubling them?

The boy returned to the sledge, and Pelask began a slower pace than before. "Light another one, Lonn," said the driver. "And stand behind me with it."

The boy obeyed quickly and soon a broader swath of illumination surrounded the sledge. The Vigen rose, clutched a lashing pole, and peered out into the forest. All he could see was the snow's unmarred surface, sculpted into troughs and heaps by the wind.

"Torged was cutting in the northwest section," said Watnojat. "You'll want to turn soon."

The fisherman grunted. The glassmaker wondered whether Torged's tracks would still be visible. The snow, though persistent, had not yet left a heavy coat. But on this main track there were so many blade ruts and hoof marks that no one could say whether Torged had passed.

Reaching a crossroads marked by a snow-dusted rock cairn, Pelask turned north. Here was a less-traveled path, and down the center, partially covered by new powder, ran a single pair of ruts.

"Soso," called Pelask to the ponies. Then one of the boys jumped down to kneel in the snow and gauge the track.

"Not deep, Father," said the young son. "An empty sled, I'd say."

That made the case for Torged's passing strong. There was no pair of returning, deeper ruts.

The boy scrambled back to the sledge, but before Pelask could start again the ponies began to whinny and snort—a sound that raised hairs on the Vigen's arms. This was the animals' fear call, and Pelask was reaching for the spears even before the first sound of baying became audible. "Take the reins!" he called to one lad. While the boy came forward to control the panicked animals, Watnojat threw his gloves to the floor and reached for his belt pouch with fingers that were already stiffening from cold. *Time,* he thought. *Will there be time?*

The baying grew louder. The Vigen knew that some of the wild packs held a dozen dogs or more. Even with spears and arrows the men could not kill them quickly enough. In moments the beasts would be on them.

"Bows ready!" cried the fisherman.

"Father, the ponies will run!"

Watnojat held his shaking fingers to the light. *Why, this time, am I afraid?* He had faced more than one wild pack in his treks through the forests. Yet he almost dropped the pouch with its precious contents. *It is for Torged that I tremble.* He fumbled for the talismans he needed and finally extracted three balls of differing amber shades strung on a tether. The sledge lurched sideways. The Vigen fell, but with his pouch clutched to his chest.

The baying filled his ears. He rolled to a sitting position and saw the gleam of teeth emerge from the darkness. An arrow felled one dog, then another. The Vigen pulled against the bench, dragging his bruised shoulders close to the lamp. The ponies were jerking the sledge crazily, first forward and then to the side. The air darkened as the torches pitched into the snow.

The Vigen tightened his grip on the bench. With his free hand he moved the beads toward the swaying lantern, the last source of light and heat. *If that goes out too, we are lost,* he thought. The dogs were rushing Pelask's spear. "Scatter!" Watnojat shouted to the pack. This was no waste of words, for he held talismans that matched the colors of their eyes. "Run, or feel Ormek's wrath." For just a moment, he touched the beads to the hot cover of the lamp.

Suddenly the baying gave way to whimpers of pain. The lead animals backed off while those behind them turned to bypass the sledge. A few dogs lingered to snarl, but when Watnojat again touched the beads to heat they plunged into the forest. The boys shot arrows blindly in the direction of the fleeing dogs, and a yelp indicated that they had planted at least one more shaft. In moments the pack was gone.

Pelask hurried to the ponies and tried to calm them. They stopped their aimless bucking at last, but muscles still trembled along their flanks. One boy picked up the fallen torches and lit a fresh one for the ponies' socket.

"Vigen, those are powerful charms you carry," Pelask said with measured awe when he returned to the sledge. "You take credit for our victory. I only hope that my son is as well protected."

"Torged carries such beads," Watnojat assured him, his seeming calm hiding the turmoil within. He knew that dog packs were not the only hazard of the night. "Many of the townsfolk carry them," the Vigen added in a chastening tone. For he felt certain that the fisherman must possess at least one dog's eye.

"Forgive me, Vigen," said Pelask. "I'm a man of the sea, not the woods. Though my son is trained in your art, I lack his faith." He looked down at the weapon in his hand. "I feel safe only with an iron point in front of me."

The Vigen nodded; he had met others with such views. The truth might even be worse than the fisherman expected. Against some enemies, Watnojat feared, neither his beads nor Pelask's iron might prevail.

"Come!" Pelask called them back to the sledge. All returned to their places, and with some coaxing the ponies began to advance. They had reached such a dense part of the forest that snow did not penetrate easily. Instead of a spray of fine powder, occasional torrents dropped as snow heaped on branches collapsed and tumbled to the ground. The lead ponies, still skittish, reared as a brief cascade crossed their backs. They began to race forward, and the other two were obliged to follow. Pelask stood up, crying "soso" and tugging at the reins. Then the animals whinnied, twisted, and nearly toppled the sledge as they brought themselves up short.

The way was blocked by another sledge and four lifeless grays sprawled in the snow.

Pelask rushed toward the wood-laden sledge. Watnojat followed, heading for the figure that had fallen across the driver's bench. Above the dead man his lantern still burned, illuminating his open mouth in his final expression of astonishment and defiance. *Torged!* A spear lay beside him, its point blood smeared and matted with coarse hair that could only have come from a Lame One's coat. As Pelask lifted the torch, his mourning wail already pouring from his throat, the Vigen saw the string of talismans—the Lame Ones' eyes—clenched tightly in Torged's fist.

Then the mourning wail poured from all four throats and no one stood watch for a return of the attackers. Indeed, had the Lame Ones reappeared, they would have found four easy victims plus the ponies. Watnojat knew his protection to be as weak as had been Torged's.

The Vigen gently brushed the snow from the dead one's brow and cheeks. Torged's face was untouched. Watnojat averted his gaze from the ruined midsection where the beasts had fed. *He died with his beliefs broken,* Watnojat knew, as he took one last look at the cold eyes and mouth. *And I am to blame, only I.* The beads had failed, even with the heat of the lamp to charge them! The Vigen turned away and staggered back to Pelask's sledge.

After a while the wailing ended, and then the Vigen heard Pelask shouting orders to his boys. Watnojat remained seated with his eyes closed. Just then he did not care what became of his own sledge. Soon he felt Pelask return. The ponies snorted and began to move.

No words were spoken. The snow blew harder than before, but the Vigen barely felt the cold. The ride seemed endless, down a mountain that had no bottom. The switchbacks across the slope were numberless. How far up had they come? The glassmaker clutched at the pole and clenched his teeth. All he could hear was the whining wind and the runners against the snow. He did not open his eyes until the fisherman shook him roughly and put him off at Balin's cottage.

Only a few hours remained until dawn. Watnojat, faced with a choice of rousing someone to let him in or spending the remainder of the night in the storm, considered the latter as preferable in his current state of mind. He was about to huddle in the doorway, knowing well that he probably would not awaken, when the door flew open and Balin pulled him inside.

"I am lost, Balin," he said, the sounds coming from his lips in a hoarse whisper.

"Warm yourself, first, and then tell me about it," she answered firmly as she led him toward the hearth.

# Chapter 2

Watnojat was still sitting before the fire when sunlight began to creep across the plank floor. By then the entire household had learned of the loss of Torged. But the Vigen's apprentice had been neither friend nor kin to any of them, and there were none to grieve with the glassmaker. The others had breakfasted and then set off for their morning tasks. The Vigen remained on the hard bench staring at the glowing embers.

Mulling over the past was too painful. He had done enough of that with Balin; now he must deal with the future. The Lame Ones had killed one man. Seeing that the beads had not harmed them, they would attack again. How would the town be protected? Some of the residents might be safe. Some from the old families still possessed astablak beads made by Reslunin, the previous Vigen. Those who held Watnojat's works were less fortunate. The truth was that the supply of astablak had run out during Watnojat's first years as Vigen. He had made many tedious journeys to the mountains without obtaining any more of the precious substance. In the end he had been forced to try other pigments, mixing his powders to create beads of a dark color and fiery sheen nearly identical to that of the original. He had believed the match to be sufficiently close. Had he doubted the strength of this substitute, would he have trusted Torged's life and his own to the new beads? The genuine astablaks were all gone from his supplies. Only the powerless beads remained.

Now his task was clear. He had failed the town and the surrounding towns that relied on his craft for protection. He had thrown away the life of one who might have continued his good work. These errors could not be undone, yet amends must be made. With so little time left, he must begin at once. But how? He shook his head in dismay.

"Tem Watnojat!" Outside Balin pounded the door. The Vigen rose stiffly and met her at the entranceway. Her face was red, and not, he was certain, because of the cold. "He has done his worst, Tem Vigen!" she shouted.

"Pelask?" The glassmaker expected some show of the fisherman's anger and grief, but had not guessed the form his fury might take.

"He has hung the rope of shame on your door. And pillaged the workshop too."

"The shop . . ." Watnojat reeled from the doorway. "It is enough," he said in a whisper, the sounds barely emerging from his throat. "It is enough that I lost Torged."

"Pelask is a cruel and stupid man," Balin said. "He is gone now. Come, I will help you clean up after him. Dress yourself."

Watnojat did not respond at once, then suddenly he felt one of his arms being pulled through a sleeve of his parka. "Vigen, are you coming?" She helped with the other arm. Then he was trudging along after her through the newly fallen snow. *At least the storm is over,* he thought, as he squinted against the glare of the bright sun. *But the storm within is barely started.*

The shop door stood slightly ajar, the end of a short piece of fisherman's rope fixed by a spike to the center plank. The rest of the rope, greasy and rank, had been dipped in pitch and then smeared with fish guts. Balin stood aside and let the glassmaker enter first. He pushed open the door, caring little for the seaman's mark of dishonor. All that mattered lay inside.

"My kiln!" The stones had been pulled apart and scattered, some chipped, others broken. The hide lung of his great bellows had been torn. But stones could be replaced, hides could be sewn. What of his precious pigments?

The shelves were a shambles, and drawers had been pulled out everywhere. Vials had been scattered onto the workbench and floor. "Balin..." The Vigen sank to his knees, painful as that position was for him, and tried to assess his losses. Bottles lay smashed, their contents spilled out on bench tops and floorboards. Some had contained raw minerals, while others held fragments of colored glasses that he had prepared for later use. "These pigments cannot be replaced. Not in my remaining days. Perhaps not ever."

She opened the door wider to let in the morning light. "Tem Watnojat, do not touch anything," she said. "Look. Look carefully at what is left." She knelt beside him. Despite the open door and the light through the windows, many parts of the floor lay in shadow. "Do you see, Tem Watnojat? It is possible to gather up some of these spills. With a brush and a broad knife blade you may recover many of your colorings."

The Vigen's knees ached. "Is it possible with these old joints?" He closed his eyes and thought of the innumerable journeys he had made over difficult paths, and of long days digging under the summer sun. Then he recalled the winter nights he'd spent casting the colored batches, long nights which he otherwise would have spent by his wife's side.

"Vigen, do not despair." Watnojat opened his eyes and sighed deeply. Balin had spoken sensibly, he knew. If only he could muster the strength to follow her words. He reached up to pull open one of the undisturbed drawers and found within a selection of empty vials. If he could do as she suggested, brush the powders onto a blade and pour them into fresh vials, then something might be saved after all.

"Kyala will help us," Balin said suddenly. "She has good eyes and supple joints. We are both too old to be crawling about on floors."

"Kyala!" The Vigen struggled to his feet and leaned against the workbench. "She is half imp and half snow hare."

"Don't judge her too harshly, Vigen. Though she teases, she really does care a great deal for you. It's her youth that makes her behave so."

Watnojat shook his head. "Younger girls than Kyala are already wed, yet she still acts a child." He offered Balin his hand and helped her rise. "I don't think she has the patience."

"Give her a chance, Vigen. She has a good eye for color, and that should help. My boys are too clumsy. And Mara is unfit for any kind of careful work."

The glassmaker rubbed his nose, feeling the scars from times he had bent too close to the kiln. "Colors, did you say?"

"She always comes with me to the dye shop. One time I was halfway through a sweater when I ran out of red wool. Kyala found a matching skein."

"A good sign," he said. He closed his eyes for a moment, trying to imagine Kyala working in his shop. He could only hear her teasing voice.

"Give her a chance, Watnojat. You can always send her home again."

The glassmaker sighed. "If she can be serious for a little while, then perhaps she can help me after all." And so, with misgivings, he consented to Kyala's assistance.

She arrived at his shop with a lit lantern and, to his surprise, made no spiteful remarks as she carried it to a corner of the room. She took from his hands a brush of pony hair and a wide-bladed knife so that she could begin the tedious work. Some of the spilled fragments and powders were mingled with others. Some had simply vanished—blown into the air and settled elsewhere as dust. "Uncle," she said after she had labored for some time, "you are a silly old sheep but I don't think Pelask should have done this. You're not to blame for Torged."

*Ah, if only you knew,* the Vigen thought. For he suspected that somewhere in the mountains, in some distant range he'd never reached, one might find astablak. He blamed himself for never having obtained the mineral that would have saved Torged from the Lame Ones. He blamed himself also for the foolish confidence he had placed in a substitute whose power had never been tested.

"I was responsible for Torged," the glassmaker said hoarsely. "And I am responsible for all the towns and villages in this region. There is no other Vigen hereabouts."

"Uncle, you take too much on yourself." The knifeblade clicked softly against the mouth of the bottle as the last of an ochre powder dropped inside. "It is the Magistrate who must protect the town."

"Magistrate?" Watnojat shook his head. "Sendor is too busy pickling fish. So long as the Lame Ones don't touch his barrels, he'll be content. No, it is *I* who must keep the Lame Ones at bay."

Kyala gave him a puzzled look, then returned to her work. They kept silent awhile, and as the Vigen watched her he grew ever more surprised at her patience and care. Was this the Kyala who had woven his beard into a nest while he slept? Only last spring he had awakened to find a tiny blue egg nestled within the white pocket she had made. Yet this sturdy youngster was Balin's offspring; someday she might display her mother's qualities. The childishness would end, and then, perhaps, she would become the center of a fine household.

Yet her future troubled him because she was unlikely to attract a husband. Her candle of a nose was accentuated by the narrowness of her face. She possessed the thinnest of lips, and she lacked her mother's ample breasts. True, there were men who cared little about a woman's appearance. But the girl had shown no interest in the skills prized in a wife: sewing, cooking, caring for children. As if these problems were not enough, her sharp tongue was sure to rout the rare youth who called upon her.

Watnojat mused on, only dimly aware of Kyala's progress. One by one, she handed him filled vials. Here was a bottle of brilliant red fragments from a copper mixture he had cast long ago. And here was the powder from one of his best batches of amethyst glass—how his wife had admired that color! And here . . . here was raw mineral, a rare copper blue from his final journey to the mountains. The top of his workbench was crowded with vials.

"Uncle, it is finished," Kyala said, interrupting his reverie, "and I'm very hungry." The girl stood up and stretched herself, flexing one leg and then the other.

The glassmaker rubbed his eyes and saw that indeed she had salvaged most of his precious powders and that his floor had been cleared of all the spills. The kiln remained wrecked, but much of Pelask's ill work had been undone. "Kyala, you have helped me more than you know." He touched his lips to her cheek. She whirled away, laughing, then opened the door and ran out.

He followed her to the doorway. "Uncle has a briar bush on his face," she shouted back, "and the top of his head is a shiny rock!" Kicking up loose snow with her boots, she raced for home. He smiled at her display of energy, feeling a brief respite from care before his troubles crowded back around him.

Watnojat had eaten nothing that day, yet he felt no hunger. Before he could follow Kyala to Balin's house he decided that he must speak with the Magistrate. He could not keep the truth from Sendor, though he felt great shame over what he must disclose. So he stepped out onto the shadow-crossed path toward Sendor's house.

Even before he reached the door, he was assaulted by the odors of pickling brine from the curing shed that stood behind the house. After hanging up the Vigen's furs, Sendor's wife went to fetch the Magistrate. The Vigen sat alone on a bench by the hearth, formulating the words he must say.

A thudding of boots sounded behind him. "Tem Watnojat, your loss pains me," said the thin man in a nervous tone. Sendor's graying beard was neatly trimmed, and his parka, though stained from work, was trimmed with fine fox pelts. He did not remove his outer garment; he merely loosened the fastenings, as if in a hurry to return outside. "As for Pelask's misfortune, that's almost beyond bearing. So don't judge the man harshly for his temper."

*He knows about the damage,* thought Watnojat. *The whole town must know.* "I did not come, Tem Sendor, to complain about the ransacking of my shop. I'm not asking for justice."

The Magistrate seemed relieved by the glassmaker's denial. "Then how may I aid you, Vigen? If it's about a new apprentice, I can recommend several candidates."

"Your offer is appreciated, Tem Sendor. I will think on the matter." He looked into the embers, at the coals that were Ormek's gift to men. He saw only his own pyre in those coals. Could he still train a successor, and live to see the lad a full-fledged Vigen? For the moment he felt too old to hope. He must give his warning to the Magistrate and nothing more. "Perhaps I'll take no apprentice. My art may die with me."

"Watnojat, do not say that." Sendor's tone carried genuine concern.

"Be wary of too much faith in my art, Tem Sendor. There are limits to the power of beads. That's what I learned last night. If the formulation is not perfect, the talismans fail."

"Vigen?" The Magistrate stepped closer.

"We have been fortunate. For years the Lame Ones stayed away. Reslunin's beads were powerful, and the Lame Ones learned to fear his glass."

"But your own works are equally renowned."

Watnojat rubbed at his cheek. Now he must confess his knowledge. "Except for Lame Ones' eyes, my beads are sound. My glass is powerful."

"Yes?"

The Vigen struggled for the words he had practiced to himself. "But this is what you must know, Magistrate. Only . . . only the astablak talismans from the Vigen Reslunin are certain against Lame Ones. You must find the families who hold these and ask their assistance in protecting the other townspeople."

"But can you not make new glass against Lame Ones?"

"If only I could." Watnojat rose to leave, for he felt that he must end the conversation here. The Magistrate was known to lose interest quickly in any subject other than women or preserving fish. "Tem Sendor, I'm truly sorry, but I cannot help you. Just as you cannot pickle herrings if you have no herrings, I cannot make astablak beads without astablak. The talismans that Reslunin made are the only protection you'll have against Lame Ones."

"But, Vigen . . ." The man's tone turned to one of pleading. The glassmaker had thrown responsibility onto his shoulders, and it was evident that he did not care for the burden. Watnojat wasted no time; he hurried into his furs and stepped out of Sendor's warm house into a biting wind. He knew, as he trudged forth into the dusk, that much of the respect the Magistrate had held for him was gone. Past successes were wiped away by this one defeat. But he had done what he was obliged to do, and he felt relief that the interview was finished.

Evening came, and the Vigen sat at Balin's table. With some coaxing, he swallowed a bit of soup, but he did not taste the food. Torged's burning would be soon; Watnojat had seen men building the pyre in the market clearing. Joyful as he would be at the young man's ascent to Ormek, he dreaded another encounter with Pelask.

When the time came, however, Watnojat stood at the front of the crowd. Torged's body was dressed in a fisherman's garb of sealskin, as if his father now repudiated the career his son had followed. He lay on a bier of pine boughs atop the pile of split oak, facing toward the stars that were

Ormek's dreams. Pelask held a torch—and something else. A packet that he lifted above his head gave off an odor of the sea and of death as he paraded around the bier. Then he stopped directly in front of the Vigen.

"My son was a brave fisherman," he said in a voice that all could hear. "He was a man of the sea. That is all you need recall of him. I burn this token to Etma so that all of you will be saved from my fate. Beware this Vigen, this false maker of glass. His works are worthless. Stay clear of him, I say. And if any man sends him a son, let him suffer as I have. Let him lose that son."

Pelask placed on Torged's chest his offering to the sea demon. Then he touched the flame to the pitch-soaked wood below. The other watchers edged back from the sudden burst of flame, but the Vigen stood firm though the smoke stung his eyes and the heat pained his face. The oak logs crackled as the heat spread. Torged burned, and his ashes flew to Ormek. And the other thing that burned; what of it? What was that strange and foul smell that mixed with the smoke from Torged's flesh? Watnojat wanted to dismiss the curse as merely a seaman's superstition, but it was widely held that Etma could intervene with Ormek. True or not, many townsfolk would be troubled by Pelask's words. Watnojat fretted over the consequences as he watched the pyre collapse into embers.

At last the Vigen felt a tug of his arm and saw that Balin was urging him home. He turned his back on the glowing remains and went to his first sleep since Torged's fatal journey.

By morning the glassmaker had made a decision. He could not sit idle while the town and all the neighboring towns lay vulnerable. He must travel again, to find the astablak that had so long eluded him. But this feat he could not do alone. "I'll need a new apprentice," he told Balin. Pushing aside for the moment the fisherman's warning, the Vigen went out to find Sendor.

The day was gloomy, overcast as if another storm was coming. Watnojat passed several townspeople as he approached the Magistrate's house, and none greeted him. They turned their faces away or even shielded their eyes when he passed. The Vigen was stunned; everyone in the town had always trusted him. Did they think he would deal with them as with animals, using talismans to control their wills? It was acceptable for a Vigen to briefly call the spirit of a departed one, and talismans also had their uses in healing. But to control a person for any other reason was a grave misuse of the art.

The Magistrate did not come to greet him inside his house, and Watnojat was obliged to seek him in his pickling shed. Sendor's assistants were gutting mackerels on a table, and the odor of the place made the glassmaker's stomach threaten to return his breakfast. "I'm sorry, Vigen, I can do nothing for you," said Sendor, who had retreated to a dimly lit corner of the shed. "You know how superstitious people are. They have faith in your beads, even if they did fail against Lame Ones. But they fear the old sea curses. You won't find an apprentice."

"But, Tem Sendor." The Vigen could scarcely form his words. "You told me I must pass on my art. If I have no assistant—"

Sendor raised his hand. "Certainly you must pass on your art, and surely you must have a new apprentice. But I can do nothing for you now. In time Pelask's words will be forgotten. Wait a year, maybe two. Then I'll make inquiries."

"A *year*? How long do you expect these bones to hold together? I do not think Ormek will grant me the time to wait."

The Magistrate, walking sideways, edged along the wall of the shed as if trying to keep his distance from the approaching glassmaker. "Be patient, Tem Watnojat. Go to the herb-healer. Tell him you need extra years."

"Extra years? Wait until you are my age. You'll trade ten

barrels of fish for his rheumatism cure that does no good."

"I have work to do, Vigen."

"So you do."

Watnojat fled from the disagreeable smells and returned to the town streets. He did not believe that everyone feared Pelask's curse. There were many friends he could call upon. The ironsmith Arod, for example, spent frequent evenings in Watnojat's shop, and often showed interest in the Vigen's art. Moreover, Arod had three sons whose careers were yet uncertain.

After a short walk, Watnojat came to Arod's shop, where he watched the sparks scatter as the smith hammered out a spearpoint on his anvil. His cheeks were smeared with soot and his blond beard darkened by smoke. Arod glanced up at his visitor, then made a few more clanging blows before setting down his hammer.

"Watnojat, I'm sorry to see you today." The glowing point hissed as Arod quenched it in his bucket. "I know why you're here." The smith did not look up from his work. "And I know what Pelask did to your shop. If you need help rebuilding the kiln, I'll come. I'll do what I can for you. But don't ask for my sons."

Watnojat spread his arms. "Do you fear the fisherman's demon?"

Arod showed a troubled look and did not answer directly. "Think of my work, Vigen," he said. "Half my trade is with seamen. What can I do?" He kicked his boot at a length of chain. "Will they want my hooks and my anchors if they think me cursed?"

"I see, Arod. I see." Watnojat glanced about the room at the piles of finished pieces—spikes and harpoons and grappling irons—tools of the sea. Even if the demon were powerless, the beliefs of men gave Etma influence over other men's acts. Could Watnojat ask the smith to lose his livelihood? "At least do not hide your eyes from me, Arod. That's the worst pain of all."

The ironsmith sheepishly raised his face and looked openly

at the glassmaker. "Time will help you, Watnojat. We can't do without a Vigen, and people will forget Pelask's words. Wait awhile and ask me again. I'll consider sending you my youngest son, Denet. But for now, I think you'll have no apprentice."

Watnojat did not give up that easily. He called on another friend, a farmer idled by winter, and then on a woodcarver of his acquaintance, but wherever he went he found excuses and apologies. Whether it was fear of the curse or more practical considerations that lay at the root of each decision, he could find no man who would consider apprenticing him a son.

# Chapter 3

Though disheartened, the Vigen woke the next day with a new plan. In a two-pony sledge he had borrowed from Balin, he set off for a neighboring village. The path to Wekerval ran first along the coast, then turned inland to cross a series of low hills. He passed few travelers that morning. A snow hare at the side of the road sat up and stared at him as his grays trotted past.

Then the first stone cottages appeared, with snowdrifts piled against walls and chimney smoke drifting toward the clouded sky. Frequently he passed barns and stables, and once he saw girls returning from their milking. *No fishermen here*, thought the Vigen with satisfaction as he approached the quiet center of the village. Wekerval was a place of farmers and weavers. The Magistrate himself was a renowned weaver, whose rugs decorated the most prosperous houses of the region. *Lanado is a man who will sympathize with my plight.*

Watnojat's optimism continued as he waited inside the doorway of the man's shop. Lanado had two assistants working the looms. The weaver's wife had notified her husband of the visitor, but he remained preoccupied. The Vigen could see only the short man's back as he bent over the closer of his two workers. A strong smell of wool and dyes filled the shop. The looms creaked as the men worked, and the glassmaker grew impatient. But he knew that he must not disturb a craftsman at his art.

Then Lanado finished his instruction, and Watnojat glimpsed his puffy face and bristle of reddish beard. "Tem Vigen, your works are well known in this region," said the Magistrate. "We had trouble here some years back, as you may recall. Weasels getting at our farmers' chickens. My predecessor went to you for help."

"I remember," said the Vigen. "Ten summers past. Or perhaps twelve."

"And it was *your* predecessor long ago," Lanado continued, "who rid us of Lame Ones. So the Vigen of Darst is always welcome in this place."

Watnojat murmured his thanks, but he knew that now he must humble himself again, and this was especially painful after the good words from the Magistrate. "Tem Lanado, the problem with Lame Ones is not yet ended."

The weaver nodded. "I've heard rumors. They say it was your apprentice..."

"Yes. So I came in the first place to warn you. If any of your villagers hold Lame Ones' eyes from Reslunin, then you must arrange that they be shared. If new attacks come, only the old beads offer sure protection."

"That's unpleasant news, Vigen. You have my sympathies for your loss. But we've seen no Lame Ones here in many years."

"I cannot say if they'll come here. You're farther from the river than we are. But be forewarned, Magistrate. Be certain you have defenses."

"I thank you for the warning." Lanado glanced aside and Watnojat followed his gaze. One assistant was standing up and spreading his arms in a gesture of helplessness. Lanado apologized to the glassmaker, and rushed over to see to the difficulties. He was gone for some minutes.

"Have we anything else to discuss, Vigen?" asked the Magistrate, still standing, at his return. "It is a busy morning for me."

Watnojat cleared his throat. "Tem Lanado, as you know, I need a new apprentice. I've come to ask for your recommendations. Perhaps there are lads in your village who would be interested in learning my art."

The Magistrate raised his eyebrows. "A surprising honor you bestow on us, Vigen. I certainly would like to assist."

"You understand that certain tests must be given. A boy may be willing, but he must show talent."

"Naturally, Vigen. I've faced that matter myself." He nodded in the direction of his assistants. "One cannot test too carefully," he confided in a lowered voice. "And so I'll find you several candidates. But I have no answer today." He scratched at his bristle. "Let me speak with my wife this evening about it. She can tell me likely names. She knows every youngster in the vicinity. In a few days, I'll send you a message."

*At least he does not ask why I seek outside my town,* thought Watnojat. "Your offer is generous, Magistrate. Due to my advanced age, I must get a quick start on this new boy's training."

"So it must be. You can trust that I'll give the matter my attention."

Watnojat could ask nothing more, so he left the busy shop. He returned as he had come, riding the sleigh over the hilly road, past curious snow hares and occasional sledges traveling from Darst. He regretted having no definite answer from Lanado, but he had preparations to make in the coming days while he waited for a message from the Magistrate.

The Vigen returned to his shop and there, after pulling out many dusty drawers, found the maps he had used in his trips to the mountains. The sheepskins were well annotated with information he'd gleaned on each journey. He ran his finger along the route of his last trip—past the Fanged Peaks and halfway to the foothills of the Sentinels. Beyond that point, so far as he knew, no man had ever traveled.

Might one find astablak in the high cliffs of the Sentinels? Watnojat could not say, but he wondered if he had the fortitude to reach even their foothills. And what about the southern route, past the inland sea that was called Ormek's Footprint? With the local boatmen, he once sailed to the sea's eastern extremities and traded with savage forest dwellers there. The barefoot hunters had long known of the Vigen's needs and had provided him with quantities of ochres and blues. But none had found astablak. Watnojat shook his head. The southern area did not look promising.

The glassmaker sighed as he looked at the places on the map that he or his predecessors had thoroughly combed. He had followed many a rumor and tale in his travels with no success, and yet the map was large and the terrain varied. Perhaps some possibility lay yet untouched.

As his eyes roamed over the maps, again and again he found himself staring at the hamlet of Wintersgate that lay to the southeast at the edge of the Winterkill range. When he recalled what he'd heard of the place, goosebumps rose on his arms. There were tales that he had never dared verify, of a Vigen who abused his powers. The glassmaker of Wintersgate, it was said, held the greatest store of pigments of any Vigen in the region. He had gotten his treasure by forcing men to work against their wills in his mountain diggings. Though Watnojat shuddered at the method of collection, he could not help wondering about this mysterious Vigen's store of astablak.

In the next few days Watnojat began to equip himself for his journey. He dipped into his store of silver coins and purchased four ponies to replace the team that the Lame Ones had destroyed. The farmers took his money, but bypassed even the usual haggling in their haste to be done with the transactions. And whenever he walked in the town, the glassmaker felt the discomfort of being shunned.

"You aren't safe, Vigen," said Arod on the night he helped Watnojat with the kiln. "If a child sickens, they blame you for having glanced in its direction. If a pot boils over, they say it's because of Etma's anger."

"Superstition," said Watnojat with a grunt as he lifted one of the heavy stones.

"Superstition or not, there are some who mutter about putting you out of the way before some disaster befalls the town."

"And do you think I'm frightened by such talk? But I have my own reasons for haste. I've not much time. Come; let us finish." He dropped the stone in its new position, then stepped back to study his work. With Arod's aid, he had reassembled his stones into a much smaller kiln, one that could be quickly taken apart for transporting on the sledge. "Now I can train my apprentice anywhere," the Vigen said with satisfaction. Arod did not reply.

Within a few days the last of the preparations were complete. All Watnojat lacked was Lanado's list of candidates. The glassmaker could think only of the message, often asking Balin if anyone had come looking for him. As day after day passed, the Vigen became more and more anxious about Lanado's reply. By then the man or his wife had had time to canvass every family of Wekerval. Were they also deterred by Pelask's curse? A good deal of commerce passed between their village and Darst—fish were traded for grain, firewood for woolens. So the events surrounding Torged's passing by now must be well known in the inland village. The Vigen sat alone in his workshop one cloudy afternoon and admitted to himself that no answer would come from Wekerval.

Watnojat needed advice, and only his old mentor Reslunin might help him. With a heavy feeling, the glassmaker rose from his stool and approached his secret storage place. He kneeled to push aside a bulky crock of sand, then pulled up a loose floorboard and lifted out his personal box of beads. "Reslunin," he said softly. "I do not call on you without cause."

The beads lay in no particular order in the bottom of the box. Many were wrapped in small cloths, with names embroidered on each piece of fabric. The Vigen unwrapped the hazel-colored glass of his mentor, the eye he had cast from memory on the evening of Reslunin's burning. He sat down at the workbench with the bead in his palm and felt the distinctive vibration that was as much a part of the glass as the visible pigment. He could feel its color even as he closed his fist.

*Take heat,* he thought. He squeezed the glass orb in his palm to bring it life. When he was certain that it was warmed through, he set it down for a moment and picked up a knife blade. He jabbed his thumb and squeezed the flesh until a drop of blood fell onto the talisman. "Reslunin, I am alone. I have no apprentice. Must your knowledge die with me?"

He picked up the glossy bead and cupped it in his hand again. Then Watnojat closed his eyes and waited. Each time he had called on the old Vigen's spirit, it had taken longer and longer for the voice to arrive. Some day Reslunin would be one with Ormek and no longer respond to the power of the bead. Watnojat did not know if this threshold already had been reached.

"Reslunin, I need your aid," he called. "Return to me this last time and I'll not trouble you again."

A familiar feeling of gooseflesh ran down his arms as the shop became quiet. Moments before, he had heard children playing outside. Now he did not even hear the wind.

"Reslunin, is it you? I hear nothing. Nothing at all."

He listened to the silence. Even the whistling that sometimes troubled his hearing was gone. He called upon Reslunin once more, reminding him of his pledge to help Watnojat as long as he was able. "I hold you to your oath even now," said the Vigen. "Answer me."

Then there was a rustling that changed to a hiss and at last became a voice, a hoarse whisper. A single word repeated: "Watnojat. Watnojat. Watnojat." A sour taste came onto the Vigen's tongue. "Do not call me again," said the voice. "Do not call me. Do not."

The Vigen struggled, as he always did in such times, to form his words clearly. "Reslunin, do you understand my plight?"

"I cannot stay here. I cannot. You ... You are your master."

"Master of none but myself. I can find no apprentice. Reslunin?"

"Vigen, I am. I am gone."

"Reslunin!" Watnojat reached for his knife and gashed his other thumb. Blood ran freely onto the bead, smearing his palm with red. The sour taste, momentarily gone, began to return."

"Watnojat. Watnojat. You must release me. Ormek. Ormek angers."

But the glassmaker would not relent. "What of my apprentice? Does Ormek want my precious knowledge lost?"

"Apprentice," the voice whispered. "Apprentice. Apprentice." The whisper grew so soft that the Vigen feared losing it again.

"Reslunin!" he shouted. "The fisherman's curse has frightened everyone in the towns. Tell me where I must seek."

A faint whisper returned. The glassmaker couldn't make out the words. "Louder, please! You are drifting away."

"Watnojat, listen. Listen." The voice strengthened for a moment. "Balin. Go to Balin. She will help you."

"But, Reslunin." Watnojat could make no sense of that advice. Ilak was already apprenticed to a potter, and the younger boy was pledged to a baker. "Balin's sons are spoken for," he protested.

"Daughter. Yes, Balin's daughter. Quickly. I am gone."

"Reslunin, please!" But then Watnojat lost the spirit taste

entirely. He heard the sounds of the outside flood back into the shop. Once more he cut his finger and called his mentor's name, but this time there was no response. It was over. He would get no more from the departed Vigen.

The glassmaker opened his eyes, stared at his blood-stained palm. He had wanted to ask other questions, but Reslunin could not wait. The one answer that the old Vigen had given was unacceptable. Watnojat scowled while he recalled again Reslunin's parting words. He had heard the voice say *daughter*. Yet he began to doubt his memory. Kyala, his apprentice? Watnojat puzzled over how such a thing might be possible.

He was not aware of a woman having ever been a Vigen. The work was often hard—felling trees and splitting logs, gathering sacks of sand, digging for minerals. Kyala was strong; he had seen her swinging an axe at the woodpile when her brothers were away. But more than mere strength was needed. She would be entering a craft that had always been the province of men.

Watnojat puzzled over the matter while he pressed his cut thumbs together. When the bleeding stopped, he cleaned Reslunin's bead, then replaced it in its box. He did not expect to use the talisman again. In fact, he now regretted this final call on his mentor. Never had Reslunin been so reluctant to come and so eager to depart. Was it possible that he gave a false answer to gain release? One normally did not doubt the word of a spirit, but in this case...

The Vigen shook his head; he could not accept Reslunin's advice. He acknowledged that he would find no one immediately, but with patience he would have a suitable apprentice. Arod's son, Denet, seemed his best candidate. Perhaps as early as the spring, the ironsmith would consent. So he must pursue that possibility, at least to the point of learning whether the boy had talent for the work. If Denet was qualified, then surely the other matters would resolve themselves.

Eager to settle that question at once, the Vigen unfastened his belt pouch and spilled its store of beads onto his workbench. For a test, these would not be enough. From his box he selected others, lining them up across the bench as he contemplated the talents that must be checked. Then he closed the box with its remaining talismans and hid it under the heavy crock.

Arod was working on a length of chain when the Vigen approached his smoky forge. By then little daylight remained outside, but Watnojat was determined to have his trial. The smith did not cease work. Watnojat spoke his words slowly, interspersing them between clangs of the hammer. "You have said, Arod, that some day you might send me your son."

The smith frowned, but did not answer. He continued to beat at an iron rod.

"I am willing to wait, only I beg your permission to test Denet."

Arod halted for a moment and wiped the perspiration from his forehead with a sooty rag. "Test him?"

"To see if he has talent, for working glass."

The smith shook his head. "I don't want the boy thinking about your art," he said. "If I let you do this and later don't send him to you, he'll be disappointed."

"It's merely a trial," the Vigen protested. "I . . . I won't tell him the results. I'll just say it is a game."

"And what if he shows well? Then you'll have an extra argument to use on me. You are a wily old Vigen."

"Arod, please. I'll test him and say no more about it. Rely on this. I'll not undo a promise and lose your friendship."

The smith waved his hammer toward the rear door of the shop. "Go then. Find him in the house. But be brief so he doesn't think much about it afterward."

Watnojat nodded and went quickly in search of the boy. The house was but a few steps from the shop. A smell of roasting venison came from its wide chimney. He found Arod's son outside, bringing water from the well, walking along a path where the snow had been cleared down to the hard ground. Denet's appearance shocked the glassmaker for a moment; he had forgotten the resemblance between this boy and the young Torged. The twelve-year-old's hair was blond and cut short. His face was well rounded like his father's. "How many chores have you?" the Vigen asked.

"Just this." The boy raised his laden hands slightly.

"Arod says you can play a game with me for a short while."

Denet's eyebrows rose in surprise, but he said nothing more until he'd left the buckets in the house. Watnojat glanced up and was glad to see a break in the clouds. Some late sunlight fell between the shadows in the snowy yard. "This is a bead game," said the Vigen, opening his pouch carefully.

"Those are *eyes!*" the boy exclaimed.

"For today they are merely things of color."

"Color?" Denet scowled and wrinkled his nose.

"It's only a matter of looking and touching. See?" The glassmaker took out the first pair of beads that he wanted the boy to examine. "I have here two that were colored with blue earth." He held a pair of irregular spheres in his palm and extended them toward Denet. "One is darker than the other; can you tell which?" The narrow band of sunlight gleamed on his weathered hand and on its glossy contents.

Denet picked out the darker shade at once, then stared at the Vigen as if he had posed him a foolish question. When Watnojat brought out a third bead, the boy correctly told which of the first two most closely matched its color. *A good start,* Watnojat thought. But he said nothing to the boy except that his answers were correct.

Then the Vigen brought out some talismans tinted with iron pigments. For some reason the boy's responses were slower now. Denet made one outright error, misranking two closely matched siennas. But that test a full-fledged Vigen might have failed. Watnojat could no longer see the difference; only by his memory of the shapes did he know which had the darker shade.

So he progressed to the sense of touch, which in some instances proved more sensitive than vision. With his back to the Vigen, the boy distinguished, by the warmth of the glass, Allig's green from cupric and even charcoal from smoke. His small hands cupped the beads carefully and he answered with assurance. Watnojat congratulated himself on his good fortune. The boy's abilities seemed almost as good as those of young Torged!

"I have two lynx eyes here," said the glassmaker, offering his final test. "And two of cliff cats. You may turn around."

The boy stared at the golden yellows with their narrow pupils, then poked at them with his index finger.

"I do not expect you to know which is which, Denet. But can you separate the pairs?"

The boy hesitated.

"You may use touch if you wish," said the Vigen.

Denet, scowling, took the beads into his own hands, first one at a time and then in pairs. He seemed about to answer, then took a different pair to hold. He lifted the glass to the light, squinted, and finally chose.

"That is the hardest game I'll show you," said Watnojat, concealing his disappointment. "One that takes practice." Indeed, he wondered whether he had offered an unreasonable test. He opened the pouch and let the boy drop the cat eyes in with the others. "Perhaps we'll play this again soon." Then the Vigen, rather than taking his leave of Arod, passed through the gate directly out to the street. He did not want the smith to share his doubts.

Watnojat looked at the sky and saw that sunset was approaching. He had not climbed to his knoll since the day he had watched for Torged, but he knew he would not go there today. Watching the sunset was for old men, and he dared not think of himself as aged anymore. He had much to do, and time was passing. Spring would come and find him still without an apprentice.

"Vigen, watch the road!"

Someone pushed him roughly, toppling him into a snow pile. The cold bit his cheek. Then he heard the breathing of ponies and the hiss of runners. "You nearly were trampled, Tem Watnojat." A young man of his acquaintance, a brewer's apprentice, bent over him. "If I hadn't happened by..." The youth helped the Vigen rise and then brushed the snow from his clothing.

"I did not see the sledge," said the glassmaker with embarrassment. "You were quick witted, Erlen. For that I thank you."

"Are you all right, Tem Watnojat? Maybe I should help you into your shop."

"I'm just shaken." He looked at the ruts where the sledge had just passed. "I thank you again, Erlen. There's no need for you to linger."

The young man shrugged and continued on his way. The Vigen paused to get his breath. He leaned against a hitching post and looked along the street at the rows of stone houses. Had the incident truly been an accident? Arod had warned him. Perhaps they were already trying to rid themselves of their old glassmaker.

Watnojat furrowed his brow. The townspeople were foolish at times, and he could hardly blame them for their ignorance. At that moment he felt little affection for most of them, but his obligations remained clear. He would not abandon the town that had supported him all his life.

But how was it to end? After the incident with the sled, he no longer felt comfortable in postponing his journey. He stamped his boots angrily, thinking for a moment of the reward that had been taken from him. He should be enjoying himself by the fire now while Torged managed the shop. Instead, he must end his life questing for what he had never found in his youth. Worse, if he made the wrong choice of apprentice, his precious Vigen's knowledge could be lost. *Ormek, guide my hand,* he thought as he turned in the direction of Balin's hearth.

# Chapter 4

The glassmaker kept his thoughts to himself throughout the meal. But at last the table had been cleared and the cleaning finished. Balin remained alone, tinkering with a pot handle that needed mending. Watnojat approached her cautiously, but could quiet himself no longer. "I must test her," he blurted out.

"Test? What are you saying, Tem Vigen?" Balin put down the pot and stared at him.

"You told me that Kyala is good with colors," he explained in a rush. "You urged me to let her help salvage my pigments, and I agreed. Maybe she can help me more than you think."

"Watnojat?"

He felt his cheeks flush. He knew that Balin was concerned about her daughter's poor marriage prospects, but he could not predict how she would view an apprenticeship for the girl. "I have some beads I'd like to show her. To see if she has the Vigens' talent. But don't tell her that."

"Watnojat!" Balin's eyes widened.

"Would you allow it?" he said in a tone that showed no eagerness.

"Kyala as your apprentice? You can be sure that I'd welcome the chance."

"Then let her think this is a game. Don't set much store in it yourself, either. The talent is not common. Had I no recommendation—" But he caught himself. He did not want to give her unreasonable hopes.

While the Vigen seated himself at the large table, Balin went to find her daughter. Watnojat brought out his pouch of beads and heard the talismans click softly against each other. Carefully he spilled some beads onto the tabletop, cupping his hand to keep any from rolling.

Kyala arrived with a glum face and nervous steps. "Uncle, why can't you get some hairs to grow on top of your head," she said, forcing a gaiety she clearly did not feel. "You have so many below."

The glassmaker smiled and rubbed his bare head. "Like a mountaintop," he said, giving the usual response. "No soil, so no grass."

"I think, Uncle, that the goats have eaten all the grass," she answered, still trying to maintain a show of merriment. But her voice quavered and she barely spoke the last word. *Her mother has said too much*, he thought ruefully. But now he could only continue.

Balin set two lamps down on the table. The light flickered on the talismans and reflected dim colors. *It was not proper to study beads except in daylight*, the glassmaker thought, starting to regret his haste. But he picked up two copper blues.

"You've seen my beads before," he said to Kyala. "Now I'm curious to know how carefully you can look at them. Here. Take these two. One is darker than the other; can you tell which?"

Kyala picked out the darker piece. Watnojat nodded, then offered another pair. "And which of these is darker?" Her answers were quick and correct. Certainly she could do the easy tasks. Nearly anyone in the village could do as much.

He switched to iron pigments, recalling how the boy had erred on the closely matched siennas. The "hairs-breadth" pair was the first he thrust at the girl. *Unfair,* a voice cried within himself, but he gave her the talismans. She lifted a lamp so that the light was cast evenly on each. "That one is darker," she said thoughtfully. Watnojat nodded. She had one chance in two, he reflected, to guess the correct answer. Had she really seen the difference? But soon there remained no more pairs to show her; she had correctly judged them all.

*What now?* He turned to the problem of color touching. "In some people," he explained, "the fingers can do as well as or better than the eyes." Kyala indicated some surprise at that revelation, but she was willing to try. She turned her back to him with her palms extended behind.

"It's . . . it's like bedstones in the morning," she said when she held the two beads, one in each hand. "They still have some heat when you take them out of the bag. And one of these beads feels cooler than the other. Does that mean a darker shade?"

"It does," the Vigen assured her. With that knowledge, she duplicated Denet's successes. He wondered if she could do even more. Again he gave her the siennas, his most difficult pair, and again she chose correctly. He watched her fingers with amazement. He had never paid much notice to Kyala's hands. They were not delicate, but well proportioned and seemingly strong—and evidently sensitive!

Finding her faultless, Watnojat tried to fool her with perfectly matched ochres. Now her head hung down as she passed the beads back and forth between her hands. The Vigen became ashamed for his trick, but he waited for her decision. "Uncle, they feel the same."

Watnojat's heart began to race. "There is one more exercise," he said. "Color memory. Difficult for the inexperienced, but let us try it." This was a test he had not even considered for Denet.

She turned to face him. He showed her a deep yellow, then mixed it in with a handful of similar yellows before closing his hand. He paused, wondering how long she could keep the first in her mind. He counted to himself slowly, marking the time. Kyala stared at him but said nothing. Then, when he opened his hand, she picked out the one he had first shown her. She was able to repeat the task using touch instead of sight. ·

As he searched once more through his store of beads, he asked himself if his idea for one final test was too cruel. She had yet to err; he was determined to learn her limits. He rose and walked to the end of the table where Balin sat silently. He whispered his request and Balin, with a puzzled expression, turned to a small chest by the side of the hearth.

"Has she seen this?" the Vigen asked as Balin unwrapped from its cloth the talisman he had cast years earlier, at the time of her husband's final illness.

"No."

The glassmaker felt the bead's soft vibrations in his hand as he studied the color carefully. Then he returned to the table and picked out three others of a similar smoky hue. "Kyala," he said in a gentle voice. "Kyala, I know it has been five years. You were a child then. But do you recall your father's eyes?" Balin's talisman he mixed with the three beads of his own. She lifted the lamp again as he opened his hand.

Watnojat saw tears forming as Kyala reached unhesitatingly for her father's bead. The Vigen could not speak. He looked up at Balin, still standing by the table, and then at her remarkable daughter. *I could not have done that,* Watnojat thought. *Not after five years.* Perhaps the Vigen of legend, the great Kolpern, might have managed such a feat.

"Return the bead to your mother," the Vigen said hoarsely. Then he slowly put away his talismans. He laced up the pouch and remained staring at his hands as they lay on the smooth tabletop. "Balin," he said at last, "your daughter has great talent. I had planned to wait for Denet, but now my decision is much more difficult."

"Denet? But Vigen, if she has the talent..."

"It is not so easy, Balin. Can I throw over all the years of tradition?"

"I see. Now I do see. The legends are what trouble you. The Vigen Kolpern and all the others."

Watnojat nodded. "You know the stories. The Vigen is always a brawny fellow who can drop a tree with one blow and batter a Lame One with the trunk."

"Isn't it the power of the beads rather than the strength of the Vigen that wins out?"

"It is both." Watnojat tugged at his beard, pulling the hairs until they hurt, as if the pain might clear his mind of confusion. He had doubted Reslunin, and yet the test had proved the master's words. Why did he hesitate? Because he must be certain. If Kyala was to become Vigen, she would have to prove herself twice over.

"Perhaps you are right, Balin. Perhaps we are misled by our legends. Perhaps we need new ones." He stood up and looked toward the door. "It is late now, but I would like to show Kyala something in my shop."

Balin, asking for no explanation, gave them a pair of lanterns, and within a short time they were trudging through the quiet streets, their boots falling softly on the well-trod paths. The sky was clear, and overhead the dreams of Ormek glittered in their ageless patterns. The night air invigorated the glassmaker after the long session indoors; he felt charged with new enthusiasm. "There, do you see?" he said, pointing to the cluster that every child knew: the Vigen who forever chased the Lame One across the sky. He wondered, for a moment, whether some day children might think of Kyala when they viewed those stars. *New legends?* Perhaps.

In the workroom, Watnojat lit a fire in his reconstructed kiln, which now vented its smoke through the old chimney pipe. He brought out a small mold and his mixing board, and then he held the lantern to Kyala's face. "Have you studied your reflection?" he asked.

She nodded with a shy smile.

"Then you will understand," he said. Carefully he pulled the wooden stoppers from several vials. Greens and blues and a touch of milk glass he mixed together on the board. He placed the makings of one talisman into the center hole, inserted a thread of copper metal, then slid the mold into the kiln.

"You may pump, Kyala. It is not such a difficult chore." His large bellows, still damaged, lay to the side. He had obtained a fireplace bellows from a cooper, and this would be adequate for the smaller kiln. He showed her how to push the end against the kiln's breathing hole, and how to pace herself when her arms grew tired. She squeezed the handles together, and when she heard the first rush of air into the fire she began to grin. "Keep a steady rhythm," he told her. She started to pump; the small kiln heated quickly. Watnojat added more wood. The room grew warm and Kyala soon shed her parka.

This must be taken slowly, Watnojat knew. He rested on a stool and mused over his own first days at the task. How Reslunin had worked him, firing batch after batch of glass with no respite between. He remembered the many vials of rare earths, now long expended, and the colors that only Reslunin could coax from them.

The air hissed through the bellows, each time slower than the last. "May I rest?" Kyala asked, her brow damp with sweat.

"Talisman making is not something you take up and put down like a piece of knitting."

Kyala frowned, but continued. He wondered whether she could finish. No, she must do more than finish—she must prove herself before he dared accept her into his art. There would be trouble enough for evading Pelask's curse, for choosing a daughter instead of a son. But the real test would come when Watnojat was gone, when Kyala tried to serve as Vigen. Would people believe in her beads? Would they trust the power of her glass? If the colors were true, if the glass was properly set, then they would have reason for trust.

"How much longer does this take, Uncle?" she asked when her cheeks had turned red with exertion. "I don't think I can go on."

"A bit more," he answered. "You must work awhile longer." He brought her water and held the cup to her lips. But his reply was the same each time she asked.

"I am finished, Uncle. Truly, I must quit." Her breathing was heavy and her rhythm irregular.

"Not yet, Kyala. The night is long."

"Shall I continue 'til dawn?" Her pumping had slowed, and he thought that surely she would stop. *If she lacks the strength*, he thought, *then her chance is ended*. But he did not speak his doubts. "Until the star Vigen has slipped across the sky. Until the Lame One is gone."

To his surprise she struggled on, though at times he was certain that she would topple from exhaustion. He fed log after log to the fire, and brought her cool water when she asked, but he did not let her cease. At last he went outside to check the sky, and when he returned he told her that the work was done.

"Do you know what you've made?" With his long poker, he knocked a few stones away from the kiln's opening. He was as eager as she to glimpse the results, but glass must cool slowly, so he did not remove the bead at once. The heat of summer rose from the kiln and bathed their faces. He urged her to kneel and see what lay within.

"That is *your* bead, Kyala, the one that matches your eyes and controls your spirit. You must keep it with you always, so that you are the guardian of your own fate."

Kyala moved closer to the kiln, but the Vigen pulled her back. "Wait until it cools properly," he said. "Then we'll attach it to a tether."

Light from the coals reflected from her face as she continued to watch the talisman. The Vigen glanced from the girl's eyes to the bead she had fused. The glass glowed with an intensity that he did not credit to his powders.

"Uncle, is this my first lesson?"

"Lesson? Have I not discouraged you from this calling?"

"I'll be a Vigen—if you'll let me. I don't mind the work."

Watnojat rubbed at his beard. "You have proved that to me. I did what I could to dissuade you, but I failed."

"Yes?"

"Yes. I've run out of excuses. If you wish, you may be my apprentice."

"Then Uncle, let me tell you something." She looked up at him and smiled weakly. "After this, you must trim your beard if you want to teach me anything. Otherwise I'll laugh every time I see the bristle patch. And I'll call you an old sheep. And that's not proper talk for an apprentice."

"Apprentices are beaten for less," he answered, but the corners of his mouth twitched, and he sensed that she did not believe him. Suddenly he felt a lightening of his burden, an easing of the cares that had come with Torged's death. Yes, he could see the girl's viewpoint. He had glanced at his reflection and she was right—he did look like a sheep. He ran his fingers through the tangled growth, and his lips twitched uncontrollably. Throwing his head back, he began to laugh.

Kyala made a snipping motion with her fingers. "At least we can make it tidy," she said. "Come. Mother has shears."

# Chapter 5

There was such a brisk wind at their backs that Watnojat thought Ormek must be speeding them on their way. The Vigen's new grays stepped smartly, their broad hooves kicking up small white clouds of powder. He would not soon forget the ponies he'd lost to the Lame Ones, but these new animals would serve well. They moved with grace along the snowy track and required little guidance. The Vigen found the gentle rhythm of the sledge soothing, the relative idleness of driving enjoyable after his days of preparation for the journey.

"Kyala?" Watnojat glanced sideways at his assistant, who stared grimly ahead at the passing clumps of icy bushes. One of her hands clutched a lashing pole and the other hung limp by her side. The Vigen did not know what to make of this change in her temperament. Before departing, she had been full of her usual gaiety, rushing off with youthful abandon whenever he released her from chores. But now that the journey had started, all was changed.

Wekerval lay behind them and the white peaks of the Buttresses could be glimpsed almost directly ahead. The morning was nearly gone, but since leaving Darst, Kyala had said not a word. "Where are your good spirits?" he asked at last. "Must I watch you sulk for a whole day?"

"Uncle, I'm ready to go back home," she said quietly. "I didn't know we were coming so far."

"So *far?* We're like the hare who has put one whisker outside his hole. Do you know how distant is the Winterkill Range? And if we fail there, we will be but halfway to the Teeth of Dawn."

"It's not the same as when you showed me the maps. Then you just moved a finger from one place to the next."

"Aren't you warm enough in your new parka?" He glanced briefly at Balin's fine present to her daughter—fleece outside and lined with rabbit fur.

"Vigen, don't you see? Everything I know is in Darst. You're taking me into a country of strange things."

"Kyala, I've been traveling many seasons. I have survived all these things you call *strange.*"

"But you've not been to the Winterkills."

"No, but I've passed near them. Along the Worm, on my way to Ormek's Footprint, I saw the peaks."

"Uncle, you are full of names. Now tell me why someone chose to call mountains the Winterkills."

The glassmaker smiled. "Don't let names frighten you. There's a village called Etma's Pit along the coast just below Hesh. You'd think it a place of sea evil, but it's a quiet settlement overlooking the cove."

"Then why call it a *pit?* Such a place should be filled with demons."

"They wish to keep travelers away, that's all. The people of Etma's Pit don't want to share their fine village with newcomers. The land is rich, and the nearby harbor is a boon to fishermen. They'd like to keep it all to themselves."

"Ah, then they're an unfriendly lot. But should I think the Winterkill Range is equally pleasant? Who would want to keep entire mountains to themselves?"

Watnojat laughed at the question, but was not quick to

judge its foolishness. Untmur, the Vigen of Wintersgate, might well claim the range as his own. The tales of Untmur's abuses had kept Watnojat away from those mountains, and he doubted that other Vigens had been eager to travel there. "Let's take the journey as it comes, Balin's daughter. I don't think we'll gain anything by fretting in advance." But from Kyala's tightened lips, he gathered that she remained unconvinced.

Her reservations about the journey did not surprise him. He remembered his own apprenticeship, when Reslunin had taken him on his first long excursion, along the Asep River and up into the Fanged Peaks. Watnojat recalled dreaming every night of home. His face each morning was damp with tears. But Reslunin taught him how to read the clouds and how to build shelters in the wilderness and where to find promising diggings in the hills. Soon the new knowledge filled his thoughts, and his bouts of homesickness became less frequent.

"Kyala, do you see the cottages?" Watnojat asked as they reached the top of a rise. "Look, down there is Torsplain." A vast flat valley lay below, its white expanse dotted with blocky gray houses. A cluster of buildings marked the town itself, sledges moving slowly in and out along the connecting roads.

"Torsplain!" she exclaimed. "My father came from there. He told me about working in the barley fields. But that's all I know of the place."

"I've come down this road in springtime to see the whole valley sprouting. Now that's a sight no one forgets."

"Will we stop here, Uncle?"

"To rest the ponies, yes. But by evening we must reach Eastplain. I've acquaintances there."

Soon they paused at a waystation. The grays drank fresh well water at a trough. Where the water sloshed over the sides, a thick coating of ice had built up. Watnojat slipped half a copper to the boy who tended the well, then dipped a ladle for his own thirst from the bucket. Kyala wandered off to tend to her needs, while the Vigen found a place behind a crude fence of poles. His steaming urine spattered softly into a hole of yellow ice. Such poor comforts as this will seem luxuries before we're done, he thought.

After Torsplain they reached rolling countryside, with spruce forests spreading in every direction. The animals negotiated several tight switchbacks as they climbed some of the steeper hills. Watnojat had always traversed this country in warmer weather. Its winter appearance was new to him, and he was much taken with the views of dark conifers scattered over white hillsides. The afternoon passed quickly for the Vigen, though Kyala offered little conversation.

At last, with the waning sun at their backs, they came down into the long valley of Eastplain. The Buttresses, closer now, glistened in the last reddish light. The town itself was already in shadow as the Vigen drove the ponies into the large barn that stood behind the inn. A boy took charge of the animals, and the Vigen led Kyala to the squat stone building that fronted the road.

"Watnojat, is it you?" A bald man with plump cheeks greeted the travelers at the doorway. The smell of roasting fat filled the air. The innkeeper's leather apron was stained with grease. "I thought your traveling was over."

"So I had hoped, Dalba. But now I am in search of minerals again. Tell me, how are your sons?"

"They don't change," the innkeeper answered with a smile. Then he lowered his voice and added in a confidential tone, "Tem Vigen." Watnojat understood the need to keep his calling to himself. Strange Vigens made people uneasy.

"Those lads would rather spend their nights drinking up my ale," Dalba continued. "Better that, they say, than answering to a wife. I can't argue the point." Dalba laughed. His questioning gaze moved to Kyala and his brow furrowed.

"Torged's dead, Dalba," Watnojat explained in a soft voice. "An accident in the woods. Now I've a new apprentice."

*"Apprentice?"* Dalba's scrutiny of Kyala began at her face. Even with her hood thrown back, her appearance was not feminine—hair cut short and neck bare rather than circled by the band of cloth that most young women wore. In the dim light she appeared to be a boy. The Vigen had no cause to correct that impression. "For a moment..." Dalba hesitated, then seemed to think better of pursuing his observations. "Yes, Tem Watnojat," was all he said. "I sympathize with your loss. I remember Torged. We had a laugh or two over ale."

"We'll overnight here, Dalba. Early tomorrow we continue toward the east."

"It will be a privilege." Dalba motioned for the two to follow him as he stepped toward a curtained doorway. A stout youth stood guard, loosely holding a pikestaff while he watched the noisy patrons in the tavern. Dalba's strongroom was windowless, lit by a guttering candle. A rug with a motif of a rearing white horse hung across the narrow wall. The innkeeper made change; coins clinked within a wooden chest set on a tabletop.

Passing back through the curtain, Dalba led them to a place at the end of a long table and at once caught the attention of the serving boys. It was not long before platters of steaming sausage, a loaf of barley bread, and mugs of ale were set between the travelers. Kyala raised her eyebrows and reached for the ale. At home, Watnojat knew well, her mother watered whatever brew she served Kyala. More often it was goat's milk that filled her daughter's cup. But the Vigen could do nothing now. He watched with curiosity as his assistant drained her mug.

Kyala's mood improved quickly, and Watnojat was grateful for a respite from the bleak face she had shown him all day. Glancing about the low-ceilinged room, with its disks of Ormek suspended from many beams, the glassmaker observed the high spirits of the other patrons. The farmers and woodcutters of the district chatted and joked, and occasionally he picked out a strand of their conversations.

There was talk of the Mej from time to time, and talk of taxes to support his militia.

"Let him pay his own taxes," said one man.

"Out of one purse and into another," laughed someone else. "He's got enough of 'em."

Understandably there was resentment, for there was doubt that the Mej's soldiers benefited the outlying villages and towns. Watnojat knew that before Reslunin's time the present Mej's grandfather had been petitioned for aid against Lame Ones. A year later three horsemen in leather armor had gone into the forest and shortly afterward two of them had been seen fleeing along the coastal road. Bones of the third were eventually found. The Mej never sent aid again.

Watnojat glanced back at Kyala, whose lips were shiny with grease. Using a two-tined fork, she stuffed another piece of meat into her mouth. "We won't always have such fare," Watnojat said. "You may as well enjoy yourself while you can."

He took a swallow of Dalba's good ale, then put down his mug when he noticed a peculiar stirring in the room. The hubbub of conversation changed to a hiss of whispers as heads bent toward each other. Whatever news was being passed reached the group of sheepskin-clad farmers at the far end of Watnojat's table. They picked up their mugs and platters and began searching for other places to sit, all the while averting their eyes from the Vigen. Within a few moments the tables surrounding the pair from Darst were empty.

"Curse the barnboy!" Watnojat growled, slamming his mug down to clatter on the tabletop. Kyala looked about nervously, then to the glassmaker for an explanation.

"The barnboy saw the kiln stones and must have poked around in our belongings. Now they're all afraid of us." Watnojat stood up. "Dalba will show you the room," he said quickly. "Put down the bar when you go in and don't open it 'til you hear my voice. I'll stay with the sledge tonight."

"But, Uncle—"

"They won't touch anything else if I'm there. Dalba will take care of you. Finish your dinner." Then, with an angry tread, he went out to the barn.

Night had fallen, but lamps at the big doorway showed him the way. The boy turned from the Vigen when he came in. Watnojat, saying nothing, took up a lantern and raised it above his head. The animal smell grew stronger as he trudged over the thick covering of straw that aided the runners to slide across the floor. The barn was crowded, grays penned or tethered along the walls while the sledges stood side by side in the center. Ponies stirred as the glassmaker approached, shuffling softly in the straw. After a brief search, he found his own equipment and climbed up to the cluttered rear section.

Several hides that covered his belongings had been disturbed. He pulled up corners to see that some of his sand mixture had been spilled from its crock; but the thick cover of the clay jar was now secure. What else had been opened? With trembling fingers he pulled up another hide, then lifted the lamp above the chest that held his pigment vials. The leather straps were all fastened as he had left them, interlaced in a manner that would be difficult for another to untangle. He checked the food stocks next, and then was satisfied that no thieving had been done.

Behind the benches of the sledge was a clear space where he could sleep. Watnojat climbed down to the barn floor and wearily lifted up handfuls of straw to make himself a bed. He covered himself with a pair of fur rugs from one of the trunks, then blew out the lantern and lay down. His breathing slowed as he heard all about him the quiet creaking of the stalls and the rustling of straw. *I have slept in worse beds*, he thought, feeling the hard places beneath his back. Outside the wind struck and the boards of the barn began to rattle against each other. Some of the animals snorted. Watnojat raised his head for a moment, but the sounds quickly died down. He felt sleep coming.

"Uncle!"

The Vigen shielded his eyes from the lantern that hung over his face.

"Uncle, I can't stay in that room. It makes me itchy."

The glassmaker was still groggy from his first sleep. "Kyala, this is far worse than Dalba's beds," he said, slapping at the floorboards. "Go back."

"I don't like it in there. The walls are so close they make my head hurt."

"Kyala!" Watnojat groaned, wondering how he could get enough rest that night to continue the journey. "Kyala, I must sleep. You can bring up some straw if you want. You know where the furs are packed. But don't wake me again before dawn."

He closed his eyes and heard her shuffling about. Before she settled down, he drifted off.

"Uncle!"

*Was it dawn already?* Watnojat rubbed at his eyes and looked up. A faint light showed through the cracks in the barn roof. "Uncle, someone's here."

*Someone?* The glassmaker's back was stiff and sore. He pushed himself slowly to a sitting position. In the gloom he could just make out the pinched features of a thin little man standing beside the sledge.

"Vigen?"

"Who disturbs a man at his rest?"

"A patron of your art, Vigen. An admirer of your talents."

"I am Watnojat of Darst, and I have yet to hear what you're called."

"My name . . ." The intruder coughed. "Call me laden-with-silver." He raised a purse he'd been clutching and shook it so that the coins within jingled their unmistakable message.

"Give your silver to the ponies," said Watnojat. "They'll do as much for you as I will."

"But Vigen, Tem Vigen—I need a talisman. I . . . I heard

you carry kiln stones. Couldn't you work your craft for me?"

"What? To give you some power over your neighbor? Or is there a village girl you lust after?"

"Vigen . . . Vigen, no. Don't think ill of me. The problem's with my wife. She does what she pleases. She lets me go hungry when she's not inclined to cook, and she won't mend my clothes."

"Let me feel the purse," said Watnojat. The man proffered it eagerly. The Vigen hefted the weight and smiled. "Kyala, hold this for a moment," he said. "Learn how much my art is worth." The girl's mouth opened as the coins weighed down her hands. "Shall I help this man?" he asked her in a mock serious tone. Then he turned his attention to the visitor. "You, stranger. Tell me why you don't hire a servant? There's enough here, I'm sure, to pay wages for years." Watnojat returned the purse, but the man did not leave.

"I tried what you said, Vigen. I hired a servant. But nothing she did would satisfy my wife. So the girl ran off, and now I'm as helpless as before."

"I can do nothing for you. Try another servant. A boy this time. Now be off."

"You turn me down so quickly. Who else do you think will do business with you? You—with a *girl* for apprentice. They'll laugh you out of every village! Be reasonable." He offered the purse once again; the Vigen tore the heavy sack from his hands and tossed it to the floor.

"Go, before I get a better look at your face!"

"Vigen!" The visitor dropped to his knees to search for his lost treasure in the straw. "Have you a light?" he said. Then, thinking better of the idea, he added, "No, no light. I can find it."

Watnojat turned away as the man continued to scuttle about the barn floor. Kyala peered over at the stranger and stared back at the Vigen, her mouth open in an expression midway between astonishment and delight.

"We'll see more of his kind," the glassmaker told her in a dark voice. "You should know that a Vigen never betrays his art. We do not make beads to control *people*. Never forget that."

The girl nodded. "Y-yes."

"Help me stand, Kyala. We must hitch the ponies and move on."

The glassmaker rose painfully, brushing the wisps from his clothing. As he climbed down from the sledge he saw the intruder clutching his purse with two hands while he ran awkwardly from the barn. "You see why it's best not to be recognized," he said. "Now go find out if there's hot bread in the kitchen. I'll hitch the ponies."

# Chapter 6

"It's time to begin your lessons," said Watnojat as they drove out of Dalba's yard. The morning was gray and cold; the Vigen's steamy breath blew against his face when he talked. "We'll start at once. I must teach you in a season what Torged spent ten years learning."

"In a season?" Kyala, still sleepy eyed, handed him a chunk of the innkeeper's bread. "When we're back in Darst, you'll have time—"

"Don't think about Darst. I am old, Kyala. Learn from me now while I still have wits." He bit into the loaf, already cold against his lips.

"I'd go back home today," she said. "I'd forget about astablak."

"And what would you do about the Lame Ones?"

"I'd . . . I'd get all the men together in the square. Women, too. Everyone who can hold a spear. We'd stand together and fight the beasts."

Watnojat smiled. "I'd like to see that. I'd like to see Sendor standing in front. I'm afraid he'd be hiding in one

71

of his pickling kegs. We don't have many heroes in Darst."

"Then I hope we find astablak tomorrow. Then we can go home."

Watnojat shook his head sadly, knowing they might never find the pigment. *The lessons would serve two purposes,* he thought. They would teach her the craft, and they would keep her mind occupied during the months of travel. "First, you must learn the Eighteen Fires," he said. "There are six grades of wood, and each can be burned in three ways." He went through the list, naming each combination and giving an example of its use. For a while he lingered on smoky fires, explaining their effect on the colors produced in new glass. There was so much she had to know.

The travelers continued toward the southeast along a track that would bring them near the Buttresses. They passed one town, but as dark approached they found themselves in open country. The travelers stopped at a crude shelter with a single wall and a roof of branches. Under this Watnojat parked the sledge, tethering the ponies to the side. After a cold meal of dried meat and hard bread, he brought out talismans— eyes of wild dogs and great mountain cats.

"You'll learn to recognize these by touch," he said. "These are our protection." He held up each talisman and named the animal it would control. Then he asked her to do the same.

"Bear . . . No." She rubbed at her eyes.

"Try it again," he said.

Yawning, she took up the handful of glass pieces and began to recite the names. This time she made only two errors, confusing two similar cats. "No more, Uncle," she pleaded.

"Then tell me the Eighteen Fires," he asked. "After that, you can sleep."

While she stumbled over the list, Watnojat arranged the talismans in a circle about the lantern, making sure that Ormek's heat would touch any predator that happened by while they slept. The travelers wrapped themselves in furs and tried to find comfort on thin piles of straw they had arranged on the sledge. The wind, blocked by the shelter's lone wall, hissed as it passed.

"Uncle," she said in a sleepy voice, "couldn't we light a fire?"

"Kyala, is there any wood?"

"Just the supply for the kiln."

"Then we must make the best of the furs."

She began to weep softly; and the Vigen understood her misery. Although she was older than he had been on his first journey, the conditions now were far harsher than those he had known with Reslunin. It might have been wiser to delay. If he had waited for warmer weather, she might have had an easier time of it.

"Kyala," he whispered, reaching under the furs to her sleeping place. "Kyala, tomorrow will be better." He touched her shoulder gently and then brushed his fingers against her damp, hot cheek. "Tomorrow you can drive the sledge. That's what you've been wanting."

"Uncle?" She turned toward him. In the lamplight he could see the start of a smile. "Uncle, you'll see how well I do."

Watnojat nodded. "Now sleep, Balin's daughter. So that I can have my rest."

The night seemed a long one. Many times the Vigen felt wind sweeping through the open shelter. Later he heard the panting of ponies as another traveler pulled beneath the roof. He raised his head to see a lone figure, heavily muffled, moving about on a small sledge. *A hunter,* Watnojat decided, and then he closed his eyes once more.

"So you're the Vigen they talk of." A deep voice interrupted a dream that Watnojat did not want to leave. He tried to hold onto the images of summer meadows, of grasses reaching to his knees, but the voice droned on. "I heard you were passing this way. I need a deer eye if you've got one."

"Does the news travel so fast?" Watnojat sat up and looked at the hunter. The man's long hood covered most of his face; only a mottled nose and a sparse beard showed in the light of the hunter's lamp.

"Vigen, it's dawn and I've no time to waste. I've two ermines to trade if you've got a deer eye."

"Perhaps." Watnojat had planned to save his talismans for trades that would best provision his journey. But *ermines!* The hunter was offering a high price if his skins were good; they could be traded later for the wagon he would need and for other supplies. "Let me see your furs."

"Two ermines, I told you. Did you say you had the bead?"

"I've seen ermines not fit for wiping off my runners," the Vigen replied, as he poked at Kyala with his foot. He wanted her to hear the haggling, but all she did was turn over.

"And there are eyes that won't charm a toad! Look at this." He opened his hand to show a small talisman that was riddled with cracks.

Watnojat reached under the blankets and shook Kyala vigorously. She opened her eyes and let out a quiet moan. "Wake up, apprentice," he said. "Wake up and tell me what you think of this deer eye." He had shown her some of his own deer talismans while they were still in Darst; he wondered how well she'd remember.

Kyala roused herself and leaned over to stare at the talisman. He held the bead closer to the lamp. "I think too much yellow," she replied hoarsely, blinking. "Let me hold it a moment."

"It's as much help to me as a skunk pellet." The hunter dropped it into her hand.

"Too much yellow in the iris. Yes. You need a better Vigen." She gave back the bead and the hunter, with a sudden flip of his arm, tossed it out into the snow.

"It cooled too quickly," said Watnojat. "That was why it cracked. Whose work was that bead?"

The hunter barked a short laugh. "Do I know? Some demon lost it to me in a *patna* game. Now show me the talisman you have."

"You'll need patience," said the glassmaker, "if you want to trade with me." The hunter made a rude noise but did not move away.

Watnojat told Kyala to fold up the bedding while he went to the rear of the sledge. He did not want the stranger to know what riches he carried; behind the cover of his chests he poured out the contents of his pouch onto the plank floor. The least successful of his deer eyes he picked up. This one was slightly off, the long pupil's hint of blue not quite dark enough; it might prove weak against a strong-willed creature. Some spirited bucks would elude this hunter, but he would be far better off than when he carried the charlatan's pebble.

"This is what I offer," said the glassmaker when he returned. "If your ermines are as fine as my piece then we may have something to talk about."

The hunter picked up the bead and carried it to the gray light outside the shelter. For a few moments he scrutinized the color. Then he strode back to his sledge and began to move his bundles around.

"Have you any fresh kills?" asked the Vigen.

"A few foxes," the hunter shouted back. "You can have them all for the bead."

"Keep them. But my apprentice would like to see one for instruction." Watnojat motioned to Kyala, and they both climbed down to cross the short space between the sledges. The other double-runner was badly weathered, its planks dark and warped. The ponies tethered near it had a tough and lean appearance, with many scars across their hides.

"I'm not running a school," said the stranger, as he tossed a stiff silver-haired fox at Kyala. The eyes were filmed and of little value, but Watnojat urged her to try to see the colors within. She went out to study the dead eyes in the growing daylight. "Here are your ermines," the hunter said, carefully handing the cured skins to the glassmaker. "Tell me where you've seen better."

Watnojat took one of the white pelts and stretched it

lengthwise between his hands. He rubbed his nose through the soft hair, sniffing carefully to check the curing. "What is this?" he said as he lifted the second. The black tip of the tail was missing.

"That's how I found it," grumbled the hunter. "Is it my fault the critter got his tail bit off?"

"That's fine for you to say. For a maimed skin, I'll get half price."

"Vigen, I've no time for your haggling. Maybe your bead is as worthless as the one I tossed out."

"Then return it," said Watnojat, dropping the two ermine skins back on the stranger's sled. "In the Winterkills, I'll find a better trade."

"Winterkills?" The hunter kicked at some of his baled furs, then kneeled and untied one of his bundles. "Take these then, you old thief. Here, mountain goats. You'll need something warm where you're going." He handed over the goat hides and then the ermines again. The Vigen grunted his assent to the bargain.

"Good traveling," Watnojat said in parting, but he did not smile over the trade until his back was turned to the stranger. Kyala, her studies done, was waiting for him at the sledge. "Ready the ponies," he told her as he went back to store the furs. "You said you wanted to drive."

She took her seat. Cautiously she directed the grays from the shelter back to the road. The lessons must begin again, he thought, but first he would let her gain confidence with the reins. He must hold back a bit on his teaching lest she be overwhelmed. Yet his time was running out. How could he strike the proper balance?

With his hands free, the Vigen felt idle. He tapped his boots against the kickboard and stared out over the passing landscape. Directly to the north, the great cliffs rose. Here stood the forbidding Buttresses, which no man had ever scaled. If astablak lay buried on their heights, then only the birds would know of it.

Kyala was quiet while she got the feel of the animals.

He was certain she had never handled more than a two-rig before, yet she caught on quickly. As her confidence grew, she became more talkative and the Vigen began to better enjoy the route. "Tell me, Uncle," she said as they descended a gentle rise. "Tell me about the bead you traded."

"That was one of Torged's practice pieces," he answered with a grin. "Not perfect, but the hunter will do all right with it. There's a rule of our art: 'The keener the wit, the closer must be the match.' Deer are easy to control."

"Then when will I make a deer eye, Uncle?"

Watnojat laughed. "You must start at the beginning. First you must learn how to make colored glass." And with that, he forgot his reservations and began to teach again. He spoke of combining sand and crushed shells and pot salt, and of how glass could be made soft or hard. There was so much in her head already, yet he asked her to memorize the proportions of the various mixtures. Soon he would have to let her practice, otherwise the learning would be just empty words in her mind.

At noon, as they crested a hill, they saw wooden disks of Ormek dangling from an overhanging branch. "We must stop," said Watnojat. Kyala directed the grays toward a modest shrine perched above the narrow valley. They found four mossy stone columns overlaid by a roof of logs. Kyala brushed dead leaves from the block of marble while the Vigen brought oil and a wick.

"Ormek, be thanked for your daylight," said Watnojat as he poured fish oil into the cuplike depression in the stone. He struck sparks from his flint and ironstone. The greasy wick took fire quickly from his tinder of charred cloth. "And be thanked for the hunter you sent our way, and for your heat that kept us safe from the night's dangers. We travel in your service. Allow us, if you will, to find the object of our search." He stared into the tiny flame of the offering and tried to see there the images of the journey to come. If he could discern a sign ... but Ormek showed him only a dancing light.

\* \* \*

Days passed and they reached the Hamidun lowlands. Settlements were rare here; the ground was poor for farming and the sparse vegetation harbored little wildlife. On many nights the only shelter was a covering of hides tied together on a pole frame at the front of the sledge. But the nights were not so cold as they had been in the foothills, and sometimes rain would fall, tapping gently on the shelter's roof.

During this time Kyala's lessons continued. While her talents could not be denied, he often found her an exasperating pupil. She could remember colors easily, but facts did not always stick in her head. Sometimes he found himself repeating over and over what she had seemed to know perfectly on the previous day.

When they passed through settlements, the teaching would stop. Watnojat typically tried to pass as a peddler, even making occasional small trades of cloth or spun wool that he'd brought along for that purpose. But often he found that his name had arrived ahead of him. The people in these villages had never seen a Vigen. They would surround the sledge and peer through splayed fingers at the new arrivals. The innkeepers would feed the travelers well, but inevitably would seat them in a corner with their faces toward a wall.

Kyala's spirits often were low. Only on sunny afternoons, when the melting snow turned to slush on the roads, did she show much cheer. But the weather turned cold again, bringing them back to winter. A new storm came and by midday traveling was impossible. They stopped under a three-walled shelter, lashing hides across the opening to keep out the blowing snow. *Work will keep her mind busy,* thought the Vigen. "We can have a real lesson," he said as he began to unload the kiln stones. "You proved back in Darst that you can pump. Now see if you can make a batch of glass. Any shade you wish."

That offer improved her mood. She seemed to forget the

weather as she pondered the question of color. "I'll make an amber glass," she said finally. "So that I can use it to make a fox-eye talisman." From the vials in the Vigen's trunk she selected fragments of a yellowish iron mineral. These she ground up in a small iron bowl.

"Finer," he said, looking over her shoulder. "The powder must be dust."

"Yes, Uncle," she said, channeling her annoyance at his correction into the pestle she was using to pound the stone. When the dust was as fine as she could make it, she was ready to mix the mineral with the raw ingredients of glass.

"Not from the crock," he said, when he saw her approaching his prepared glassmaking mixture. Instead he showed her the sacks of sand and black salt and ground shells that he had brought for her instruction. "I want to see you setting your own proportions. You mix everything from start."

Kyala used a small wooden paddle, counting out measures from each of the sacks. She glanced at Watnojat defiantly when she was done; his only response was to nod. She stirred the contents with the pigment, then poured the mixture into a slotted mold.

"Now think about your fire," Watnojat said. "And show me the shade you hope to produce."

Kyala searched through the vials of his crushed glass and finally handed him one containing amber fragments. "To make this color, I'll need smoky flames and a tight kiln. Yes?"

Watnojat was pleased at her planning. She began to pump, and he did not have to encourage her to maintain a steady rhythm. He let her decide when the batch was done, but he reached out to stop her when she went to open the kiln too quickly. "Have you forgotten? It must cool in a closed kiln or the glass will be tinged with blue."

Kyala dropped the poker and slumped moodily into the

heap of straw that had been cleared from about the heat.

"Don't despair, Balin's daughter. You're doing well for one so fresh."

"Fresh? Am I a slab of meat?" She turned away and did not speak to him for some time.

Later they took out the mold and scrutinized the result. The color, despite her efforts, showed streaks of violet. The mixture had fused unevenly, glassy in places but grainy in others. "Not bad for your first casting," said the Vigen. "The pot salt wasn't mixed evenly into the rest, and you didn't heat it long enough."

"And the porridge you made this morning was lumpy, Uncle," she said sullenly. "And your snoring keeps me up at night." She turned away from her handiwork, pulled back the hides, and stared out at the drifts that separated the shelter from the road.

Next morning Watnojat went out and saw ruts in the snow. "We've a path to follow," he told Kyala. "We can drive." He loaded the equipment back onto the sledge with only token help from his sulking apprentice. The weather continued clear and cold, and for two days they crossed lowlands, rising at the end into open forests. During this time Kyala seemed to recover from her disappointment. She asked to make glass again.

In early evening they set up the kiln in a stable behind a crude inn. The penned animals grunted and kicked against their stalls while Kyala worked. There was a good supply of pine in the woodpile. "It's not fully seasoned," Watnojat said. "It will give you the smoke you need."

"I can see that for myself, Uncle." She measured out her ingredients, and this time she was careful to mix them thoroughly. She heated the kiln, and he could see the same look of determination on her face that he had seen the day she had helped clean up his workshop. Watnojat was sleepy and hungry, but he did not tell her when she was long past fusing her batch. He let her pump until she felt she was done.

"It is *all* glass!" she shouted, when she finally pulled out the mold. "And the color?" She held up a lantern. "I don't see any blue. Uncle, have I matched my shade?"

Watnojat blinked. The light was poor and the glass was too hot to touch. "I think you have done it, Kyala. We'll see in daylight. Come, let's eat something." The inn's kitchen had closed by then. They stood in the stable, chewing dried meat and biscuits. From Kyala's mood she might have been feasting at the Mej's table.

They moved on the next morning. Toward noon Watnojat looked up to his first view of the Winterkills towering above the treetops. "Now you see our destination," said the glass-maker. For a moment he stopped the rig to stare up at the line of jagged ridges. *That's where Untmur's diggings lie.*

Many warm days and frigid nights passed. The mountains were always before them, as they descended hills and crossed shallow streams, or drove through small settlements in the valleys. Kyala's learning progressed at a rate better than he had hoped, but when the night winds whistled, she would cry into her bedding and talk of home. Sometimes the Vigen thought that she would desert him, attempting to find her own way back over the distances they had crossed.

She has proved she can make glass, he thought. *But I must let her mix glasses and fuse them into a talisman.* The prospect cheered Kyala, and she voiced no complaints that day. They stopped traveling before noon and pulled their sledge into an empty barn at the edge of a farm town. The place had holes in the roof and one wall had buckled. "For today, it will serve," said Watnojat. "Now show me how you will start."

First she studied his fox-eye beads, scrutinizing them in the daylight that streamed through the roof. Then she went through his powders, pouring out bits of colored glass from a dozen different vials onto the mixing board.

"This is the crucial step," he told her. "You must not waste the powders. Mix them in your mind before you make your choice."

She lingered over the board, finally taking some fragments from her own amber batch as part of the makings of the bead. For a few moments she hesitated over the results of her mixing. She looked at him for reproach, but he said nothing when she added a few grains of red. "And now for the pupil," she said. "Narrow for a fox." She dropped darker glass into the center and her preparations were complete.

Wasting no time, Kyala stocked and fired the kiln. While she began to pump, Watnojat noticed that a few people had assembled outside the barn. The visitors remained at a distance, their faces so muffled with shawls that he could not say if they were men or women. "They are curious and afraid," Watnojat said. "You'll get used to that if you want to be a Vigen."

"Uncle, it is always like this," the girl complained while she worked the bellows. "Everywhere we go it is the same."

"Where a Vigen is a stranger," he replied, "people always fear the worst."

"But why is that, Uncle? In Darst no one thought ill of glassmakers."

She complained so that he felt obliged to tell her of legendary Hestafos, of a man whose tale she evidently did not know. "There have been Vigens who abused their powers. Or so it is said. The people who remember such tales are the ones who fear us."

"Tell me."

"About Hestafos? I wish I could forget him."

"He made beads..."

"Of those who trusted him. Yes, he knew all the colors of the villagers' eyes. First he sent one man to kill his neighbor. And then he charmed the dead one's wife into his own bed. When he tired of her..." The glassmaker sighed. "Must I recite the whole of it? I think you understand."

"What did the people do about him?"

"What could they do? Those who still had their own wills left that village. In the end there was no one but the old Vigen living alone among the dead cottages."

"But, Uncle. Was there really such a person?"

"Tales, Kyala. Was there really a Kolpern? Was there ever a Lame One who could talk?" He shrugged. "This much is certain. One who holds power can be tempted to misuse it." But he had yet to say anything to her of Untmur.

Kyala produced that day the first talisman of her own mixing. By evening it was cool. She stared at it in the lamplight, turning it over and over as if she could not believe it to be her handiwork. Then she offered her creation to Watnojat.

He could feel the colors between his fingers. Though the talisman was not perfect, it was a decent piece of work for an apprentice. The barn was dark except for the Vigen's lamps. In the faint illumination that reached outside, he saw the shapes of onlookers who still lingered near the doorway. "What am I offered for this fox eye?" asked Watnojat of his audience, holding up the new talisman proudly between thumb and forefinger.

"Uncle, no!" Kyala protested. The Vigen gave her a smile and a wink. He stepped toward the opening and every one of the visitors slipped away into the darkness. Watnojat looked out into the empty yard and then up at the sky of stars.

"I'll keep this then," he said loudly. "For I think the farmers in this region aren't troubled at all by foxes." He tucked the talisman into his pouch.

In the days that followed Kyala talked less about Darst and more often of the land that lay ahead. *At last,* thought Watnojat, *she is reconciled to the journey.* They were not far from the foothills, and that meant their first destination was at hand.

In all the settlements along the way, Watnojat had looked and listened for signs of Untmur's activities and had found none. For many days he had not seen glass in any form, outside of his own. Were the rumors false?

"Wintersgate!" shouted Watnojat one gray afternoon as

they passed the whitewashed poles that marked the approach road to the town. *Now I will know the truth.* He clutched the reins nervously. The road was more mud than slush as the ponies strained to pull them up a rise. Then the first log cottages appeared, small square houses with steeply pitched roofs and eaves that reached halfway to the ground. The few windows were of stretched bladder skins. How could this be the center of Untmur's territory? He headed for the one building of substance—a long, log-walled inn that stood at the center of the settlement.

"So the news runs ahead of us again," he said unhappily, watching the barnboy turn away as the rig halted at the doorway. "See that nothing is touched," the Vigen said to the cringing youth.

The travelers left the sledge. Kyala bent to a pile of soggy snow, packed together a small ball, and tossed it at the boy's head. Startled, he turned toward her. "Too late!" she shouted, as he brought up his hand for concealment. "I saw your eyes. I saw. They're mossy green. Now you can stop hiding."

The boy, unconvinced, ran into the barn.

"Uncle, I am tired of this." Kyala, her momentary enthusiasm spent, followed Watnojat listlessly toward the building. The inn, too, he noticed, had skins in its tiny windows.

A short young man of gentle features greeted them, introducing himself as Nedomin. The proprietor, in his immaculate woven trousers, seemed out of place within bark-covered log walls. Though he did not overtly conceal his eyes, he made a point of keeping his face in shadow.

"Your town figures in some fanciful tales," said Watnojat to the youthful innkeeper. "Perhaps they are exaggerated."

Nedomin stroked his neatly trimmed beard and replied cautiously. "Tales? Perhaps from Grandfather's time. This is a quiet place. Our guests feel safe in their beds."

"Yet the stories are too numerous to be entirely false. Is

there no glassmaker named Untmur living in these parts? Perhaps by now he is dead."

The proprietor backed away deeper into the shadows. "Let us hope he is dead," he said in a low voice. "Glassmakers have no friends in these mountains." He glanced nervously at Watnojat. "But of course I respect your art, Tem. I would not turn you away from a night's rest."

"So it *is* true. There was a Vigen here who betrayed Ormek's trust." He heard Kyala sucking in her breath, but did not look at her.

"Nobody speaks of him now," said Nedomin. "I'm too young to remember. The others prefer to forget."

Watnojat shuffled his feet, but kept his gaze on the proprietor. "I came to see the man, but I am not so disappointed to find him gone. I may still accomplish something, if I can find someone to lead me to his diggings. You know the people here. Will you help me find a guide?"

"Guide? As you can guess, few here would care to aid a glassmaker." The innkeeper's voice trailed off, as if he regretted his choice of words. "Though I would surely help you if I could," he added hurriedly.

"I have never harmed a person with my art," Watnojat said in a rising tone. "I need to make talismans against Lame Ones. I have no other purpose."

Nedomin shook his head. "I thought the Lame Ones were long dead."

"They are not. Surely someone in this region can guide an old man on his last journey. For Ormek's sake if for no other. And I will pay well."

The innkeeper cupped his chin in his hand. "A difficult request." His eyes closed and his brow furrowed, as if he were chasing an elusive recollection. "Let me think on it, Tem Vigen. In the meanwhile, let me offer what hospitality we have."

# Chapter 7

In the tavern the travelers were seated as usual, with their faces toward the wall. Nedomin hurried off, leaving them to the care of his serving boys.

"So it is true, Uncle," Kyala said when they finally were alone. "There have been bad Vigens."

Watnojat shifted his weight on the hard bench, trying to relieve a tender spot that had developed. "Untmur. Perhaps he was one. But thanks to Ormek, he no longer threatens the villages."

"Tell me about Untmur."

"I have told you about Hestafos. You need hear no more."

"Hestafos is a legend. But you came to *look* for Untmur."

"I thought . . . I thought he might have astablak. That is the only reason I came. He had many men working for him, men who had lost their wills. With all those helpers, he may have found rich sources."

"But he's gone, Uncle."

"He may be gone," Watnojat answered in a low voice. "The diggings remain. Perhaps in his leavings we can find the pigment we need." He motioned her to silence as the serving boy dropped a platter of scrawny fowl onto the table.

Nedomin's establishment, they quickly learned, offered drafty rooms, lumpy mattresses of straw, and meals that were barely palatable. But the travelers did not expect to stay long. The next day, while they waited for the proprietor to make his inquiries, Watnojat used the free time to instruct Kyala in selecting kilnwood. They saddled two ponies and rode through the surrounding stands of fir and oak, ash and birch. Here she could see for herself how the six grades of wood were found. Watnojat expounded at length on curing and splitting, until he felt that Kyala would listen to no more. Then they rode quietly awhile, enjoying the sight of the first green shoots emerging from mud.

"What if no one will help us, Uncle?" she asked. At the top of a low rise he halted his mount. Kyala stopped beside him. Below the buildings of the town cast shadows eastward.

"Then we'll continue toward the Teeth," he said in a discouraged tone. "We'll trade for a wagon and leave the sledge behind. The snows will be gone soon."

"And how long a journey to the Teeth of Dawn?"

"Better not to think about it, Kyala," he said with a shake of his head. "But I know of no unexplored mountains between here and that range. It will be far better if the Winterkills give us our astablak."

The afternoon was waning by the time they reached the barn. They spent some time there, brushing all four of the ponies, checking their feet, and making sure that the animals were properly fed. Then the glassmaker and his assistant plodded through the muddy yard to see if Nedomin had found them a guide.

They located the innkeeper at the doorway to the kitchen. He was joking with a wash girl, tossing one of her soiled cloths into the air and then snatching it back before she could catch it. "Ah, Tem Watnojat," he said, his expression quickly becoming solemn as he turned to the Vigen and lowered his eyelids. "Everyone within a half day's journey knows of your needs by now. I'm afraid there's only one man who might help you."

"One will do."

"His name is Stort. He . . . has a reputation for trouble-making."

"Does he know the mountains?"

"That he does, and more. He was acquainted with the man you asked about." Nedomin put a finger to his lips before Watnojat could blurt out the Vigen's name.

"Then I must speak to him."

"You'll have your chance. I sent word for him to come here tonight. But be cautious what you promise him. He's slippery as a sausage." Nedomin turned back to the kitchen girl. Watnojat, feeling a thirst after the long afternoon's ride, went off to enjoy some ale while sitting by the large stone fireplace of the tavern. *Stort,* he thought as he watched the flames. *Now I'll meet someone who can tell me the truth about Untmur.*

Evening arrived, and Kyala sat with Watnojat at their usual place in the corner of the room. The meal was a stew of unfamiliar meats. The glassmaker ate sparingly of the gamy dish, and Kyala sated her hunger with the inn's coarse barley bread. All the while they were eating, the conversation of the other patrons was a steady murmur in Watnojat's ear. Only when the sound dropped off suddenly did he turn his head in curiosity.

A large man wearing bearskin breeches and a jacket of gray wolf was walking toward the glassmaker. His face appeared misshapen, and as he drew closer Watnojat saw the bare patch above his jaw—a mass of scars where no beard grew. His nose looked as if it had been split in two and carelessly put back together.

"Vigen," the stranger said in a loud voice, planting one of his soiled boots on the glassmaker's bench. The reek of manure was strong, but Watnojat tried to ignore the man's offense. Surprisingly, the newcomer did not hide his features. He stared directly into the Vigen's eyes. "I'm Stort," he said. "If you're going to the mountains, I c'n take you."

"Sit down," said the Vigen.

"No time for chat. Come now if you're goin'." He glanced at Kyala. "That one too. And bring all y'r gear."

"What about terms?"

"*My* terms, or no guide. Well?"

"I can't work that way," Watnojat said, holding back his anger.

"Got no choice." Suddenly Stort picked up the uneaten bowl of stew. He tipped back his head and with his fingers began to shove the food into his mouth. When he was finished, he tore off a chunk of bread and sopped up the gravy from his lips and beard. "You've got t' come with me," he said after gulping down the crust. "Nobody else'll take ya. Why? Look here. Nobody else has one of these."

He reached behind his neck and pulled at a tether, bringing out a talisman pierced by a copper strand. It was a Vigen's bead, and though the light was poor, Watnojat was certain that it matched Stort's eyes. Why else would he display such confidence?

"As long as I've got this, you can't hex me," Stort said with a grin, swinging the gray orb back and forth in front of the glassmaker's face. "Now what do you say?"

"I need to find astablak. For Lame Ones' eyes. If you can show me where to dig, I'll pay you in hunters' beads— bear, deer, marten. Whatever you want."

"Beads? Do I need beads?" Stort laughed as he pulled a much-creased pouch from his belt. He spilled out the contents. The Vigen drew in a long breath when he saw what the stranger carried.

"Weasel . . . fox . . . ermine . . ." Stort called off the names of the talismans as he turned each one over with his thick, greasy fingers.

*So many!* "What do you need, then? Silver?"

Stort laughed again. "You can pay me, Vigen, but not with metal. Come with me and I'll show ya." He scooped up his talismans and poured them back into his pouch of unfamiliar leather.

Watnojat looked at Kyala's scowl and then back at Stort's mangled face. "Tell me how you came by your beads, and then I'll decide," said the Vigen.

"Untmur!" Stort spoke the word as an epithet.

The glassmaker rubbed his nose. "Nedomin said you knew him."

*"Knew* 'im?" Stort smirked. "I was his 'prentice. 'Til I broke his arm for beatin' me."

"Those beads are your work?" Watnojat already knew the answer as he looked at the hunter's leer. *Stolen from his master.*

"Vigen, do I carry you out of here?"

"Can you carry the two of us?" said Kyala. "Watch out for me. I have sharp teeth." She hooked a finger at each side of her mouth and pulled back her lips.

Stort laughed at the display, but suddenly his face became grim. "I'm wastin' time with your chatter while someone's dyin'."

"Stort, explain yourself." Watnojat touched Kyala's arm to quiet her. She dropped her hands and stared up at the hunter.

"Herb-healer needs help," the tall man continued, this time in a tone more of pleading than of demanding. "You know what I'm askin'. I need a Vigen."

The glassmaker nodded. He understood now why the man had not stated his price. "There are those who believe what you ask is against Ormek's will," Watnojat said. "There are those who would fear the consequences."

Stort started to grin again, but his expression quickly fell back to one of concern. He chewed at his lower lip. "And you?"

"I've aided healers more than once, but I do so with caution. So far as I know I've not offended the Lifegiver."

"Then what are we arguin' about?" Stort stamped his boots impatiently.

"I won't give my answer until I've seen the sick one," Watnojat said. He turned to his apprentice. "Come Kyala," he added quietly. "This man's request is fair, despite his manners. Let us see whether we can do anything for him."

A gibbous moon lit their way over a track of ice-covered mud and frozen slush. The grays strained as they pulled the sledge over the difficult course, and Watnojat regretted that he had not already made arrangements for a wagon. Stort rode impatiently ahead of them, often advancing out of sight, then doubling back to see why the sledge was so slow. He led them through a birch forest and past a lake that gleamed softly in the moonlight. Above the lake stood a squat cabin; Watnojat could discern only its blocky outline.

"You can build y'r kiln in the fireplace," said Stort, leaping up onto the sledge as soon as they halted. "I'll help with the stones."

"Not yet," said the Vigen. "I won't waste my glass if there's no hope of a cure." He told Kyala to follow him and stepped down onto the slippery ground in front of the cabin. He leaned on the door and it opened slowly. The odor of hides made him gasp as he entered the dimly lit room. To the side lay an untidy pile of skins; from the smell he guessed that many were fresh.

In the corner by the fireplace sat a woman whose long hair was braided into many thin skeins. She faced sideways, showing the Vigen a snub-nosed profile, a receding chin, lips firmly set. In her hands was a bowl, and as Watnojat approached her he saw a dark, pasty substance within. She stirred the contents slowly, chanting in a sing-song voice that formed no words. By her side, under a dozen hanging Ormek disks, lay a man on a thin pallet, his slender body covered with fur rugs.

"Herb-healer, how much time do you need?"

The woman turned her head slowly, and did not speak at once. "Y-y-you're the Vigen?" Her voice sounded like a young woman's though her face bore the wrinkles of middle age.

"Watnojat, of Darst. I'll try to hold his spirit here, if you tell me you can cure him."

"I-I-I." She lifted the spoon and touched it to the man's lips, which were already smeared with black. "I th-think two days. If y-you can hold him that long . . ."

"Two? Are you certain he can be helped?"

"If the f-fever breaks, he-he'll live."

Watnojat grunted, picked up a lamp, and knelt by the bed. The man had a roundish face. The bare patch in the center of his scalp was ringed with white hair. An old scar ran across his forehead to his ear. Gently the Vigen pulled back an eyelid. "Kyala! We must match this in lamplight, no easy task." The girl bent over to scrutinize the sick man's eye of storm-cloud gray.

"Then you will do it, Uncle?"

"I will at least try to call him. But first we must cast the bead. Study the color."

He turned to see Stort leaning in at the doorway, bending to keep his head below the lintel. "Are you ready to move stones, Vigen?" the hunter asked.

Watnojat nodded. The kiln must be brought inside. He rose from the bedside to examine the hearth, to find the best place to set up the stones. With his boot he pushed aside some sooty pots from the edge of the hearth, making a clatter of metal against stone. "Here," he said. "We'll build it at the side." He followed the big man to the sledge.

With Kyala's help, they carried in the blocks and quickly arranged them so that the kiln could vent into the chimney. Stort brought in the chest of vials and the Vigen undid his interlaced belts.

It was time to select colors. Watnojat set his mixing board on a crude table and called for light. Soon several lamps ringed his workplace beside the hearth, casting an unreliable light onto the mixing board. He held up one vial after another, finally choosing only three to be opened. "This batch is as old as you are, Kyala," he said as he poured out a small mound of crushed gray glass. "A nice shade, but not dark enough. He opened the other two vials and added a pinch from each to his mound.

When he was done mixing, he carried lamps back to the pallet and let Kyala check his work, first peering at the sick one's eye and then at the makings of the talisman. At her urging he added a touch more of shadowglass. He poured the powders into a mold, then dropped in the pupil.

"Stort, have you forgotten your training?" said Watnojat as he pumped his bellows a few times to check its action. The rush of air blew dead ashes about the base of the hearthstones.

"You have a 'prentice," Stort grumbled.

"I thought you might want a hand in the making. It's all the same to me."

Kyala began to load the kiln with wood from the hearth's pile. She pulled a brand from the fire; the kiln's fuel began to crackle and burn.

"Kyala..." Watnojat offered her the bellows, but Stort stepped in front of her and took the handles. She bent to close up the stones, and Stort leaned down to pump. The rush of air was a comforting sound in Watnojat's ears.

"This is why I quit Untmur," said the hunter after a short time. "I never liked pumping."

"I thought he threw you out," said the Vigen.

*"Him* get rid of *me?"* Stort grinned. "Breakin' his arm was easy. I could've done worse to him. Should've." Then he looked at Kyala. "Here, you do this awhile." He straightened up and flexed his shoulders while the girl took his place at the kiln.

"You haven't mentioned what finally happened to Untmur," said Watnojat cautiously.

"He's far from here. In Vanikval." The hunter spoke the name with disgust, as if the sound made a bad taste in his mouth.

Watnojat's head jerked with surprise. "Then he's not dead?"

"Not likely."

"I've never heard of Vanikval," said the glassmaker.

"To the northeast. Above the Footprint. You don't wanna go there."

Watnojat had stared at his maps for so long that he could see the markings in memory. The region mentioned was an empty space, totally unknown to him. "And does he practice his art there?"

"Does a rat hone his teeth?"

The hunter's smile made Watnojat uneasy and he put the matter aside for the moment. "Tell me something else, Stort. You claim to know these mountains. You must have gone digging with Untmur?"

"More than once."

"Then you may be able to repay my services."

The hunter shrugged in the direction of the pallet. "If this man lives, Vigen. Otherwise..."

The glassmaker nodded agreement. So long as there was hope, he felt obliged to make the attempt. Even if the man was lost, Kyala would learn something of this aspect of the craft. He turned his attention to the herb-healer, whose expression remained fixed. She stared straight ahead at the wall while she chanted softly to the dying man.

"His name is Lemp," said the hunter. "You'll need that."

"Lemp." Watnojat settled into his chair to wait. "You can relieve my apprentice if you wish," he told Stort. "I'm going to close my eyes until the wood burns down."

But the Vigen did not sleep. He listened to the hiss of the bellows as Kyala worked. About him he felt the presence of the cabin, its aged musty logs, its cache of pelts, the herb-healer with her resigned face. A sense of death surrounded him, and only the girl at the kiln stood in opposition to that feeling. Perhaps Ormek had decided Lemp's fate, and the Vigen was wrongly interfering.

"Uncle."

It was time to add more wood. The glassmaker opened his eyes and saw Stort, wielding a poker, pushing away the stones that sealed the grate. He watched as the big man quickly restocked the fire, then closed up the kiln. "Well done, Stort," said the Vigen. "Your master taught you a few things."

"And some you wouldn't want t' hear."

"Tell me about Lemp. I'll need more than his name."

"Lemp?" While Kyala continued to pump, Stort pulled a rickety bench toward the Vigen and sat down with his long legs stretched before the fire. "He's a cat hunter. Big ones. Snow cats. Two days ago he got jumped. Clawed."

"He's your kin?"

"Half-brother."

"Then tell me what he likes best in this world."

Stort laughed. "That's easy. Burnt apples."

"Apples!"

"Toasts 'em on a stick over the fire."

"No woman?"

"Lemp? Nah. Not anymore."

"Burnt apples, then." The Vigen closed his eyes once more and waited for the bead to fuse. He tried to focus on Lemp, to imagine him stalking the dangerous white creatures, but his thoughts drifted.

"His breathing's shallower." The herb-healer's voice startled the Vigen. For a moment he puzzled over the time that had passed. Was the bead ready? It was needed at once. He stood up groggily and took the poker from Stort's hand.

"It'll have to cool in a hurry," said Watnojat. He knocked away stones and was relieved to see that the melting was complete. Heedless of the damage he was doing to the glass, he knocked away more stones so that the heat could escape quickly. "This bead need not last a lifetime," he said. "You may rest now, Kyala," he added, noting the vague expression in her eyes and the sagging of her cheeks. She shuffled toward the nearest pile of straw and dropped into the crude bed.

"We've worn out my apprentice for this and used up valuable powders," said the Vigen. "I hope we'll have something to show for it." He reached into the opened kiln with tongs. The talisman adhered briefly to the mold and then came free. "Have you a heavy cloth?" he asked Stort.

The hunter rummaged about the hearth and picked up a sooty scrap that might have been bear hide. "Pot rag," he said, holding out the skin to take the hot glass.

"At least knock some of the ashes off," said the Vigen, still holding the talisman at the end of the tongs.

Stort grumbled, then slapped the pelt a few times against the stones of the chimney. Watnojat coughed as a small cloud of ash erupted. He turned his face away and nearly dropped the bead.

"This is good enough," said Stort.

The Vigen let the bead fall into the cloth, then carried it to the bedside and sat down at the edge of the pallet. A scent of burnt hair rose from the old pelt. He licked his thumb, touched it briefly to the glass, and heard the sizzling of his spittle.

*Kyala should watch this,* he thought. He glanced at where she lay motionless. "Stort, I'll need my apprentice."

The hunter lifted her, still sleeping, from the straw and dropped her roughly at the Vigen's feet. She cried out once, then opened her eyes and slowly pushed herself up from the floor.

"Kyala, you must listen while I work." The Vigen turned back to Stort. "Have you an apple? It might help." The hunter aimed a careless kick at the woodpile. "Ya need two 'prentices f'r all y'r errands," he grumbled. At last he stomped over to a barrel that sat in the corner.

"Lemp..." The glassmaker closed his eyes and began to call the wounded man. He tired to imagine him in his prime, riding up the high trails to the lairs of the great cats. He pictured a snow-white pelt drying by a fire, and the satisfied face of the man who had brought it home. "Lemp, stay with us this night," said Watnojat. "We've a cure for you. The herb-healer waits by your side."

He continued in this way, ignoring the footsteps of Stort on the rickety floor. "Lemp, we are waiting," he said, and then he blew his breath across the talisman. "Speak to me. Speak with your inner voice."

At first he heard only a soft hiss, then what sounded like a faint cry. "Louder, Lemp. You can make words if you try." The sound grew in the Vigen's ear. "Better, Lemp. That is better."

A high-pitched voice, thin, broken: "You... Who are you?"

"The Vigen of Darst. Brought here by Stort to help the healer."

"A Vigen. No. No. Away from me."

"Don't confuse me with Untmur. I've come to help you."

"Help? Help me? No. Too late. The fever."

"Take the herb-healer's food. Take it, Lemp. She says you can live."

"Ormek... Ormek calls."

"Open your lips, Lemp. You are not yet gone."

"Leave me, Vigen." The voice trailed off to a faint whisper: "Leave me..."

Watnojat opened his eyes. He looked up into Stort's twisted face. "He's afraid," said the glassmaker. "Let him rest awhile before I try again." He sent Kyala back to her makeshift bed and found some furs to rest on.

"Healer wants ya," said Stort, shaking the Vigen roughly. He had dozed. Groggily he stood up and walked toward the bed. Kyala sat cross-legged on the floor beside the healer.

The woman's ear was at Lemp's chest, her braids dangling over the edge of the pallet. "H-Heart. I-I can barely hear it."

Again the Vigen tried the talisman. He warmed it in his mouth, then tried to call the feverish hunter. This time he could get no answer at all. Had the man already passed to Ormek's realm? Watnojat shook his head. If Lemp was lost, there would be no help in Wintersgate, no chance for searching these mountains. He looked up at Stort's scowl. There was one thing more he might try.

Watnojat took the knife from his belt and pricked his thumb, dripping blood onto the glass as if he were calling a spirit. *Ormek, forgive me if I wrong you,* he thought. "Lemp," the Vigen called again. "Lemp, tell me. Where are you bound?"

A faint sound. At last, a response.

"Louder. Speak to me."

"Ormek . . . Ormek calls."

"Stay with us, Lemp."

"I . . . I." The voice faded. The glassmaker squeezed more blood onto the bead.

"Vigen, you set yourself against Him."

"Are you certain you're ready? You can still choose."

"I . . ."

"Have you forgotten the feel of a well-balanced spear? Have you lost the thrill of the chase?"

"Vigen . . ."

"Stay with us one more night. I ask this only for your brother."

"Stort . . . Stort . . . The toad-eater! I owe him something." Silence.

"What you owe, you'll need life to repay."

"What I owe the . . . scar-face he . . . won't want."

"Open your mouth, Lemp. Take the healer's food."

The Vigen raised his eyelids and watched Lemp's mouth. Was there movement? His lips seemed to part slightly and his tongue pushed forward. "Roast the apple," said the Vigen to Stort, without taking his eyes from the sick man's face.

"Thirsty. Thirsty," said Lemp's voice.

"He needs water," Watnojat said. There was a sound of shuffling and then the woman brought a dipper to Lemp's mouth.

"If you thirst, then drink," the glassmaker said.

"Can't. I can't."

"Open your lips."

"Vigen. Leave me. I'm done."

"Lemp, you must drink," he said. "Your flesh has its own will."

"Vigen . . . ah." His lips parted just a bit. The woman lifted Lemp's head, then poured a bit of water into his mouth. The blankets fell back, revealing the stained bandages about his shoulder and arm.

"Swallow, Lemp, swallow."

The muscles of his throat worked. The herb-healer tilted the dipper.

# Chapter 8

By dawn the sick man seemed slightly improved and the herb-healer left his side. Everyone needed rest. They stacked furs for mattresses and covered themselves with other skins. Watnojat lay on his back and was asleep at once.

When he awoke, the fire had burned down to embers and only light through the walls' chinks told him that it was daytime. The Vigen was hungry, and the others were still sleeping. "Kyala," he called in a loud whisper. "Kyala, will you dream 'til evening?" Hearing no reply, he pulled on his boots and shuffled toward the door.

After the gloom, the daylight was blinding. He closed his eyes, then opened them slowly. The sledge stood where he had left it. The grays, tethered before an emptied trough, looked at him expectantly and bobbed their heads. "Be patient, my ponies," he said. Then he climbed onto the sledge to see what he could find for his breakfast.

During the journey from Darst he had reacquainted himself with the basics of cookery. Not since serving Reslunin had he handled domestic matters, but Kyala barely knew how to scrub out a pot. By now he could readily take care of himself. He found a large bowl and dipped it into the sack of ground barley. *Take enough for four,* he thought, as he sized the amount in the bowl. *Or maybe five.* Behind him he heard the scraping of the cabin door.

"Uncle!"

"Kyala, it's time to make some porridge." He saw his sleepy-faced assistant shielding her eyes against the midday glare.

"How's Lemp, Uncle? I was so tired at the end that I don't remember."

"He was improving. Now take this bowl. I've got to see to the ponies."

Behind the cabin, he found a stable of sorts—a roof that jutted out from the dwelling's wall. He led the grays under the shelter and tethered each to a separate ring. "Kyala?" He heard what sounded like the creak of a windlass. At the cabin's side he found her struggling with an oversized well bucket.

"Let me help with that," said the Vigen. But before he reached her the iron-hooped pail slipped out of her grasp, and half the water spilled onto the ground. The rest splashed into a split-log sluice that led toward the stable's trough. Kyala's cooking pot was empty.

"It's too heavy," said Watnojat. "If the pail's not so full, it will be easier to handle."

"Yes, Uncle," she said irritably. She managed, on the second try, to half-fill the bucket and after that the pouring went better. She brought the cooking pot inside while Watnojat carried straw to the ponies from the sledge.

The others woke up by the time the pot was bubbling. The herb-healer shared their porridge, but Stort would not touch it. "Give mine to Lemp," he said with a laugh. Then he brought down a haunch of cured venison that hung from the rafters, sliced off a chunk with his bone-handled knife, and began to chew.

"W-We must feed Lemp again s-soon," said the herb-healer. The firelight played on her features, emphasizing the puffiness beneath her eyes. She showed no fear of the Vigen's gaze. "I-I have other medicines for him."

She squatted to rummage through the contents of a large hide sack, then brought out red clay jars with wooden stoppers. The sides of the unglazed jars were grooved with circles and crosses, symbols that the Vigen had seen often but could not interpret. The woman poured out a pinch of coarse dark powder into her bowl, then added porridge and stirred the mixture. "H-Have you the tal-talisman?" she asked Watnojat.

The Vigen nodded, then returned to his place by Lemp's head. He took the bead from his pouch and heated it in his palm. "Lemp, you are recovering," he said softly. "Now you must take food."

The man's breathing remained slow and regular. The Vigen heard no answering voice.

"Lemp, it is time to awaken." Then he turned to Kyala. "Where's the rest of that apple?" She brought the roasted fruit still impaled on its stick. "Cut me a slice," said the Vigen. He rubbed the juice over the talisman, as he had done several times during the night. "Lemp, do you hear me?"

The quiet whisper came. "Vigen . . . Vigen. I had dreams."

"Of fine hunting?"

"Of Ormek. He waits."

"Ormek is patient."

"He . . . calls."

"Lemp, we have something for you to eat. Open your lips."

The herb-healer raised the man's head. For the first time since the Vigen's arrival, Lemp's eyelids rose of their own accord. The sick one's lips trembled. "See this," said Watnojat, holding up the talisman. "It is yours. When I'm finished here, do what you want with it."

Lemp tried to speak, but no sounds came into the room. In Watnojat's ear, the voice whispered, "Don't hex me, Vigen."

"It is poorly cured," said the glassmaker, turning the talisman. "Tap it with a rock, if you wish, and make dust of it."

The herb-healer brought a spoon to Lemp's lips. He hesitated, his eyes moving from the bead to the Vigen's face and then returning to the glass. Watnojat could guess his thoughts: *Do I eat from hunger or because of this talisman?* At last, his questions unsettled, Lemp began to swallow the porridge.

Later, while the sick man rested, the Vigen left the cabin with Kyala. The sun was low and the forest unfamiliar, but the glassmaker had spent too much time in the close air of the dwelling and his head was hurting. They began to follow a muddy path that circled the lake. The surface had melted, and shallow puddles of water covered much of the ice.

"Uncle, tell me this," Kyala said as she followed him through a birch grove. "When Father was sick, your bead couldn't help him. Yet here—"

The Vigen shook his head. "There was nothing I could do for your father. He resisted my every call. Even had I wanted to risk Ormek's wrath, I could not have held him."

"And Lemp?"

"Lemp showed some hope from the start. I spoke and he answered. Even so, I may have been wrong in what I did last night. A Vigen must be cautious in meddling with a healer's work. Each case must be judged."

"Judged how?"

"I listen to the inner voice. There's a pull in each direction. If the person's drive to Ormek is strong, I cannot hold the spirit. I must release it." Lemp would have gone to Ormek gladly, Watnojat thought. But he did not want to burden her with his own doubts.

"Ah, it's fine to be wise, Uncle." Kyala leaned over the lake and pulled at a twig that was still frozen into the deep ice. "I don't know when I'll have such wisdom. How will I learn the difference between harm and good? I don't even know how much water to put in a bucket." The twig broke off and she toppled backward. Watnojat reached down and caught her before she fell.

"Uncle!" she cried, more angry than grateful as she regained her balance. "You're always here to hold me up. How can I learn from my mistakes? How can I think for myself if you always give me the answers?" She pulled away from him and ran into the woods that edged the lake. He heard branches snapping as she made her way alone back toward the cabin.

Watnojat smiled; she was still the old Kyala at times. Like a filly too long in the stall, he thought. *Let her run.* He rounded the lake just as the sun fell below the treetops.

"Vigen!" Stort was standing by the cabin door. "Healer wants ya."

The glassmaker did not see his apprentice inside as he approached the bed. The healer sat holding a bowl, her spoon raised. Lemp's eyes remained closed. "He n-needs to eat," the woman said without turning her head. "He pays me n-no heed."

Sighing, the Vigen took out the gray talisman and warmed it with his breath. Rousing Lemp's voice was easier this time.

"I'm weary, Vigen," came the response. "Don't you give a man rest?"

They argued a bit, and some coaxing was needed before Lemp complied. There was no more talk of Ormek. Nonetheless, Watnojat held the bead in his palm until the man ate and drank. All the while he fretted about Kyala's absence, but his obligation was first with the sick one.

Stort was in a corner, whittling on a stave as thick as his arm. "Your 'prentice?" he answered, when the Vigen questioned him. "Don't know. Didn't come back."

Free from his duties at last, Watnojat picked up a lamp and hurried outside. "Kyala!" Twilight was past and the moon had not yet risen. By now she could be lost in the forest. How would she find her way through blackness? He pushed as far as he could into the woods without losing sight of the cabin. Visions of snow cats prowling at the edge of the lake tormented him. *Did they hunt so close to the villages?* he wondered. "Kyala!" he called again.

He circled the cabin and found nothing. At last he went back for Stort. "I need help," he said. "Someone to search with me." The hunter kept whittling at his staff.

"Never heard of a girl 'prentice," he answered grumpily. "Y'r better off if ya lose 'er."

The glassmaker crossed the floor and pulled the stave from Stort's hands. "I'll use this for a torch. And when I bring it back, I'll scrub your teeth with it."

Stort grumbled, but made no try to retrieve his staff. "Got torches over there," he said, nodding his head. "This stick's too green."

"Too green?" The Vigen rapped his fist against the wall over Stort's head. "These logs are dry enough. If I set the cabin afire, she'll find her way back."

Stort showed no alarm over the threat. His head turned suddenly as he hearkened to rustling sounds by the door. "There's your slut!"

The Vigen dropped the stave and faced his returning apprentice. She was dragging balsam boughs through the narrow doorway. "The old hides stink in here," she said casually, as if she had just come back from the well. "These'll help."

"Kyala, you should be beaten for running off. These woods..." But he did not let her see his tears. He crawled under the furs on his makeshift bed and lay there, face to the wall, while she and the herb-healer rattled pots at the hearth. *She wants to make her own mistakes,* he thought ruefully. *And for that, I must risk losing her.*

By the following noon, Lemp was sitting up and feeding himself. Stort took the healer back to wherever he had found her and did not return. Kyala went out to care for the ponies while the glassmaker sat restlessly on a bench and watched Lemp.

*Have I angered Ormek for this man?* he wondered again. He had done more than was right. He had called back one who was almost in the Lifegiver's lap.

Lemp put down his spoon and stared at the Vigen. "What did Stort promise ye? Whatever, y' won't get it. I'll be left to pay."

"We need a guide into the mountains. To look for minerals. Stort says he went digging with Untmur."

"Untmur? Pah! Thirty summers past. How much can he remember?" Lemp shook his head while he stirred the gruel in his bowl. "From the start I told 'im t' stay away from that Vigen."

"You must know the trails."

"Better than Stort." He tapped his shoulder where the lumpy dressings lay beneath the cloths. "Where the cats hunt, I follow. Places where they got no trails. And I can show you some of Untmur's mines, though I heard they're all worked out."

"What I'm looking for isn't found deep in the earth. The minerals weather on the rock faces and wash down into the meadows. Have you seen a tiny red flower on a thin stalk? The Maiden's Kiss, we call it. It blooms early in the spring, just about now. The flower closes at dusk and the whole droops 'til dawn." Watnojat traced in the air with a bent finger the wilting of the flower.

Lemp smiled. "I think I know y'r bloom. We used t' pluck and dry 'em. Brought 'em back and made a kind of tea. Such a drink!" He winked. "That was the way to get *more* than a kiss."

The Vigen leaned forward. "You *do* know the flower."

"When Stort was a young 'un—still suckin' at Ma's teat—I used to go huntin' the Kiss. All the boys went."

"That plant grows only near deposits of astablak. Can you find me the flowers?"

Lemp laughed. "They were gone before Stort got any good out of 'em."

"Flowers gone. Does that mean Untmur dug up all the astablak?"

"Maybe we picked too many flowers." Lemp grinned.

Watnojat did not smile. "I'll go there anyway. If you can find the place. Over the years a bit more might have washed down."

The old hunter leaned his head back against the log wall. "The trails are changed. Trees grown up in places that were meadows. Woods burned out by lightning. It's not the same as it was."

"But can you find it?" The glassmaker approached the bed.

"Vigen!" Suddenly the man brought up his hand in fright.

"Do you think I still want to hex you?" Watnojat pulled the gray talisman from his pouch. "Here. Take this if you don't trust me. Now you're as safe as Stort."

Lemp grabbed the bead and squeezed it tightly in one hand. "You brought me back with this?" He stared at the piece of glass, his lips curled in disbelief.

"That, and a roasted apple. And some blood from my thumb." The Vigen held up the scarred finger, still paining a bit from the cuts.

"After Untmur, I thought Vigens were no better'n pit demons."

"Untmur's not one of us. If I believe the tales, then he has no right to call himself Vigen."

"I've seen his trickery for myself. When Stort was a pup. Whatever ya heard is likely so."

"Tell me. From your own experiences."

"Ha. I'll give ya just one. I knew a prankster lad. Would put a balsam crown on a pony or toss a dead rat in front of a lady walkin' in town. Once the lad pranked Untmur. Smeared tar on his workshop windows. Those windows were the best sheets of glass a Vigen could make. Untmur cast a bead and told 'im to stand all night in the snow. You know how cold it gets in these hills. I found the lad in the morning—stiff as a tree."

"You make this man a living Hestafos."

"He was. Likely still is."

"Still is?" The thought troubled Watnojat. Somewhere a glassmaker still lived who abused his powers. But what could he do about such a demon? He sat down on the edge of the pallet. "At least he's far from here. And I've a problem of my own. Do you know the Lame Ones?"

Lemp smiled. "Tales for children."

"Near Darst, they survive. In the deep caves, north of Asep River. Sometimes they cross."

"Untmur used to say we needed 'im to keep the Lame Ones off. Never saw any, though."

"Maybe he did his job in that respect."

"Never saw a pelt or a claw of one."

"It's easier to chase the beasts away than to kill them."

"Never seen one. Not since Untmur left either. Twenty-five winters."

Watnojat could not keep the old memories from flooding back. "Lemp," he said quietly. "Believe me when I say they are real. They came into our village when I was a boy. I still dream of those days, and I wake up trembling. But we were safe in Darst after the old Vigen came. The beasts stayed on the far side of the river. Now they've attacked a man—my friend. I saw his face. I watched the pyre take what was left of him. That's why I need the astablak."

Lemp's voice was hoarse. "I won't dispute you, Vigen. For your sake, I'll search out the old places. I'll pay Stort's debt." He set the bowl down on the floor and closed his eyes. "Give me two days of rest. That's all."

The Vigen and Kyala made preparations. They packed his vials and laid the kiln stones in their places at the rear of the sledge. The two returned to the inn by moonlight as they had come, their runners crunching through the fresh ice of the roadways. In comparison with the cabin, Nedomin's establishment now seemed luxurious. The meat pies from his kitchen had somehow acquired a rich flavor. The tepid water in his bathhouse had turned steamy. And the straw beds were as soft as Balin's feather-stuffed mattresses.

Much of the Vigen's belongings they left in the innkeeper's care: the chest of vials, the ermine skins, and other valuables. Nedomin locked these in his storehouse, safe behind his casks of wine.

They returned with all four of the grays, riding two and leading two. One was loaded with shovels and picks, spears and provisions. The fourth would be Lemp's mount, since his own had been killed by the snow cat. The morning air was damp and cold as they reached the hunters' cabin.

Stort and Lemp were shouting at each other when the Vigen came through the door. Lemp was dressed for travel, his wolfskins laced up and his boots secured. Stort, as usual, was carelessly garbed, his coat open and his boots off.

"What do I need *you* f'r, skunk-ass?" Stort said. "You think I don't know the way?"

"You couldn't find a dead muskrat if I didn't point your nose at it," retorted Lemp.

"And you're nothin' but cats' meat."

"Enough!" said Watnojat. "My ears hurt from your bickering. I don't care if I have one guide or two." Looking at the men side by side, the Vigen could scarcely believe that they were kin. Lemp was notably shorter and thinner than his half-brother. His face was round, his nose small and bent. He bore no resemblance to Stort's blocky features.

"He should be stretched out on the mattress," Stort said, picking up a boot and waving it toward the bed. "He's in no shape t' ride." He began to pull the leather over his foot.

"Better shape than you, scarface. I *slept* for two nights. How much rest did *she* give ya?"

Stort grinned. "She has herbs you'd like t' try. You won't get the chance, geezer."

"Wait'll *you* get clawed!"

At last Stort stomped out to ready his mount, a thick-necked pony of mountain breed. Watnojat helped load the lumpy sacks of gear onto the pack pony, and then they were ready to leave.

The mists began to clear as the followed a trail that rose above the lake. Stort led, always well ahead of the rest, taking risks with his roan on the narrow path. Lemp was next, followed by Kyala. The Vigen rose last, the pack pony behind him. All morning they climbed through scrubby forests and across ledges wet with melting snow. Kyala complained about hunger, but the mountaineers did not slow the pace. They continued into the afternoon, crossing a gap, then rising to a narrow plateau that held a small meadow.

Watnojat glanced around at the fresh grass sprouting between last year's dead stalks. In such a place he could always hope for astablak. Patches of snow still dotted the ground, but the Kiss was known to poke its head through melting drifts. Stort did not even look about. He crossed the meadow quickly and continued up another rocky trail.

Not until dusk did Stort halt at a shallow valley between two granite outcroppings. Watnojat was so stiff and sore that he could barely walk. He leaned against the pony and tried to flex his cramped legs. Behind him he heard Kyala groaning about her own pains and discomforts, but he could not turn his head to look at her.

The meal that evening was cold meat and biscuits. Later Lemp found enough dry wood to start a smoky fire. They chose watches by lighting slivers off pine. Lemp dropped his taper first and so, to Stort's amusement, took first watch. The shorter brother sucked his singed fingers moodily as he watched the Vigen and Kyala and then Stort let their tapers fall to the wet ground.

The next day was more of the same. At times, when trails diverged, Stort and Lemp would argue vigorously over the choice of direction; generally it was Stort who prevailed. Watnojat watched their indecision and lost hope of finding the places they once had known. But his own observations might prove useful. As they traveled he scanned the terrain for signs of minerals. He looked for tell-tale stains and odd patterns of vegetation. In midafternoon the Vigen shouted in surprise: "Diggings!" He turned from the main path toward a heap of broken rocks. Then he saw the remains of an old smelting pit.

Waving for Kyala to follow him, Watnojat dismounted and hastily tied his pony to a bush. Lemp rode up behind the Vigen but stayed on his mount. "This wasn't Untmur's," said the hunter.

"We must look away," Watnojat answered. Already he could see hints of blue on the pile of tailings. "There are minerals here, Kyala. Coppers. Look for yourself."

She rushed ahead and began to pick up small pieces of jagged rock.

"They pulled good metal out of these stones," said Watnojat, taking from her hand a piece that showed a streak of green. "Pot metal. But we'll get no use out of these. We call this one Vigen's curse. And this"—he showed her a powdery coating of blue—"this is demon sky. Some fools have been known to drag home a wagonload of it."

"Why fools, Uncle? Won't these color glass?"

"The best you can get from them is a muddy shade, useless for beads. These common ores are for smiths only." He tossed the stone back onto the heap.

"But how will I know the useful pigments?" She bent to study other fragments.

"There's one sure test. You try some in the kiln. But if you should ever find a large heap of any mineral, you can be sure you've got demon stones. The pigments that breed true colors only appear in small pockets."

Kyala looked down at the large heap of rocks. "Might there be small pockets among the others?"

"One can always hope." Watnojat began to circle the pile, watching for any signs of the glossy fragments that had ever been the object of his searches. He had often pored over mine dumps such as this one, sometimes with success.

But fresh diggings were best. Others had surely picked through these tailings.

"Let's ride!" shouted Stort. Watnojat ignored him and continued to study the loose stones. It was a good place for instructing Kyala, and so he lingered until he feared the hunters would ride off without them.

Stort led as they continued their journey. They came to a shaded side of the mountain where snow still lay heaped beside the trail. Watnojat saw something unexpected up ahead, dark patches against the white ground. Stort halted, and the others came up beside him. It was a moment before the Vigen recognized the scattered bones and torn furs of what once had been a hunter. Lemp dismounted and began to search through the scraps of clothing. Some of the remains were still snow buried. He poked about in the slush with a stick but did not find anything of interest. "No pouch," he said grumpily, kicking the jaw bone into the center of the trail.

The Vigen looked at the shredded garments and only wanted to know what beast had torn them. Stort seemed to follow his thoughts. "Cats," said the younger man. "Lurras. The same as got Lemp."

The Vigen shook his head. He had known mountain cats in other ranges, but never had seen such destruction. Evidently the creature had devoured every edible scrap. "Have you talismans against these lurras?" he asked Stort. "I don't know if mine will serve."

"We're safe." Stort pulled back his sleeve to reveal a string of beads wrapped about his forearm. Watnojat rode closer and bent to study the colors. "This one," said Stort, pointing to a golden-green eye.

That evening, while they camped beneath an overhanging ledge, they heard the coughs and grunts of the creatures. "They're huntin'," said Lemp, tightening his grip on a spear. "I could get one tonight. Get even for this." He touched his shoulder where the old wounds were healing. His voice quavered as he talked, and the Vigen doubted he was truly eager for another meeting with the beasts.

Kyala held a spear also, as did the others. All four weapons might be needed if a cat approached the camp. Stort's bead lay at the rim of the fire, within Watnojat's reach. He wondered if its strength would suffice. "Cats can be strong-willed," the Vigen told Kyala as Lemp fed the fire. "If the color is a shade off, they might get past the beads. And if they're as hungry as the ones who found that hunter..."

Lemp laughed nervously. "I've been doin' *without* beads f'r all this time. What do I care?"

The girl sat upright, her back against the stone, her spear pointing out toward the darkness.

"We'll get no rest this night," the Vigen said. He ran his thumb carefully over the spearhead, testing the sharpness of the barbs. *Arod's gift,* he thought. *Tonight you may taste flesh.*

The grunting grew louder. Lemp tossed another log onto the fire. The Vigen thought he saw something, squinted, then moved his head away from the fire. "There!" He picked up the talisman, dropped it, picked it up again. The beast was slinking toward them on its belly. Its head was huge; the two fangs glowed red in the firelight. "Out," he said, dangling the bead over the flames. "Go with the night, or die."

The beast held steady. It made no move to attack or to flee.

He lowered the glass closer to the flame. "Away!" said the Vigen. Then, seeing no reaction, he touched the bead directly to a hot coal.

The great cat hissed, but showed no signs of the pain that the heat should have caused. Then its bulk rose up, its body arched. Watnojat forgot the talisman.

The cat landed to the side, close to the ponies and well clear of the fire. The grays whinnied in panic. Watnojat saw Stort knocked down with a blow of the creature's paw. Lemp seemed frozen, his spear unused at his side. The Vigen stepped past him, aimed at the throat, and lunged with what strength he had. The lurra reared, dislodging the shaft from Watnojat's hand.

Stort recovered and attacked the cat from the side. He succeeded only in angering the beast, holding its attention as it clawed the air in search of his quick-moving weapon. Lemp recovered his wits and stepped into the fight, but his thrust merely took out an eye. Watnojat was helpless, his own spear still lodged in the creature's throat.

Then Kyala ran forward. Watnojat wanted to stop her, to pull the weapon from her grip and send her back to safety, but she was too quick for him. The cat snarled and reared up as Stort slashed and Lemp prodded. Kyala plunged in as the body began to fall again. The writhing cat landed on top of her, roaring, flashing its fangs. The Vigen still had no weapon. He rushed closer—the shaft was tossing about like a branch in the wind. He grasped the wood, but the point had gone deep and would not come free. The white fur was stained with gouts of the creature's blood. *She is lost!* He would not release the shaft though it nearly tore off his arm.

The lurra screamed and spat; its body shook in great spasms. Then the struggling ebbed and the creature sank to the ground. Only the limbs twitched as blood dribbled from the neck wound onto the slick ground. Watnojat could not understand. How had the beast been stopped?

"Kyala!" Stort and Lemp rolled the cat aside to free the girl. She was covered with blood, her unmoving face wet and shiny. "Kyala!" They carried her to the fire.

"Uncle . . . Uncle, I . . ."

Stort poured water on her face from a skin. The Vigen wiped her gently with his sleeve and saw no gashes. Quickly he unlaced her jacket, and when he pulled that open, there were no stains on the goatskins within. "Kyala, are you hurt?"

"Uncle, I—I think I killed it."

Watnojat glanced at the carcass and only then noticed the

rip in the belly from Kyala's spear. The blood on the girl was lurra blood. The Vigen probed gently for broken bones, but found none. "He'll . . . he'll make a good coat, Uncle," she said. "Let me look." Shakily she rose and went to kneel by the long body. Watnojat lifted the head to examine the remaining eye. He went back to the fire for a brand, then looked again under the brighter light. "Kyala, do you see this?" The girl came to his side as he gaped at the blue-green color. "I've never known such a shade in an animal's eye. No wonder the bead failed."

Stort looked at the eye, muttered something about Unt-mur, then stalked away. Lemp brought out his flaying knife. "Who needs talismans," he said. "Can't trust 'em anyway." Slit from neck to tail along the belly, the pelt stripped off smoothly. The hunter raised it in triumph, as if it were he, rather than Kyala, who had overcome the creature.

They built up the fire and began to roast the choicest parts. Lemp scooped out the brains and ate them uncooked. Stort, joking about roasted apples, toasted the lurra's "apples" on the end of a stick. "He won't need 'em," the big man said with his mouth full of meat. Watnojat took the tongue, broiled it slowly, then ate it in thin slices.

Kyala was offered the liver and the heart and sampled both. She passed the rest back to the men. Despite her seeming good spirits, Watnojat saw that she was still trembling. She rushed from the fire, and he heard her retching at the edge of camp.

The Vigen remained seated, wanting to go comfort her but forcing himself to stay. *Let her remember this night with its pain,* he thought. Kyala wanted to make her own choices. He must allow her that freedom, for soon she would be on her own. Perhaps Ormek would take special care of her. That was a hope. Perhaps, in her besting of the cat, the Bright One had given a sign.

# Chapter 9

In the morning Kyala seemed recovered from her encounter with the snow cat. She even aided Lemp with packing up the rest of the meat, balking only at helping him stuff the entrails into a small sack. All would keep in the chilly air, he said. They left the carcass behind, with enough left on it to attract a horde of scavengers.

Now that Lemp had revenged himself, he was as eager as the others to leave cat country. All morning the trail wound toward the lower elevations. They halted at a faint trail that crossed the main path. Lemp and Stort discussed the route and decided to take the narrower downhill track. At midday they reached another small meadow, this one on a mountainside that dropped gently to a long valley. The Vigen squinted as he scrutinized the dark cliffs above the meadow. Here was a place with promise.

Lemp waved at Watnojat and began to ride across the emerging grass, zigzagging as he scanned the ground. The Vigen turned loose the pack pony and urged his own gray to catch up with the hunter. "The Kiss?" he shouted, wondering if they had finally reached the place of Lemp's memories. "Have you found it?"

"This is the spot I knew," Lemp called back. "Maybe it's too early f'r the flowers. Maybe they never did come back after we picked 'em all."

*Or maybe Untmur was here.* "Do you recall where they grew thickest?" asked Watnojat.

Lemp continued downhill, approaching the sheer face of rock that rose at the edge of the meadow. The glassmaker looked about at the fresh greenery but saw nothing resembling the tall stems he sought.

"Here," said the hunter, halting by a rounded boulder that lay half buried in dirt. "We'd sit up here and look down on all those sweet red lips. Think about the real ones waitin' for us at home." But only grass now grew about the stone.

The Vigen, undaunted, rushed back to get Kyala and the equipment. There was once astablak here; that knowledge was enough to spur him on. They took down the shovels and began to turn over the brown soil, searching with great care for the elusive pockets of dark earth. Watnojat's arms ached from wrenching at the spear, and he could only dig slowly. Stort grew impatient and rode off, but Lemp seemed content to sit on his rock and watch. The sky cleared and the Vigen grew warm; he shed his heavy coat. *I am too old for such labor,* he thought, but he went back to the shovel anyway, ignoring the pain.

By the time they rested, the area all about the rock had been turned over. Kyala and Watnojat shared some of the cold charred lurra meat with Lemp, and drank thirstily from the skin of spring water. "I think Untmur knew about this place," Lemp said in a discouraged tone as he gazed out toward the digging. "Maybe he came here and took what y'r after."

Watnojat was not ready to quit. He rested after each swing of the shovel, wiping his brow frequently, but keeping at the work. Kyala showed no sign of tiring; methodically she dug up the ground, progressing along neat rows, paying special attention to the areas at the base of the cliff. Sometimes she would call the Vigen to inspect a dark lump of soil, but nothing she found resembled the gritty texture and intensely dark color of the mineral. Just before sundown she pulled a flat, rusted object from the ground. The glassmaker recognized it as a piece of broken shovel blade. "You're right, Lemp. Untmur's been here." The Vigen threw down his own shovel and staggered over to the sitting place.

Stort had not returned. The three made camp, and Lemp insisted on protecting the area by rubbing the cat entrails he'd saved over the surrounding rocks and bushes. The scent had ripened. "Uncle, I think every beast in the mountains must know a lurra died."

"That's for the best," said Lemp. "They won't bother us tonight."

Kyala rolled herself in blankets and was asleep before the stars emerged. The Vigen, weary as he was from digging, sat with Lemp while the cat's haunch roasted. "Is there no other place for astablak?" he asked. "Was this the only meadow?"

"One more place I remember, Vigen. And maybe Stort can find another one. If Untmur got those . . . Well, y'll just have to go to Untmur to get y'r astablak."

By morning Stort had returned. Watnojat saw a couple of fresh fox pelts dangling over his roan's rump. The younger hunter was growing impatient, already looking for diversions along the trail. Yet they had made no progress toward Watnojat's goal.

They left in search of the second meadow. Lemp took the lead, taking them up a streambed that ran through a narrow canyon. The water was running high from the snow melt, and the footing at the edge was slippery. The canyon narrowed until the rushing stream touched both rock walls.

Lemp rode through the gap. Watnojat glanced down to

see the water foaming about his mount's legs, and swirling around rocks and tree stumps that were covered by the flow. The roar grew, but still Lemp continued. Then they were looking up at a waterfall that sent spray like a rain squall into their faces. There was no way forward. The Vigen turned his gray at once, squeezed past the nervous pack pony, and slowly brought it around to follow him. Whatever was said between the brothers, the Vigen did not hear. But Stort took the lead for the rest of that day and well into the next.

At last they came to what was thought to be another place for astablak. Here they dug also, turning up the ground for an entire afternoon. Kyala worked with unflagging energy, but soon Watnojat found his arms too heavy to lift the shovel. He could only follow her about, looking at any promising handfuls of earth she chose to show him.

There was nothing in that place.

At the Vigen's insistence they continued the search, exploring other meadows, places that the hunters did not recognize. Nowhere did they see the Kiss. Higher and higher they climbed until snows choked the trails and sent them back to lower elevations. Along the way they saw numerous promising cliffs. Watnojat and Kyala spent many a morning walking along a rocky base, scanning for dark stains or for the elusive flower. Each day the glassmaker felt more weary, but he was not willing to concede these mountains. "Surely there must be a trace of the mineral somewhere," he said.

But as the days passed, Kyala became despondent. "Uncle, I think there is nothing here," she told him while they stood at a ledge and gazed over the sweep of valley below. Stort had vanished again, perhaps not to return at all, and even Lemp was losing interest in their search. Watnojat looked down at the fresh green of the distant fields. The earth was renewing itself, but his own life was dry and brittle and ready for the flames. He would never have the strength for another journey such as this one. "Kyala, you are my hope," he said. "You will be Vigen after me. You will find astablak as I could not."

"Uncle, there will be other places," she said.

"You are still young enough to find them."

Watnojat turned and asked Lemp to guide them back to Wintersgate. They rode endlessly, the Vigen weak and sore, Kyala moody. Only Lemp's spirits seemed high. Perhaps he was merely happy to be alive.

Where would they go next? The Teeth of Dawn were too distant, too steep, too wild. All the unexplored regions seemed hopelessly out of reach. But to Vanikval, to Untmur's present home—that was a journey even an old Vigen might make. He had set out to see Untmur; he had found only his shovel blade. But the man and his ill-gotten pigments might still be located.

# Chapter 10

The washhouse smelled of soap and damp wood. Kyala dipped a tattered cloth into the lukewarm water of the bucket, then wiped her face.

"Come a long way, have ya?" Beside her a plump woman knelt at a wooden basin, rubbing clothes against a ridged board set into the water.

"From Wintersgate," Kyala answered. "And before that..." She paused as if the memories were as distant as the place. "Before that from Darst." She rubbed her shoulders with the chilly cloth and shivered.

"Wintersgate. I've heard of that." The sound of washing and the slap of wet garments interrupted the woman's talk. "Goin' north from here, I take it."

"North?" Kyala dipped her cloth again, then pushed her amulet aside while wiping about her neck. Trembling with cold, she quickly washed her middle and then her legs.

"North, sure," said the woman. "Where else would y' go from here?"

"Where?" Kyala hurried into her goatskin trousers. "Why to Van-Vanikval. That's where we're headed." The rhythmic sound of rubbing ended. Kyala turned to see the woman stopped in midaction, holding a child's pair of stockings that streamed water into the tub.

"Not Vanikval. No. Nobody goes there." The woman dropped her laundry and made the sign of Ormek, a circle of thumb and forefinger.

"I'm not afraid of an old Vigen." Kyala finished lacing up her jacket, then sat on a three-legged stool to pull on her boots.

The woman remained silent, but continued to hold the sign of Ormek. Kyala was about to say more, but she caught herself. *Watnojat is afraid, but I'm not.* "Tell me then why no one goes to Vanikval."

"B-Because nobody comes back from there."

"I've heard such tales."

"Not tales. My brother learned of work there for carpenters. Told us he'd send for his wife. We never got back a word. After a year she went to look for 'im. We never saw *her* again either."

"Maybe they liked it so much they stayed. Maybe it's a good place—"

"*Good?* If my brother was doin' well, wouldn't he send word back with a peddler? Trouble is, even peddlers don't come out of Vanikval. Now you tell me what you want in such a place."

"My ... My uncle's a peddler," she said in a faltering voice. "We've heard of a spring festival there. They'll be needing things."

"Things indeed. But not what you're peddling. Go north, I say. Forget Vanikval. There's Southbog and Middlebog and all those swamp towns." She wrinkled her nose. "Bad smells there they say, but better'n Vanikval."

"I've no use for swamps." Kyala knew the Vigen was waiting for her outside, but the woman's talk had made her curious. "Tell me, do you know anything about this Vanikval festival? In Darst we had Ormek's Feast at this time of year."

"Untmur's festival isn't any you know." She made the

Sun sign again. "He feasts, all right. Gulps the souls of the living."

*Souls!* Kyala tore her gaze from the glistening dark eyes. The woman's words were frightening and she did not want to hear more. "Good day, then," Kyala said hurriedly. "Good day and thanks." She pulled open the door on its creaky leather hinges and saw Watnojat waiting in the wagon. The morning shadows of the ponies stretched across the bare yard.

"Uncle, I talked to a woman in the shed," the apprentice told him when she reached the wagon. She saw the Vigen's weary look and knew he had already heard too much of what lay ahead. "She says . . . she says the festival is Untmur's. I don't know how a Vigen has such a thing to himself."

"Do you wish to find out?" He handed her the reins, and slid over so that she could drive.

"If it will get us home the quicker."

Watnojat sighed. "Then let's be off."

"Uncle, are you worrying again? Untmur will be glad to trade with us. Think of all your rare colors."

"Ah, Balin's daughter, I fear he'll be all too eager to trade."

Kyala frowned. They had been over this point more than once, yet Watnojat kept bringing up the matter in different ways.

"But do I dare offer coppery blues," he said, "or mossy greens? Think what such pigments are good for."

"Calling spirits, healing, and yes . . ." Her voice fell. "If Lemp's tales are true."

"I'll offer Untmur trade. But I'll give him only what he needs for animal talismans. If those shades won't do, then we'll seek our astablak elsewhere. We'll *have* to try elsewhere. Even if we must climb the Teeth."

She turned for a moment and saw Watnojat's weary face and his downcast eyes. She had watched him weaken slowly as they came through the Winterkills and down across the flatlands. She did not think him capable of another mountain passage. "Uncle, we won't give him colorings for any cruel purpose. Now let's not talk of it anymore."

That evening they reached a simple inn, a long building of logs at the edge of a fallow field. Inside they found a large room with a row of beds at one end and a single table by the hearth at the far wall. A thin little man, the proprietor, dished out stew to the guests from a dented cauldron.

There were only two other guests that night—a traveling blacksmith dressed in sooty goatskins and a peddler garbed in woolens. These two exchanged brief words with the Vigen, then pushed aside their bowls just as the newcomers began to eat. The peddler brought out a patna pouch and the smith agreed to a game. The play started at once, each in turn shaking the small skin of pebbles and then releasing his thumb from the opening so that one stone, either dark or light, could fall to the table. Copper coins clinked against each other as they were passed back and forth.

Kyala watched the game while she ate. Occasionally the smith would win, but the peddler's heap of coins grew steadily. The blacksmith's face darkened, and when he lost six times in succession he stood up and pounded the table with his hairy fist.

"You've a demon in y'r sack!" he said. The peddler protested as the larger man tore the pouch from his hands and took it close to the fire. "What's this?" he said after turning the leather piece and inspecting it from all sides. *"Two* holes?" He pulled a knife from his belt and in a moment sliced open the pouch. Then he held it out so that Watnojat and Kyala could see the trickery—two compartments within and a separate hole for each. The peddler had shaken stones from the favorable hole while the smith's stones had fallen from the other. The peddler tried to sweep up his coins, but the smith calmly grabbed him by the shoulder and held the point of the knife to his throat.

The peddler swallowed. "I . . . I was gathering your . . . your winnings."

The innkeeper began to bang loudly with a poker on his

iron pot. The smith drew his knife slowly downward, slicing through the lacings of the peddler's jacket and taking no care with the point. The peddler screamed. A stout youth, evidently answering the innkeeper's alarm, rushed in with a stave and knocked the smith sharply on the side of his head. The big man grunted once, then fell back and lay on the floor with his legs caught on the bench, his boots pointing to the roof.

"Put both of 'em outside," said the innkeeper to the youngster, who appeared to be his son.

"I'm cut," the peddler wailed. "And there's no other lodgings in these parts. Where'll I go?" He pulled out a rag and mopped at the line of blood that ran down his chest.

"Take the big one first," said the innkeeper. The smith's boots fell heavily to the floor as the young man dragged him away from the table.

"Can y' help me?" the peddler asked, staring anxiously at Kyala. "I got ointments and such. In a box on my cart. Look under the seat." The blood was welling in his cuts and running down into his dark woolen trousers.

Kyala looked at Watnojat, who made no sign. Should she help the man? The peddler was a scoundrel, but she felt sorry for him. She put down her bowl and went out to find his wagon.

A single lantern was lit in the open-walled stable. The peddler's cart was unmistakable, heaped with weathered barrels and warped chests. Beneath the seat she found a small wooden box bound with a leather strap. The scent of herbs rose from the wood. She brought the box inside and found the man still mopping at his chest.

"There's a jar in there," he said in a worried voice. She unbuckled the strap and found inside a collection of packets and clay jars that would be the envy of an herb-dealer. "That one," said the wounded man. Kyala pulled out the stopper and handed him the open jar. His hands were so shaky that the container fell into his lap. "Please," he said. She dipped her finger into the cold yellow salve. The peddler winced as she rubbed it on the wound, but the bleeding slowed. "Good. That's good." She continued the yellow smear almost to his navel.

As she was finishing, the youth returned and leaned over as if to lift the peddler. "I'll split open again if I move," he protested.

"Father?" The young man hesitated, turning to the innkeeper.

"You'll have a corpse on your hands," the peddler added. *"Then* you'll have something to explain to the Magistrate."

Surely he exaggerates, thought Kyala. For a moment a grin crossed her face and the young man, seeing her expression, grinned back. She hadn't noticed before the pleasing line of his jaw where his new beard sprouted.

"Let him sit awhile," said the innkeeper. "But he sleeps outside. I'll have none of his kind in my beds."

The youth nodded and left the room, presumably returning to his post guarding the stable. The peddler's features relaxed a bit. He thanked Kyala for her aid. She wiped her fingers clean on the man's rag, then closed up his box of medicines. Watnojat was still toying with his dinner when she returned to sit beside him. The gravy had congealed in her own bowl and she pushed it aside.

The innkeeper, who had been waiting impatiently for them to finish, grabbed up all the utensils and flung them into a wash basin. "If y' need anything else, just bang on the kettle," he said gruffly before walking back to a curtain at the end of the row of beds.

Watnojat turned to the unhappy traveler, who was trying to pull the remains of his jacket closed. "You seem as much a stranger here as we are," the Vigen observed. "Are you from the south?"

"South. North. What does it matter? If y' trade with Vanikval, it does somethin' to ya. It *makes* ya strange."

"You trade in Vanikval?" Watnojat pushed his bowl next to Kyala's.

"I trade *with* Vanikval," the peddler said. "Never been *in* the town. Wouldn't want to be."

"We've heard about a festival," said Kyala.

"That's not for you," said the peddler. "Don't need to go in there to grade with 'em. If y' want to do business with those folks, you stay this side of the well."

"Well?"

"Half a day's journey." He started to point, but winced and dropped his hand. "Half a day from here. Broken-down well. Dead bushes all around it. That's where I always stop."

Kyala leaned forward. "Then you know what sorts of things they trade for. Maybe you know what Untmur needs now."

The peddler licked his lips and looked away. "Hard to say." His expression suddenly became guarded.

"Pigments? Colored glass?" she asked.

"Now where would I get such as that?" He shrank from Kyala's demands, trying to hitch to the end of the bench.

Suddenly her sympathy for the man was gone. She picked up the box of salves from the table and held it beyond his reach. "We can use some of these. What we don't need, we can trade. Maybe they want medicines in Vanikval."

The traveler's face grew red. He made a fainthearted grab at the box, but the pain of his movements made him fall back into his seat. "He's got his wants," he said in a whining tone. "It's not for me to question. I bring what they ask for, and then I turn right around."

"Tell!"

"You won't believe me anyway." The man looked at the floor and spoke so softly she could barely hear him. "It was seashells I last brought him. Left a sackful. Couldn't please 'em with anything else."

*Shells!* She turned to see the Vigen nod. *Sand and pot salt and ground shells.* How often she had recited the proportions of the mixtures. "Untmur still practices his art, then," said Watnojat.

"Art? I don't know what he does with 'em. Pays me in coppers and that's all I care about. But don't think you can steal my trade. He won't need more for a while, and the coast's a long way from here."

"I'll trade him no shells." The Vigen fell silent and stared at his fingers. "Tell me how you deal at this well. Does Untmur himself come?"

"What does he look like?"

Watnojat shrugged. "I've never seen him."

"Doesn't matter anyway, it's always someone new. This time it was a boy. Small fellow. Sleepy looking like they always are. And they don't even haggle," he added with a sly grin. "If you got what they want, they pay." He looked at Kyala, who was still holding the medicines. Satisfied that he had told all he could, she dropped the box carelessly onto the table, half hoping that a jar inside would crack.

Shortly they left the peddler by the fire. Carrying sooty warming pouches with them, they crawled into the narrow beds at the far end of the room. The blankets reeked, and the straw poked sharp ends into Kyala's back. It was almost worse than sleeping on the wagon. After awhile she dozed, but later woke to hear unfamiliar snores from several other beds. Late arrivals, she thought, and then began to fret about the contents of the wagon. Unable to sleep, she lifted the door bar, slipped out, and headed to the stable. The proprietor's son was at his post, amusing himself by throwing a knife at a roof pole. Above the sky was clear, filled with Ormek's dreams. Though winter was long over, Kyala shivered in her open coat.

"Ho," said the youth. "You comin' to steal somethin'? I'll have to whack you." He picked up his stave and rapped it against the pole.

"Just looking after our wagon. That peddler would steal the whiskers off a fish." She walked closer. The young man was broad cheeked. He had a smile in the lamplight that heated her like a taste of her mother's wine.

"Come over here."

"I can see well enough."

"Come warm me. It's a long night to stay up alone."

"Alone? You've got someone waiting for you in a hayloft. Soon as you get a chance, you'll go to her."

"I've got nobody. I'm just waiting for you." He had a voice that drew her to him. She stepped closer. He reached inside her coat and pulled her against his chest. "Inside," he said moistly into her ear. "Old Carlo won't see us." He led her back beside the wagons. Then she felt him fumbling with the drawstring to her trousers. His fingers were chilly against her stomach, but she did not pull away.

Her garment fell from her hips. He pried apart her legs and lifted her from the ground. She found a crude pleasure in his touch and felt herself soften. This was so different from the way that she had played at lovemaking with Jelor in the barn behind his father's house. They had hugged and teased for hours, it seemed, before he thrust himself into her. Already she felt the huge knob parting her, forcing her open. The youth slipped deeper and the pain was drowned by a joy that made her gasp. She did not forget herself; in a moment it would be too late.

"Turn me loose," she said, slapping his face. She pulled free just as his stream erupted. She clutched at her fallen trousers with one hand, evading his grasp as he spurted in a high arc onto the floor. He called her a foul name, but she laughed while she tied her drawstring. He looked a fool with his bottom bare, his goatskins about his ankles.

"Now you're all ready, let's try it again," he said, slightly out of breath. He pulled up his trousers to keep from tripping on them.

Kyala shook her head. When he came at her, she dodged and raced back into the inn. He shouted the ugly name again but she didn't care.

Inside she barred the door and then went to warm herself at the embers of the hearth. The peddler was still there, stretched out on the table, asleep on his back. Kyala did not feel sleepy at all. She could think of nothing but the boy's moist breath against her face and his hard hands against her skin. She felt warm inside, a pleasant irritation. *But I won't go back to him,* she thought. *He's no substitute for Jelor.* So she added a few sticks to the fire and sat awhile, thinking of afternoons when the odors of cows and hay mingled with Jelor's scent. If only she could keep away the bitterness, the thoughts of their last afternoons together. She had refused to become his wife. "I'll do something else. I'll not be a mother." He could not understand.

She returned to bed for a short nap before dawn. The peddler was gone by the time that Watnojat and Kyala sat down to their breakfast of sausage and cold bread. She said nothing to the Vigen of her experience in the stable. *Uncle still views me as a child,* she thought. When the youth appeared briefly, he avoided her gaze. Yes, he was a handsome fellow, she admitted to herself, but there were plenty like him. They wanted women to cook for them and raise their children, with no life beyond the duties of the cottage. That was not the future she wanted.

When it was time to leave, she took the reins eagerly. Ahead lay the peddler's well—and beyond that, Vanikval. She paid little attention to anything but the road. From time to time she glanced to the side and noted the scarcity of dwellings and the poor quality of the soil. Even weeds did poorly in the gray earth. Trees were stunted and bore few new leaves.

Around noon they reached the trading site. Tumbled stones ringed the well. The boy they expected was there, pulling up a frayed rope hand-over-hand until a bucket of muddy water emerged from the hole. He drank directly from the bucket, wetting his chin. Water dribbled down his neck, and he did not bother to wipe the dampness away. "What you got to trade?" he asked dreamily.

"Pigments," said Watnojat. "Colored glass. Golds. Yellows. Ambers."

The boy rubbed his eyes and looked at the travelers. "He wants spices . . . and aged cheese."

"What about colorings?"

"He wants cheese." The boy spoke dreamily, his eyes wandering.

"We'll go see Untmur. Show him what we've got."

"No." The youngster scowled and suddenly became alert. He picked up a jagged rock. "Nobody goes. You stop here."

Watnojat touched her arm. "Kyala, drive!"

She clucked to the ponies, and they pulled away. The rock struck the back of the wagon, and Kyala felt its jolt. "You stop!" called the boy, but to no avail. The ponies sped on. Kyala leaned forward, eager to see the mysteries of the town ahead.

# Chapter 11

The grays were panting, but Kyala didn't ease the pace until the boy's cries had long stopped echoing in her ears. She pulled off the road at a cottage that might once have served as a waystation. A long hitching rail in front sagged on weathered posts. Branches were nailed crisscross over the small windows.

"There's a trough," she said, climbing down to inspect the old well and its surroundings. "Cracked." She kicked at the basin's side, and the rotten wood broke apart. Pulling on the well rope, she drew up a bucket that streamed water from half a dozen holes. It was empty before she could bring it to the ponies.

"We'll try a farmhouse," said Watnojat. "Down the road there's sure to be someone."

Kyala tossed aside the bucket. "The peddler was right. This is no road for travelers." She let the thirsty grays set a moderate pace.

"There," said the glassmaker after a long stretch of untilled fields. A barn with a sagging roof lay just ahead.

Kyala turned in at a track that led to a tiny cottage. Clad in a ragged sheepskin that hung to his knees, a man was crossing the yard. She watched him carry a few handfuls of hay to a skinny horse tethered by the cottage door. He did not look at the approaching travelers.

"Can you spare some water?" asked Watnojat.

The man didn't answer. The horse ate the offered hay at once, and the man returned to the barn. Several times he repeated the long walk, always returning with just a few wisps of food.

Kyala could hold back the ponies no longer. She let them pull close to the narrow basin so that two could drink. Watnojat drew the water. He turned the windlass slowly, its squeals piercing the quiet air. When the first two animals were finished, she made a great turn about the yard, bringing the other two grays close to the trough.

The drinking done, Watnojat approached the farmer as he fed yet another meager offering to his horse. "Tell me," the glassmaker said. "Tell me why you don't carry a larger bundle of hay. Or if that's too heavy for you, why don't you bring your horse to the barn?"

The man noticed the Vigen at last. He stared at him as if his words made no sense. When he answered, he spoke slowly as if half asleep. "Don't you see, stranger? He'll want more if he gets it all at once. More and more. Then he'll eat too much." He blinked a few times and cocked his head to look at Watnojat. The farmer's expression was vacant.

"But he'll be worth nothing to you if he doesn't get enough."

The farmer shook his head. "What matters to a horse . . . What matters is how much *time* he spends eating. He chews a bit, and then a bit more, and after a while he feels full. This one knows it's time to stop now."

"I've never heard of such an idea."

"It's the same with people." He patted his belly under

the torn coat. "Chew and chew until y' feel full." Kyala realized that he was as skinny as his animal. Beyond the buildings she could see the poor start he had made on his spring plowing. *This year's crops would be scanty,* she thought, *if he did not apply himself soon.*

"I think you're mistaken," said the glassmaker. "But I've no time to argue about it." They left the yard and rode on past more ill-kept farms and crumbling cottages. In places mud-smeared children stood in the roadway and did not seem to hear the approaching rig. Kyala shouted at them to no avail. They stared at her without moving and she was forced to steer around them, the wagon pitching as wheels on one side bounced over rocks and stubble.

The travelers came to the edge of town, where buildings leaned against each other with no space between. The people here resembled the farmer, thin and bedraggled. They walked with fixed expressions; nobody turned to observe the newcomers.

Kyala noticed a haze over the street ahead. The smell of smoke grew stronger. This was more than hearth smoke. Houses on fire? She slowed the ponies, fearful that frenzied people might blunder across her path. But soon she saw figures moving slowly beneath the cloud. There was no panic here.

The travelers arrived at the edge of a muddy town square. A heap of firewood, a pile of thin logs and spindly branches, lay to the side of an odd stone structure. Glancing at the walls, Kyala thought first of a small outbuilding, too low to stand up in but with an enormous chimney.

"It's a *kiln!*" cried Watnojat. "I've never seen one this size." It was built of dark blocks, neatly chiseled. At each of three sides a man leaned over a large pair of bellows that rested on the ground. A fourth man kept time for them, striking a copper pot with a stick. At each beat they pumped in unison.

Kyala halted behind the taskmaster. Beside him, on the

ground, lay numerous molds of clay. These were many times the size of the molds in Watnojat's shop. Each of the glass disks that lay within them, she guessed, would fill her hand. She turned to Watnojat. "Uncle?"

"He is making glass as we thought. But for what? Look at the color!"

Even from a distance, Kyala knew the color to be strange. It was a pale tint, like watery wine.

"Could that be Untmur?" she whispered, pointing to the man beating the pot. Nobody else seemed to be supervising the work. But the taskmaster was young, with stringy black hair that hung to his shoulders. Surely Untmur would be aged and gray by now.

"The Vigen must be elsewhere," said the glassmaker. Since the people continued to ignore their presence, they moved the wagon to the edge of the square and walked back to study the work more closely. Kyala crouched at the molds and touched a finger briefly to one of the smooth disks. It was warm, but not hot. Gently she pried it loose. "Look," she said, as she turned it to see the imprint from the mold. "It's like a disk of Ormek, but the sun sign is changed. It's . . . a face."

Suddenly her head felt light. She began to lose her balance, falling forward toward the damp ground. This was not like any illness she had known. Something unfamiliar had touched her—a force that could leave her helpless. *The disk*, she thought. She flung it from her, but could not keep her balance.

"Kyala!"

Watnojat helped her up. "Get away from the disks," she said. She took a few weak steps. The dizziness did not subside fully until she had moved several paces away from the molds. Watnojat rubbed at his eyes. "Did you feel it, Uncle?"

"There is something there I don't like." He stared at the colored glass from a distance. The piece she had discarded lay in the dirt, and nobody seemed to care. The men worked steadily at the kiln and ignored the intruders.

"That face," said Kyala. "It may be Untmur's." She had glimpsed the imprint for only a moment, but she could still picture the man's high forehead, his fat nostrils, his prominent lips. Surely she would recognize a man with such features.

"Whatever these disks are for, there will be enough of them to supply the whole town," Watnojat said.

"Untmur should be here to supervise the work." She looked more closely at the people in the square. Two women were filling molds from a barrel of coarse powder. Several men had just arrived with loads of wood on their backs. So far as she could tell, the notorious Vigen was not present.

Another man caught her attention. Everyone else she had seen that morning was intent on his or her own concerns, but this tall youth's gaze was constantly in motion. He arrived walking quickly, his head jerking as he looked first at one person and then at another. Each he scrutinized for a few heartbeats before turning to the next. Then he looked at Kyala, staring at her with sad, intent eyes. Surely he had singled her out. He did not turn away.

"He is coming," said Kyala.

"Untmur?" Her mentor had been watching the kiln.

"No. Someone who's curious about us."

The youth approached, his gait stiff legged. "I don't know you," he said in a voice that was too high pitched for one of his size and age. "I don't know you."

"We come to trade with your Vigen," said Watnojat. "We offer rare colorings for his glass."

"Where are you from?"

"Darst. Can you take us to Untmur?"

The young man's face was blank. "What do you want here?"

"We want to see the Vigen. The one responsible for all this." He swept his hand toward the kiln.

"Why do you seek him?"

"To trade with him!" Watnojat's voice rose. "I said that already." Kyala touched his arm, wishing he would not lose patience so quickly.

"See Untmur." The questioner digested that, then blinked a few times. "Untmur does not greet strangers. I'm the one to greet strangers."

"We're not looking for greetings. Tell him a Vigen has come. Another glassmaker from a distant town."

"Untmur is Vigen." The youth cocked his head and half-closed his eyes. "Untmur is Vigen and he does not see anyone."

"No. Listen. *I* also am a glassmaker. I'm Watnojat of Darst."

"No. There is only one. There is just one Vigen."

Watnojat seized the youth's arm and shook him. "Can you at least remember a message? Don't worry about its meaning."

The young man had not heard them. He only said: "You don't belong here. Why are you in Vanikval?"

Watnojat stamped his boots in disgust.

"Uncle, I have a thought." Kyala leaned closer to whisper in his ear. "This one's too stupid to take a message in words. Give him something solid—something that Untmur will recognize."

The glassmaker hesitated, then nodded. "Yes. I see I must waste a bead on this messenger." He opened his pouch and Kyala saw him consider one talisman and then another. At last he chose an odd piece, a reddish brown eye from a wild pig. "I can spare this one," he said with a faint smile. He offered it to the youth.

"What is this?"

"Take it to your Vigen."

The young man's brow furrowed. It was the first indication Kyala had seen that he was capable of thinking. "I have seen something like this."

"Untmur will want it. Tell him where you got it."

The youth turned the glossy talisman several times. "You don't belong here," he said in a less certain voice. Then he loosened the drawstring on a small pouch that dangled from his belt and dropped in the bead. He stared at the newcomers for a moment more before stalking off into the streets of the town.

"I don't know if he'll show it to Untmur," said Kyala, looking in the direction the youth had taken.

"I should have hung it about his neck with a long tether." Watnojat sighed. "If this fails, he'll be back and we can try something else. Meanwhile, we can do nothing but wait."

All afternoon the visitors sat on their wagon and watched the work at the kiln. The slow-moving townsmen packed the disks in straw-filled baskets and carried them away on their backs. Other men arrived carrying wood to replace what was consumed. Only occasionally did the kiln workers stop for a swallow of water or to wipe their faces.

"The glass doesn't seem to affect the others as it did me," Kyala observed.

"The dizziness? I think I understand that now. It was the power in Untmur's glass fighting the protection of your own bead."

"Then the disks . . ."

"Somehow he uses them for control. I think that each household will get one of these new talismans. Just as in other towns they hang disks of Ormek."

"If he does this every year?"

"Then the cottages must have disks hanging from every rafter. And his power over their lives must be great."

They watched the work continue as the sun dropped. The one who had taken the talisman did not return, and no others arrived to question their presence. At last a rider came, a short-haired, burly man on a mottled stallion, his shadow sweeping across the square. He rode toward the visitors. Kyala recalled the profile on the disk. The rider's features were too broad; this was not Untmur.

"Come with me." The rider waved his arm in a broad half circle.

"To see the Vigen?"

"If he wishes."

"And if he does not?"

"Then you've wasted your journey and my time. And possibly saved yourselves from something worse."

Undeterred by his words, Kyala took the reins, following the rider through the dirty streets. They climbed a long hill to a house built of the same chiseled stones as the kiln. From what she could see, the house was enormous, four times the size of the biggest in Darst. It was surrounded by a wall of stone. To the rear stood a smaller building, possibly a workshop, built of the same dark blocks. But it was not the house that drew Kyala's attention.

Colored shards lay on the ground everywhere. "Glass!" Watnojat marveled. "Colored glass! This man can throw his leavings into the yard."

Wherever she looked, Kyala saw bits of greens and blues and browns. How could a man who tossed away such riches care for Watnojat's meager offerings?

The fragments crunched under the wheels of the wagon. Kyala feared for the ponies' hooves, but it was too late to stop them. The thirsty animals headed for the trough. She freed them from their traces and tethered them where they could drink at will. The guide waved the visitors on impatiently.

Watnojat carried his box of vials before him as they entered a side door into a dark hallway.

"This way," said Untmur's man.

The air felt colder than it had outside. Kyala shivered as she followed by sound, feeling her way by touching the rough stones. Behind her Watnojat's vials rattled at each bump, and the Vigen swore softly. They came to a large room lit by a single lamp on a stand in the middle of a long dining table. Watnojat set down the chest.

"Here we'll talk." The guide produced the talisman that

Watnojat had given the youth and laid it beneath the light. He pulled back a carved chair for himself. "Sit," he said. "This is the reason you're here. Now tell me how you got this piece."

The visitors remained standing. "I cast it in my kiln," said Watnojat. "Do you think that Untmur is this world's only Vigen?"

The man picked up the bead and examined it under the lamp. "I'm informed that this is neatly cast. Not up to my master's work, of course, but acceptable. Possibly stolen, who can be sure? So if you're a glassmaker, tell me who was your mentor."

"Reslunin."

"The name means nothing to me. And who was Reslunin's master?"

Another voice interrupted. "Enough, Potil. I know of Reslunin." A stout figure appeared in the doorway. The speaker wore a long, open coat of leather, with an apron beneath that fell to his boot tops. A leather cap covered the top of his head, and a string of crystals hung from his neck. As the face emerged from shadow, Kyala recognized the features—the thick lips, the close-cropped beard of gray. "I am Untmur. I know of Reslunin by reputation. My old master spoke of him with respect. And so it pleases me to meet Reslunin's successor."

"I am Watnojat of Darst."

"Greetings, Vigen. Welcome to Vanikval. And what do you call this one?" Untmur came closer with a heavy tread.

"I'm Kyala—one day to be Watnojat's successor."

"Kyala?" He did not address her, but turned to Watnojat. "Is this your apprentice?" He reached out a thumb and forefinger and gripped her chin tightly, almost painfully. His hand smelled of ashes and burnt hair. "What are you saying? Kyala is not a name for a Vigen."

"And why not?" asked Darst's glassmaker. "She has the talent."

"Talent? I think, Watnojat, that we are among the last.

The last of our kind who matter." He shook his head. "A sad end to it all. I have no one to continue my work. No one at all. And you . . . You have *her*." He released his grip, but still she felt the pressure of his touch. "Kyala? Pah. How can a girl be a Vigen?"

"She has skills you might envy," said Watnojat. "And there are Vigens in other towns. Our work will go on, though the number of practitioners dwindles."

"It will end," said Untmur. "The farmers today raise plenty of cattle and pigs and goats. The weavers make warm cloth. Where is the need for hunters? And with no hunters, there is no use for our beads."

"A Vigen does more than make hunters' talismans."

"Healing, then? I haven't had a call for such aid since I came to Vanikval."

Kyala gritted her teeth. *What fool would trust this man to heal someone?* she wondered.

"Tem Vigen," said Watnojat. "The people still need protection in the forest. Near the outlying towns, one finds dangerous beasts."

"And so you spend your days making talismans against wild pigs?" Untmur snorted. "A fine use of your talent!"

"Vigen, let us not argue about the purposes of our craft. I came because of the difficulties of obtaining pigments. I came to offer you trade, so that each of us may benefit."

"Trade? I need nothing. I have stores of pigments that I cannot find ways to use. I have shelves full of glass that I cannot remember casting. So that's a foolish notion. But tell me anyway what you want."

"Astablak."

Untmur laughed. "When you talked of protection, I thought dogs, bears. But Lame Ones? They should all be dead by now."

Watnojat shook his head. "I lost my first apprentice to them, and my astablak ran out long ago. I've spent many years searching, and have found none. Even the Winterkills have been stripped."

Untmur smiled. "There was astablak there once."

"Then you have some?"

"Of course."

"In that case, since you have no Lame Ones here..."

"But what will you offer me in return, Vigen?" Untmur glanced down at the table. "I've been casting glass for forty years. Do you think your chest there carries colorings that I don't own?"

"Perhaps one of Reslunin's batches. Some of his tints that I could never reproduce."

"Hmmm." Untmur stared at the box. "Reslunin's batches might be interesting. I would like to see what that old man wrung from the minerals." He rubbed his hands together. "There's no use trying to show me them under the lamp. I'll want to see what you have in daylight. Tomorrow, then. For now, I leave you to Potil for hospitality." He turned slowly, as if engrossed in thought, and left the room.

The burly one turned to Watnojat. "You refused my invitation to sit. Now Untmur has made you his guests. I'll have dinner brought in, and you may eat it standing for all I care."

"So we are to stay here the night?" asked Watnojat.

"We can hardly let guests sleep in the stable."

"The ponies," Kyala said.

"They'll be stabled and fed. Don't fret for your beasts."

Potil vanished through the doorway that Untmur had taken, leaving them alone in the cold room. They stared at each other, not daring to whisper. A servant appeared and quickly built a fire in the huge hearth. Another servant, a wrinkled little woman, served them a meat pie with a rich crust. Kyala had not eaten such a delicacy since leaving her mother's table. The bread was fresh, and the ale was finely brewed. "Untmur is a fair host," she said quietly. But she could not forget the feel of his grip on her face.

The fire did little to warm the large room and the silence of the place disturbed her. Where were the others of the household? Why had she and Watnojat been isolated in this hall?

Potil came later and showed them to a chilly bedchamber. Watnojat slept with his arms about the chest of vials. Kyala sank into the softness of the bed; after the previous night's lack of sleep, even her misgivings about Untmur could not keep her awake.

When she opened her eyes, a tiny window high on the wall showed that morning had arrived. She shook Watnojat. "I'll go check the rig," she said. He blinked at her sleepily. She went out without waiting for his reply.

Peering down the corridor, she tried to remember the path they had taken from the dining room. She walked one way and saw nothing familiar, only rows of closed doors. The doors were of oak and intricately carved, but she had no time to examine them. Turning back, she passed the room she had slept in, recognizable by the fact that the door was slightly ajar.

"Kyala?"

The nasal voice startled her. Untmur was standing at the end of the corridor with a window at his back. She could see only the bulky outline of his body. "You slept late, Kyala. A Vigen must rise with the birds."

"If you want your guests up early, offer harder beds," she said. "And now I want to see our ponies."

"They were well fed." His voice echoed in the long hallway.

"I want to see them." This man possessed what she and Watnojat had sought for so many months. She dared not anger him by confessing her mistrust. "They will miss my touch."

"Do I look to you like one who robs his guests? Come, if you wish." He motioned for her to follow. Her face burned at his words, but she went on after him. What else could she do?

Untmur's path twisted through several new passageways, finally emerging in the yard directly across from the stable. "In there are your beasts and all the rest."

Refusing to drop her pretext, she climbed onto the wagon in search of a currycomb. She knew at once that her suspicions had been well founded. Even in the dim light she could see that the belongings had been disturbed. The trunks and hides were not as she had left them, and underfoot she felt telltale grit. At the least, someone had opened the crock of sand mixture, and she felt certain that everything had been searched. "Who has been here?" she shouted, forgetting in her fury the need to be courteous to this Vigen.

"Only the stableboy. And he is completely trustworthy."

"Trustworthy for you." She climbed down to find Untmur waiting for her by the front of the wagon. "For me he is a thief."

"He took nothing. And now it's your turn to give answers. I want to know why you're here. Play no games with me."

"We came for astablak. Watnojat told you that already."

"And I bake cakes in my kiln." Untmur laughed and grabbed her chin, this time squeezing so hard that tears came to her eyes. "I bake sweet cakes to give to the little children. And they always obey me. Just like you will do. Now tell me about this talent of yours. Tell me how you got the old fool to make you his apprentice."

"Tell me why your nose is so fat!" She twisted and broke free of him, rushed out of the stable toward the door to the main house, and did not stop.

# Chapter 12

Kyala thought she could find her way back to Watnojat, but the corridors all looked alike. She heard Untmur's voice calling, but from which direction? Left? Right? Was he just behind her? She ran, turned a corner, and found the leather-clad Vigen standing in the middle of the passageway. "So you come to me of your own accord," he said.

She was faster, but he knew the turnings. Dodging his grasp, she raced past a dozen doorways. Sounds of footsteps came from all directions. No way seemed safe. Had Untmur multiplied himself? Out of breath, she paused at a corner, her hand resting on the sharp edge where two walls met.

"Kyala." The name echoed through the passageways until it became meaningless, no longer connected with herself. "Kyala." She spun on her heels and rushed through another series of passageways, but surely she had been through these before. An arm reached out for her from an alcove.

"Don't!" she cried, but there was no arm, only a trick of the shadows. Her heart thudded, and the noise of her breathing covered all sounds of pursuit. He could be just behind her. . . .

Ahead she saw a chink of light. Then a face peered out. This was no shadow! She turned to flee, but the voice was Watnojat's.

"What are you doing, Balin's daughter?"

"The Vigen." She rushed toward him, uncertain of what to say. "Untmur doesn't—" She struggled for breath and tried to lower her voice at the same time. "Doesn't trust us. Thinks we mean him harm... We've got to... leave here. Leave as quick as we can."

"We have work to do, Kyala."

"We came for astablak. Nothing more. Make him believe that."

"If only it were true." Watnojat led her back into the room. "It was easy to discount the tales. But now I've seen for myself how the craft has been misused. He slanders the name of all honorable Vigens."

She glanced behind her, expecting the leather-clad glass-maker to charge through the doorway. "He's... He's coming after me."

Watnojat put a comforting hand on her shoulder. "Kyala, please listen. He has forced the whole town to his will, and we've seen how the people suffer for it."

"But, Uncle. There are just the two of us. We can hardly change things here."

He picked up the chest carefully. "I don't know what we can do," he answered in a low and faltering voice. "But I won't flee from this Hestafos. First we must have our astablak. After that, we'll seek a way to stop his tyranny."

Kyala heard a hopeless determination in his words. Untmur had abused his powers. A true Vigen must preserve the high purpose of the craft. But what could two outsiders do against a man who held a whole town under his control?

Emerging from the room, they found Untmur watching them from the end of the corridor. His face showed nothing of his recent anger. "You agreed to see my colorings!" Darst's Vigen shouted when he saw the man. "The sun is high."

"I would be a poor host if I asked you to trade with me on an empty stomach."

Watnojat shook his head. "We appreciate your hospitality, but our time is short. Let us get on with it."

Untmur pondered the reply for an instant, his eyelids lowering. "As you wish." He led them outside and across the shard-strewn ground toward the structure that Kyala had identified as his shop. By the doorway to the smaller building stood a block of white marble, waist-high, its top smooth and level as a tabletop. "Here is where I lay out my pigments."

Watnojat set down the chest and slowly undid the straps. Kyala watched Untmur's face as the box was opened; his eyes widened and he moistened his lips. Glancing back down at the table, she saw Watnojat pull several containers from the straw packing, lining the bottles up along the edge of the marble block. The colors showed faintly through the thick glass walls. Watnojat hunted for the vials he needed, holding each high to catch the light, selecting a few to stand close to Untmur. "These are the best I have to offer."

"Spill them out."

"One at a time, Tem Vigen." Watnojat unstopped the first and poured out a heap of richer amber fragments. Kyala leaned closer, noting a warmth that she had not seen in other amber shades. These would give lifelike fire to an animal eye.

"Interesting work," said Untmur. "Reslunin's?"

"Mine."

"Achieved with a slow oak fire, no doubt. A bit of Endella's earth in the mixture."

Watnojat nodded. To Kyala's eyes he concealed his disappointment in Untmur's response. He took out a brush and a scrap of hide, quickly swept the fragments up, and poured them back into the vial. He opened another. "Perhaps this gold will interest you. The technique is quite complex."

"Gold? I have more shades than I can classify. That one? That I have in abundance."

"And this umber? I made this batch, but never could reproduce it." Opening one bottle after another, Watnojat showed his pigments. But if Untmur didn't already know how to create the color, he sneered at its value.

"What use is that? Do I make beads to snare rabbits? Do I live in this fine house because of rabbit pelts?"

"Here is one of Reslunin's most remarkable tints." Watnojat poured out a buttercup yellow so brilliant that she was forced to squint.

Untmur waved it away. "You show me no blues, no greens, no grays. What are you holding back?" He reached toward the box, but Watnojat firmly closed the lid.

"That is all I have for you," he said softly. "If these won't do, then we cannot trade."

"I need none of the colors you've shown. There's no trade for me here." Untmur rubbed his chin thoughtfully. "And what will you do? Will you continue your search for astablak by digging up meadows?"

"If there's any place you haven't stripped." Watnojat repacked his vials and then slowly began to fasten the straps around the box.

"There's no more astablak in the ground. Not even in the Teeth. The weathering process is slow. In a hundred years, a few more grains may accumulate. Can you wait for that?"

Watnojat shook his head. "I've not seen the Teeth for myself."

"Don't waste your last days there, Vigen." Untmur rubbed the back of his hand against his nose. "I would help you if the price were fair. I've no great need for astablak. But so far you've offered me nothing I don't have."

"What else do I possess?"

He stepped closer to Kyala, and she could smell the sour odor of ashes from his garments. "You've got *her*. Let me see the so-called talents of your apprentice."

"Do you think I can trade her for a handful of earth?"

"I talk of services, Vigen." Untmur glanced at the girl;

the gray of his eyes sent shivers down her arms. "I have bottles and jars of glass, the work of many years. I've had no time to put my supplies in order."

"Then you want Kyala to work for you. Sorting your pigments."

"For a month. Surely you can spare her for that long."

Watnojat frowned and stared at his apprentice. "In exchange for..."

"All the astablak I have."

"*All?*"

"We've no Lame Ones here."

Watnojat looked at his assistant as if to offer her the choice. The notion of working with the man sickened her. The words caught in her throat. But she thought of the hopeless journey that lay ahead if Untmur turned them away.

"If... If that will bring us the mineral, then I'll do what he asks."

"Then it's agreed," said Watnojat.

"Not yet. First she must be tested," said Untmur. "With my own powders. I must know if she can do anything useful." He went into his workshop, leaving Watnojat and Kyala to exchange wordless messages. *What is this man after?* Watnojat's frown seemed to say. *Do not trust him,* was the answer that Kyala would have liked to speak aloud.

The Vigen returned with three samples in fat, wide-mouthed bottles. He spilled a bit from each onto the table—three shades of Allig's Green. He shuffled the containers. "Put each back into its proper bottle," said Untmur, handing her his own pony-hair brush and a thin sheet of silver with a crease in the middle. With moist fingers she lifted the first vial and spilled a bit of its contents. She blinked at the colors on the table; for a moment she could not tell them apart. *Close. Too close.* She glanced back and forth from one pinch of powder to the other. The reflection from the marble was so bright it hurt her eyes. Then she saw the match. She held the metal sheet at the edge of the table, brushed the fragments onto it, and poured them back into their bottle. The second sample was a bit easier; she did not look into the third bottle.

"Is she satisfactory?" asked Watnojat.

"It would have been wiser to pour samples from all three at the start," Untmur said. "Then make the choices. She might have erred."

"But she was right."

"This time, yes. Now tell me. Does she know the order of the board?"

"I do," said Kyala, seeing in her mind the sequence of colors used on the mixing board. Reds first, as in the rainbow. Oranges, yellows, greens—Watnojat had drilled her well.

"We'll see what she knows." Untmur returned to the shop and came back with a handful of fingernail-sized shards. "Rank these," he demanded, spreading them out on the surface. *Blues*. This was not what she had expected. Each was a shade of blue, with scarcely any differences between them. She must order them by their minor pigments, by the small added bits of yellow or green or gray. In her mind she must subtract the principal hue and study what was left. She laid them out across the tabletop, rearranging them several times. *What if she failed now?* she wondered. *Would Watnojat think she had purposely lost?* She arranged and rearranged until at last she was satisfied. She looked up at Untmur's pursed lips and furrowed brow.

"She'll do," he admitted. He stroked his chin for a moment. "Now let me make clear my offer."

"I thought we understood you," protested Watnojat.

"I have yet to explain fully. I am curious about you, Vigen-of-Darst. There are but a few of us left, fewer than you might think. Who has the greatest skill, I wonder. Of all living Vigens, which of us is strongest?"

"Your question has no purpose. All that matters is that a Vigen can serve."

Untmur shook his head. "Hear my offer, Watnojat. I sense

your reluctance to tarry in this place. So I'll give you a chance to end your search quickly and leave for home. There's a festival tomorrow in the town. I will compete against you there in the art of the glassmaker."

"Compete! For what purpose?"

"For the glory of Vigenhood. We'll fire our kilns and see who is the true master of glass."

"If I refuse?"

"Then no astablak for you under any conditions. If you win the contest, then the coloring is yours, and you both may leave here at once. But if you lose, Kyala must work for me for a month to earn the prize. That is my offer."

"You make simple matters complicated. First it was merely a trade of her labor for the astablak. Now you force this competition on me." Watnojat's voice faltered. His head dropped and Kyala saw that he was staring at the trunk in his hands. Surely he was wondering what pigments he would waste in the contest.

Untmur swept away his blue shards with the back of his hand. "You have no choice, Vigen. I'll see you in the square at dawn. Ready your kiln and wait for instructions." He glanced up at the cloudless sky. "The weather should be clear for us. A fine day for a festival." Then he turned to the house.

"I have not agreed," Watnojat called after him, but the other Vigen walked straight to his door and vanished. "I have not agreed," he repeated softly to Kyala. "But I must."

The two said nothing more to each other until they had passed beyond Untmur's gate. Kyala spoke first. "Uncle, I don't know what he's after. He tested me, and now he's forcing you to show your skills."

"He was impressed by your talent."

"Is it possible that he's afraid of us?"

"Even Untmur can be afraid. He doesn't know how to deal with us yet. He doesn't know what we can do to him. By tomorrow he'll have a clear measure of our strengths. Then he'll decide."

"Decide what?"

Watnojat's lips were pressed tight and he stared straight ahead as they descended the hill. "There may be trouble. I want you to carry a dagger in your boot. And watch everything he does. We'll try to defeat him in his competition. But after that, I don't know."

They returned to the square, for they had little hope of finding accommodations in Vanikval. The work at the large kiln had ended; the smoke no longer poured from its chimney and the square was deserted. They chose a space behind Untmur's kiln where a few posts would serve to tether the animals. "Here is where I'll work," the Vigen said. "And here is where we must stay until tomorrow."

They brought down the kiln stones and fitted them together. Kyala unpacked the bellows, the tongs, and the molds. All the equipment that Watnojat would need she laid out at the back of the wagon. There was no sign of Untmur's preparations. How could there be a festival on a bare patch of ground?

At noon Kyala took a brief walk about the square, peering down the streets for banners and for arriving carts. *Where would the food stalls be built?* she wondered. *Where would the dancers perform?* In Darst on the eve of Ormek's Feast, the streets would be crowded and the air filled with the sound of hammering.

It was late in the day before she saw any hint of activity. A group of bedraggled men carrying shovels arrived at the square. They walked with their heads bowed, in the slow manner of the townspeople. They halted and turned their eyes toward Untmur's house, shuffling their feet but not moving. It was Potil who rode down to direct them.

"Here," he said, pointing to the ground. One man made a mark with his shovel. "And here." Potil rode to the four points of a rectangle. When the corners had been marked, he left the men to their work. He did not stop to speak to Watnojat.

"Uncle, could that be the place for the dancing?" Kyala asked. But the men were not building a platform. They were digging a shallow pit. Why would one dance in a pit? The work went slowly until at last all the dirt lay piled to one side. The men picked up their shovels and returned as they had come.

Evening fell, and there was no further work in the square. Kyala brought an armload of wood from the big stack and built a campfire on the ground before the kiln. The town was quiet. From the sounds, they might have been camped anywhere—even in a wilderness. But the wilderness would be a dead one, for the creatures too were silent.

The travelers slept badly on the hard boards of the wagon. All through the night, Kyala heard the Vigen's heavy breathing and his restless turning. Something would happen soon; Untmur would begin whatever he had planned. The stars moved slowly, perhaps not at all.

Then she heard a sound and sat up. She held her breath to hear better, but Watnojat's wheezing covered the other noise. Footsteps? She could see nothing. Hurriedly she pulled on her boots and climbed to the ground. Now she was certain that she was hearing the sound of many feet.

It was well before dawn, but already the people were coming. From the edge of the square she saw the torches, a long procession marching toward her. In the firelight she saw the faces of the torchbearers, their drooping eyelids, their slack expressions. *Untmur's got you all!* she thought. She touched her fingers to her throat, then slid her hand down her jacket until she felt the hard talisman against her chest. Without that, Untmur might already have added her to his horde. Her lips trembled as she watched the marchers advancing.

Then she was running. She shook Watnojat, rousing him from whatever rest he had found. The glassmaker groaned as he tried to flex his stiff joints. Slowly he made his way down to stand beside her and watch the procession arrive.

"They're going to the woodpile." Kyala looked down at the embers of their campfire, wondering whether she was guilty of pilfering. Perhaps this wood had special significance. The first torchbearer reached the pile, picked up a single branch, and tossed it into the pit. Then he moved to the far end of the square and took up a position facing inward. The others followed, each dropping a piece of wood into the pit, then finding a place to stand. The ranks grew, the pit filled, and the thin branches rose above the lip.

The sky began to lighten. Soon the kiln's taskmaster arrived with his three assistants. "Prepare your fire," he told Watnojat. The sticks were too long for the small kiln; Kyala cracked the spindly branches with her boot. A torchbearer came forward from the crowd to light Untmur's kiln, but did not offer his service to Watnojat. Kyala blew up the embers of the campfire to ignite first a scrap of bark and then some kindling. The wood was dry and caught quickly, but the flames needed air.

Seeing the others leaning into their huge bellows, Kyala began to pump with her own small pair. Just as she started, a long horn blast sounded from the heights of Untmur's house. The pitch rose and fell, changed to a series of short blasts, and grew ever louder until Potil galloped into the square with the ram's horn at his lips.

"Be it known!" he shouted, trotting his horse along the front of the ranks. "Be it known that this is the twenty-fifth year of our Vigen's great works. It is Untmur who keeps us safe from the ills of the world. It is Untmur who teaches us strength and dignity. It is Untmur who preserves us from the wrath of Ormek."

"*Wrath?*" Kyala saw Watnojat scowl at the absurd phrase. To her thinking, his reaction was mild. Her mother would have dumped a pot of soup on anyone who uttered such nonsense about the Bright One.

"And it is Untmur," Potil continued, "who brings you this celebration of the greatness of his art." His tour of the onlookers completed, the horseman moved to the square's center, all the while keeping his mount turning so that his words would reach in every direction. "Today," he said, waving his horn toward Watnojat, "today, we have a special demonstration. A usurper has come to Vanikval: a visitor who claims to have the powers of a Vigen. This person is the demon Noloro in disguise. We are offered the rare treat of seeing the demon in fleshly form. Together, we'll defeat him, and Untmur's triumphs will continue for years to come."

"Uncle, are you a demon?" Kyala nearly dropped the bellows. But when she looked at the men working the other kiln, she saw no laughter on their faces.

"Kyala, say nothing." The glassmaker touched a finger to his lips. He watched Potil calmly, too calmly. Kyala wanted to scream at the man's foolishness.

As the first edge of the Sun showed, Untmur arrived driving a cart of polished wood. The wheels were spoked and rimmed with silver. The manes of his stout-necked ponies were tied with white ribbons. He followed Potil's route, riding close to the front ranks of viewers that stood on three sides of the square. Potil moved away as Untmur took the focus of attention.

The crowd stirred at the sight of their Vigen, but enthusiasm was not evident. Kyala heard a soft murmur, and saw the torches bob. A juggler on foot, she thought, would have aroused more interest in this crowd than the glassmaker in his gaudy wagon. Untmur halted and his taskmaster strode forward to take the ponies' halters. The Vigen stood on the wagon's seat and reached back to spread out the full glory of his cloak. He turned slowly so that everyone could see the glint of the crystals sewn into the black fabric, crystals the same pale wine color as Untmur's disks.

"Ormek is the Lifegiver," he said in a booming voice. "But Ormek can wax cruel, parch the land and dry up the crops. As the warm season approaches, we tremble before his heat. We shield our eyes and bend our faces to the ground." He paused and looked around at the assembled. "It is now that I, Untmur, must defy his wrath. And I must show him the power of my art. This time I will do it by besting Noloro. If I succeed, then Ormek will know my strength and he will not dare harm us." With a surprisingly agile leap, he reached the ground. The taskmaster led the ornate rig to the side while Untmur strode to the front of his kiln.

Attention turned to the edge of the square. Kyala saw Potil struggling with a boy whose hands were lashed together. The blond-haired lad showed far more energy than the other children she had seen in Vanikval; he kicked at Potil with his bare feet and tried to run, but was jerked back by the rope. As Potil began to cross the square, sometimes dragging, sometimes carrying his charge, another lad appeared behind him. The second boy, similar in appearance and similarly bound, was led by a stout man Kyala had seen on the grounds of Untmur's house. The second boy did not fight continuously against his captor, but halfway across the square he made a sudden leap for freedom. The stout man toppled, and the rope nearly slipped from his grasp. But he rose and tried to regain his dignity as he led his now-passive captive toward Watnojat.

"What is this?" Watnojat muttered. "Is training a surly boy part of my art?"

"Uncle, I don't think he's sending an assistant." Kyala saw the other youngster had been taken to Untmur and that the Vigen was now scrutinizing his eyes, holding his face to the light.

"Make a talisman for this one," said the stout man to Watnojat when he arrived with his charge. The captor bore without expression a sudden onslaught of kicks. He seized the boy's bobbing head by the hair and held him still, then slowly forced the youngster's face toward the glassmaker. The boy's mouth twisted in fear as he shut his eyes. "I can cut off your eyelids," said the man holding the rope. "Of course, my hand might slip."

The boy's lids opened halfway. He tried to bite his captor, but the stout fingers were quick. "Enough," said Untmur's man to Watnojat as he released the boy's head. "You've had your chance to see. Now make the bead." He let the boy run to the end of his rope and then proceeded to drag him toward a post near the edge of the pit.

# Chapter 13

Watnojat seemed dazed. He walked slowly to the wagon and peered over the lip at the vials and mixing board that Kyala had spread out on the floor.

"Uncle, you must not do it. You must not make the bead. If you do, you'll be no better than Untmur."

The glassmaker did not answer. He reached for one of his vials and held it to the dawn sky.

"Uncle, do you forget the rules you taught me?"

"Must I be defeated?" he asked in a quiet voice. "Must I let the tyrant have his victory?" He continued to shift his jars, and Kyala could not fathom his thoughts. At the inn, the peddler had blamed Vanikval for his thieving. Had the Vigen too been corrupted by the place?

She turned from Watnojat and peered across the square. Untmur was already at work. He had brought down a table and a stool from his cart and was comfortably seated, pouring out powders onto his mixing board. What a calm face, she thought, for one bent on defaming his art.

And the victims—the boys. These two, evidently, were not yet under Untmur's control. They glanced fearfully at

Potil, their keeper. When his attention was elsewhere, they chewed furiously at the ropes that bound their hands.

The talismans, once made, would be tested. How else to determine the strongest Vigen? Untmur had not explained the test, but Kyala's gaze lingered on the pit. Surely Watnojat guessed Untmur's intent.

Wild thoughts came into her mind. She would leap on Untmur and scatter his pigments. She would stab him with her dagger, pierce him as she had the great cat. But the jeweled Vigen sat in the middle of the square. How could she approach him without drawing attention? The glass-maker could surely hold her off until Potil and the kiln workers came to his aid.

Another thought came: defeat the Vigen with his own art. She could not reach Untmur unnoticed, but if she dared walk a shorter span . . . If she could approach his animals . . .

Untmur was busy with the pigments, his back to his wagon. She ducked behind the large kiln and saw the few paces of open ground that she must cross. *No chance to turn back now.* She stepped forward and faced the pair of ponies that pulled Untmur's rig. Their eyes were large and liquid, with irises of a rich brown hue that fixed itself in her mind. A bellows man saw her and seemed about to shout something. She was caught already, her hopes lost. But wait. *The woodpile!* She rushed forward and grabbed an armload of sticks. If the assistant did not notice that her kiln was already well supplied, she might escape. She hurried, feeling his eyes burning into her back. But the man gave no alarm.

She threw down the sticks and returned to Watnojat. He was staring at the blue and gray powdered glass he had poured onto his board. Was he planning to match the boy's eye, as he had been ordered? "Uncle, you must not choose those colors," she said. Vials shook in her hand as she searched for the ones she wanted. Then she poured out a rich umber and a deep gold.

"Kyala, I am old, but I haven't lost my sight."

"Then why do you hesitate to finish what you started?"

"I can't do it, Kyala," he said with a faltering voice. "Even to defeat Hestafos, I cannot make this bead."

"Then make a different one." She leaned over and combined the umber and gold in a square of the board. Spilling some of the fragments in her haste, she carried the mixture on a narrow paddle to the mold. "Now you may compete. Here is the bead you must cast." She added dark grains to form a long, narrow pupil. The mold was ready for firing.

Watnojat stared at her, wide eyed, and then glanced toward the other Vigen's ponies. "What you plan is madness, Kyala!"

"If I am mad, then what is Untmur?" Quickly she brought the mold to the kiln, knocking away stones from the opening. She sealed the mold inside and picked up the bellows.

"Do you understand what will happen?" Watnojat approached her slowly, his head bent and his voice hoarse.

"And what will happen if you make the bead he wants?"

Watnojat groaned. "Defeating him is one thing. Making a mockery of this contest is another. I should not have accepted his challenge. I'm to blame for my arrogance, but you'll also suffer."

"I'll finish the talisman. It is up to you what becomes of it." Kyala pumped the bellows fiercely, heaving her anger into the handles, wishing she had Untmur's head inside the kiln. *If he were Dyelo and I were Kolpern,* she thought, *I'd know how to deal with him.* The stones grew warm; the heat stung her face.

Meanwhile Untmur's bead was fusing also, hastened by a fire that was fanned by three men. But his kiln was so much larger. She doubted it would heat faster than her own. She worked until Untmur's men stopped; then she opened a gap in the stones and checked that the powders had fused. How long would the others cool their work?

They waited, wiping the perspiration from their faces

with large, tattered cloths. The many onlookers seemed tired now, their arms and bodies sagging. Yet all waited silently for the contest's end.

Potil picked up a pot of oil that had been warming by the kiln. From the pit's edge he climbed onto the pile of branches, tottering on the rickety support as he splashed the liquid over the wood. Then he went back for a fresh torch and ignited it at the opening to Untmur's kiln.

"It is ready," he called in a low voice to his Vigèn.

The cloaked one stepped forward and lifted the torch. "Now you will see Ormek's fire!" Untmur shouted. The crowd stirred, Kyala noticed, but most faces remained dull. "And now you will remember Ormek's wrath." He waved the torch toward the pit and a few onlookers edged back. "And now you will see me defeat that fury as no other man has done." He touched the brand here and there to the oil-drenched wood. The flames caught and spread; soon the pit was blanketed by fire.

All eyes were on the flames, but Kyala turned to the imprisoned boys. Evidently they had taken advantage of Potil's absence. She saw that the closer youth had freed one hand and was working to loosen the rope that bound his other to the post. He had a chance to save himself. But the second boy had made little progress. *Time. They have no more time.* Ignoring the kiln workers, she dodged behind Untmur's wagon, thinking she might reach the youngsters and cut them free. Had she foreseen this moment of distraction and started sooner, she might have succeeded. Now Potil was already rushing to his charges. Halfway to her destination Kyala turned back. A knife wouldn't help them now—not unless she could use it against Potil. But Untmur's man had allies everywhere and she had none. The boys' only hope lay in Watnojat's kiln.

Potil yanked the lads toward Untmur as the branches crackled in the pit. The oil blaze was finished; small flames now rose from every stick and limb. "They are pulling out the mold!" Watnojat shouted. "We must do the same." Kyala did not use the poker at once; she turned to watch Untmur's talisman emerge from his kiln. The jeweled Vigen picked up a pair of tongs and worked the bead free of its bed. He held it high, and began to parade with it about the edge of the square. "Here is my defiance of Ormek," he said to each group of onlookers.

Quickly Kyala pulled out Watnojat's mold. "You must take the bead as he did." She offered the tongs.

Darst's Vigen shook his head. "Kyala, perhaps I should accept my defeat. He may be content to have you sort out his colors. He may let us go after that."

"Uncle, I think not."

Watnojat sighed. "I angered Ormek. This is my punishment for bringing back Lemp. I'm sure of it." He plucked the bead of umber from the mold and raised it high. His lips moved, but Kyala barely heard his words. "I defy you, Untmur. With this talisman I mock your art."

Untmur ignored them, continuing his slow walk a full three times around the square. By the time he was finished, the thin branches had burned down to a bed of glowing embers. He returned to the place where the boys stood, and waited while Potil cut the first one's ropes. For a moment the youngster had his freedom. Then the jeweled Vigen raised the bead again. "Dance your defiance of Ormek," he commanded in a voice for all to hear. "Dance on the coals."

The boy did not run away, but neither did he obey at once. Kyala saw his mouth twist in the effort to fight the bead's compulsion. He looked at his bare feet and then at the pit. He managed to turn away from the flames and took a few slow steps toward the crowd. His face glistened with sweat as he struggled against the command. "Dance!" shouted Untmur, waving the talisman. The boy's legs, seemingly of their own accord, turned back toward the heat. He cried aloud when he saw that he could not escape the command.

Kyala tapped Watnojat's shoulder, and when he nodded his readiness she raced for Untmur's wagon. She cut the tethers that held the ponies to the rail, then waved at the glassmaker. He was speaking, but no one could hear him. He was giving his orders but the words were lost. Then he tried again, his voice louder, high-pitched but clear. "Dance," he said. "Dance on the coals!"

Watnojat's brown-eyed ponies, straining at their own tethers, remained by the post. But Untmur's animals were free to move. Still in harness, they started toward the fire. "Dance!" shouted Watnojat, and the charmed creatures could not help but obey. They charged the pit. The boy still struggled against his urges, but before he could step onto the ashes Untmur's cart was dragged in ahead of him. "Dance on the embers!" The ponies kicked and pawed and jumped in response to Watnojat's command. Untmur threw down his bead in fury and rushed forward to try to control the animals. The traces broke and the wagon keeled over, its load of baskets spilling into the fire.

Kyala reached the boy who had been under Untmur's spell. "Run," she said, shaking the dazed youngster; his companion had already vanished. "Go, before he picks up the bead!" She slapped the boy's face. He spat at her, then raced into the crowd.

Flames were licking at the fallen baskets. "The disks!" Kyala shouted, recognizing the containers from the previous day. "Untmur's disks." The assistants clustered around the pit, trying to grapple the baskets with pokers. The glass pieces spilled out, hit the coals, and cracked.

Kyala could watch no longer. Now, in the confusion, was the time to escape from Vanikval. But where was Watnojat? The onlookers had broken their ranks and were pouring into the square. She heard her Vigen's voice, but could not see him. "Look!" he shouted. "See how Ormek destroys Untmur's works. See how the heat cracks his poor glass." Were people listening? Something had weakened their obedience to Untmur. Whether it was the contest gone awry or the breaking of his medallions, Kyala could not guess. But some showed life in their faces—wide eyes, lips curled in anger. Brandishing their torches as weapons, they advanced on the jeweled Vigen and his assistants where they still struggled with the bucking animals and the burning wagon.

"Get back. All of you, back!" Now it was Untmur shouting, his huge voice carrying over the crowd. At once Kyala was aware of a change. The attackers slowed, their motions gradually becoming dreamy again. "Everyone stop. Back to your places. Now!" Untmur's power was not gone. The people halted and some began to turn.

Kyala tried to make her way through to Watnojat, but was blocked by the retreating crowds. Thick smoke from the burning wagon blew into her face. Her eyes teared, and for moments she was helpless. Then something fell on her. Rough cloth covered her face; her arms were pinioned. She kicked, connecting with what might have been a leg. "Tie her feet," said Potil's voice. "Make it tight."

She tried to cry out, but the cloth muffled the sound. They were carrying her now, bouncing her carelessly as they made their way through the crowds. She screamed again, and someone stuffed folds of the cloth into her mouth. The taste was bitter and foul. She tried vainly to clear her mouth with her tongue. "Hand her up," said a voice. She felt herself rising, and then more ropes lashed her to a hump. Her head hung down, and the hump began to move.

She was on a horse or pony, being taken—where? Soon she felt herself tilting. They were climbing a hill, and she only knew one hill above Vanikval. Where was Watnojat? Perhaps he had also been snatched by Untmur's lackeys. The talisman had succeeded all too well in humiliating the jeweled Vigen; now he would act by stealth, dispose of them quickly rather than try to dominate them with his colored glass. Kyala strained at her bonds, thinking that she might slip free before reaching the house. The animal's jostling might loosen the ropes. But, for all her efforts, she could not move. Her head ached and her stomach threatened to rebel.

*What a pair of fools we've been.* They had come for Torged's sake, to find the astablak that would spare others his fate. But there was none left in the earth—she believed Untmur on that point. So their only hope had lain with this heartless Vigen. And now they would not return at all.

How had she fallen into such mischance? She recalled the day Watnojat first came into her mother's house. With her father gone, how could she not take notice of this man who filled the empty place at the table? He was old, but his face was kind, and the people of Darst admired him. If only she could become like him, she had thought, earning respect through the skills of her hands and mind. For years the idea, unattainable as it seemed, had brightened her thoughts. Then the chance had come.

"Dump her in the shop." She felt some of the ropes loosen, but they were only the ones that bound her to the animal. Then she was dragged, her boots bouncing along what might have been the shard-strewn courtyard. A door opened with a squeal of hinges. Another door. Then she fell to a hard floor and was left alone.

She could not gauge the passage of time. There was no sound but that of her labored breathing through the cloth; there was no light at all. Her body pressed into the unyielding stone. If only she could shift her weight, turn over, she might relieve the aches. If only she could have a taste of water. Time passed, and she realized that she had been sleeping. The sound of a door scraping brought her quickly awake. She tensed for whatever was to come.

Light! A dim illumination filtered through the cloth. Then her legs were jostled and she heard a cutting sound. Roughly she was turned over and other ropes were cut. The covering was pulled from her head. "Untmur!"

"It was you who mixed the colorings." Untmur's face was bleak, his eyes narrow and his lips tight. In his hand he held the knife that had cut her free—a blade that started in a needle tip, then widened to span its handle of bone. He kept the weapon pointed at her throat. "You were the one who destroyed my festival."

"We won the contest," she blurted out. "Give us the astablak."

"Won? You won a short life with a painful end."

"*Our* victims danced. Yours didn't. So we were the winners. Your knife can't change that."

"Don't I know that ponies respond quicker than humans? They're stupid animals, and you are little smarter. Save your breath for your screams."

"Then finish it." She raised her chin to better expose her throat. "I'll be better off with Ormek. I'm thirsty and my head hurts and all my hopes are gone."

"And what were those hopes?" His lips twisted. "To be a Vigen in *Darst?* What do the people there know of fine glass? Darst and Wintersgate are one and the same, and I had my fill of Wintersgate years ago."

"Should I aspire to be a washerwoman?"

"You have talent. It's rare in a girl. Unheard of."

"How would you know that? How many girls or women are ever tested?"

He waved away her retort. "It's true what I told your Watnojat. I have no one to succeed me here. I tried testing the local boys, but the striplings were afraid. They turned pale and ran from me. I could have used talismans to keep them, but you can't get real work from a person that way."

"You've got your bellows pumpers and your pit diggers. They work for you."

"I'm talking of *thoughtful* work, not mindless labor. But I could spare you if you'd stay with me. I need an assistant or all my knowledge will be lost."

"Assistant? To help you send boys to dance barefoot on embers?"

"That's not the only way to defy Ormek."

"Ormek is the Lifegiver."

"What do you know of it?" He turned his head slightly, as if preparing to leave. The lantern he had placed on the floor cast a reddish sheen on his forehead and on the leather cap that covered his scalp. "A few days without food or water might change your mind." He reached for the lamp.

"Wait. What have you done with Watnojat?"

Untmur's lips showed the hint of a smile.

"Release him, and I'll do what you ask. Let him go home to die in his own town. Send him back to Darst."

Untmur's teeth were a sickly shade of yellow in the lamplight. "So I saved the right prize. I was going to toss him in to burn with my wagon."

"Show me that he's well if you want my cooperation."

"Show you? Come with me. You walk ahead." He stood aside and directed her to turn. The corridor was narrow and dank. Her shadow loomed ahead of her on the dusty stone floor, shifting as Untmur swung his lamp. He paused at a doorway, undid a latch, and pushed the door slightly ajar. Kyala heard the familiar wheezing, the rise and fall of breath as Watnojat slept. "There's your former master," Untmur said. "There's what's left of him." He closed the door and pinned the latch. "And now I'll show you your new quarters."

"First show me to the washhouse."

"Ahh. Yes."

There was an exit to the walkway behind the shop that led to a separate small building. Even the shop's washhouse was built of stone! Kyala glanced up at the night sky and guessed the time to be nearly midnight. She turned and glared at Untmur, who was following at her heels. "I won't run off while you have Watnojat." He handed her the light and permitted her to enter alone.

*Weapons?* She raised the lantern to see what the room might contain. But first, first she must empty her bladder. She squatted over the hole for what seemed an eternity, balancing herself with one hand while she swung the lamp with the other. There were only a few buckets and tubs, nothing of use against Untmur.

If they had not taken it, there was the knife that Watnojat had given her to carry in her boot. But what a small weapon compared with Untmur's blade. Kyala stood up, tied her drawstring hurriedly, then slipped her fingers into the boot. She felt for the sheath she had sewn into the calf, and found the small knife. A faint hope.

"Kyala!" Untmur banged on the door, and it swung open.

"My feet hurt. I'm fixing my stocking." She moved to a bench and sat with her back to the door, hoping he couldn't see what she was doing. She pulled the talisman's cord over her head and stuffed the bead of her own eye color into the top of the stocking. *That's the first thing he'll want to take from me,* she thought. Then she followed him back into the shop.

"Now you tell me how this compares with your quarters in Darst." Untmur showed her into a spacious room with a fireplace. Logs blazed in the hearth. Sheepskins covered the floor. By the bed stood a table laid out with cheese and bread. "Sit," he said. He poured wine from a jar into a glass cup. She licked her lips but did not move. Untmur picked up the glass, drained the contents, and sighed his appreciation. He poured wine into the other glass.

"It will make me lightheaded. Give me water."

Untmur frowned and pointed to a skin that hung on the wall. She tilted it to her lips. The water tasted stale, but she drank it in huge drafts. When she put aside the skin, she saw that Untmur was helping himself to the food on the table. He broke the bread with his hands and bit off chunks of cheese. There was no knife on the table, and his own weapon was out of sight. *Hidden in his cloak,* she thought. *Ready if he needs it.*

"Will you eat?"

Her mouth watered. "I'm . . . not hungry."

He pushed aside the plate. "Then come over here and I'll tell you about your duties. Your Watnojat is shrewder than I first suspected. There's some advantage in having a girl for apprentice." He reached for her where she stood backed to the wall, pulled her sharply, and tumbled her onto the bed.

"You can have any woman in Vanikval!" Kyala thrashed as he gripped her with one hand while the other searched out her fastenings. "Why choose me?"

"Mindless labor," he answered, already starting to breathe heavily. "I might as well thrust myself into a pile of straw." He reached down, tugged off her boots, and tossed them under the table. "You won't need those." His breath reeked of decaying meat.

Kyala stopped struggling. If she did not please this Vigen, then Watnojat was doomed. "I'll be dutiful as any apprentice," she forced herself to say. She tried to smile, but she was certain that she looked to him like a wild dog baring its fangs before it struck.

# Chapter 14

Untmur flung off his cloak, pitching the jeweled garment into the middle of the room. *Now we are both weaponless,* Kyala thought. *Or are we?* The Vigen stood over her, his arms, shoulders, and neck exposed by his sleeveless jerkin. Though his body hair was gray, his muscles looked firm, his skin taut.

He fell on top of her. A mass of white hair boiled up from the neck of his low-cut jerkin. She rubbed her forehead against its coarseness. Had she not rubbed against Jelor in just this way? The comparison sickened her, yet she knew her purpose. The leather jerkin was thick, but if Untmur wore his own talisman about his neck she would feel it against her face.

His weight bore her down into the thick pallet. She felt smothered under hair and leather. Where was his bead? Was this man so secure that he wore no protection against other Vigens? She gasped for a breath of air and cried out, "Don't crush me." She could barely form the words. "Don't crush me or you'll have no apprentice."

He rolled onto his side. She tried to feel behind him,

disguising her quest by pretending to rub his back. "No more of that," said the Vigen. He pulled at her trousers and cursed the fastenings. His touch made her think of the rope of shame that had hung on Watnojat's door. *Fish guts*. The drawstring came undone.

Untmur pulled the long jerkin up above his waist. *Now it must happen,* she thought. *For Watnojat, I must suffer even this*.

The Vigen drove against her. Kyala could not stop herself from screaming. She threw her hands up and clawed at his head. The cap came off, and what she felt with her fingertips nearly made her forget the battering below. *Talismans!* Glass beads set into his hairless scalp! She could feel the colors— an odd assortment of animal eyes, protection against the risks of the forest. But there must be another. *One of these. His own must be one of these*. Then she sensed a bead that had the shade of his murderous gray eyes. It was a color she could not mistake.

"Lie still, slut." Untmur raised himself on one hand and pinched her chin viciously with the other. The pain made her cry out again, but she realized that his weight was off her for a moment. Her hands were at his shoulders. As soon as he released her, she locked her arms about his neck and pushed her head out from under him so she could reach his scalp with her teeth. "Lie down!" he roared, but she was already biting into his rancid flesh. Now it was Untmur's turn to scream as she chewed at his skin. His hands thrashed wildly; she tasted his blood and raw flesh. Straining her jaw muscles, she tore the bead free. Then she pulled her legs away from him, rolled off the bed, and raced across the room.

She whirled to face him. His hand clutched his head and his face was pinched with pain, but he was swinging his legs around to come after her. The warm talisman was in her mouth. She must use it, though such use was forbidden. She must turn the bead against Untmur.

"Stop," she said, her tongue hampered by the talisman. "Hold your place."

His movements slowed when she spoke; yet he rose groggily to his feet. *The glass has power . . . but not enough!* Her pulse pounded in her ears as she watched him begin to walk. His steps were like those of a man in deep water. "I am stronger . . . than any talisman," he grunted.

Quickly she fastened her trousers, preparing to run through the doorway. But where could she hide in this place that was Untmur's own? She wedged the bead firmly in her cheek. It was heat that gave it strength—her mouth's heat ought to suffice. But Untmur wiped away the blood that trickled down his forehead and took another step.

"Hold," she said.

He extended his hand. "Return the bead, and I'll forgive you." His voice was thin but insistent.

She bent to retrieve his discarded cloak. Hastily, but gingerly, she felt for the missing knife. There were many folds, and she dared not take her eyes from him.

"You'll find nothing there for you," he said.

Her boots lay behind him now, her own weapon out of her reach. She moved closer to the door.

"Give me the bead," he said, his voice growing stronger.

He was breaking free. The talisman could not hold him. Kyala whirled to run into the hopeless dark of the corridor. *The lantern!* She snatched it from the hook. In its flame lay Ormek's power, if she dared to use it. She spat the talisman into her hand, then held the bead in her fingertips as she hesitated over what she must do. *Untmur is no more than a beast,* she thought. *I must deal with him as with any vicious creature.*

She touched the glass to the hot metal. At once the wick flared up, its glow exploding into brilliance that could not be contained. The flames extended in every direction, fearful in their intensity. *How could this be?* For a moment she was stunned, surrounded by light and heat that blotted out all else. *Ormek!* He was the source! She felt His fire about her, His power flowing into her spirit. And from that power, the talisman drew strength.

"No!" shouted Untmur. The light faded, and Kyala heard the moisture on the bead hiss into steam. Untmur clapped his hands to his eyes and sank to the floor. "Enough," he rasped. "Enough."

She pulled back the talisman, but could not speak at once. What had happened when she touched the glass to the lamp? Watnojat hadn't prepared her for such an experience. When the Vigen had used a flame against the great cat, she had seen no upwelling of light. But now she felt Ormek within her, and suddenly her purpose put words to her lips. "Give me the astablak we won. That's the first thing you must do for me."

"Go to the workroom." Untmur's voice was barely audible. Slowly he rose and turned toward the corridor; she moved aside to let him pass. Then she grabbed up her boots and pulled them on before following his shuffling footsteps.

Her lantern lit up but one corner of the huge workroom. Untmur lit another lamp, yet still the room had dark corners. She saw that he had not exaggerated his need for an assistant. Bottles and jars stood in disarray everywhere, even on the floor. Containers lay on their sides, their precious powders poured out and mixed with common dust. Her gaze fell on some slender vials, out of place amongst the wide-mouthed bottles that Untmur used in such numbers. Then, pushed under a bench, she saw Watnojat's chest. "Thief!" she shouted.

"He would not trade the blues," Untmur said softly.

"You have blues enough to master ten Vanikvals. Put them back in the chest before I use the lamp again." Then she spotted Watnojat's bead pouch, its contents spilled out at one corner of the table. "Those too!" she shouted. "Pack them quickly."

Untmur moved to obey, but again he was slow. What if Potil should arrive before he finished? "Hurry," she said.

She could not wait. While he replaced the vials in the box, she scooped up the spilled talismans and poured them back into Watnojat's pouch. "And the astablak?"

"Ah, yes. It is here somewhere. Surely it's here."

Kyala moved the bead nearer to the heat, and suddenly Untmur began to search in earnest. "These are my darkest pigments," he said quickly. He brought down the first jar from a high shelf and dropped it carelessly into the chest.

"Show me the color," Kyala said. She had never seen true astablak, only Watnojat's substitute. Untmur, at her insistence, poured out a bit of the powder. "Stand away," she said. She brought the lantern closer and stared at the fragments of glass. *Richer ... Darker ...* Even under lamplight she could see about each grain a hint of fire, a red glow cloaking the blackness. Now she understood the difference between this and Watnojat's replacement. But if Lame Ones required such an accurate match, she thought, didn't that make them more intelligent than any animal?

"Where is the rest of it?" she demanded.

"There is no more."

"There must be more. We saw the fields where the Kiss once grew. You dug up those fields."

"Dug, yes," he said wearily. "But I found only a few pockets."

"There must have been other diggings. You had workers all over those mountains."

"One or two other places. All the sites were poor. I made talismans with the rest of the astablak I had. People wanted protection."

Kyala stamped her boot in anger. "Protection against what? You said that the Lame Ones in these parts were all dead."

A faint smile touched Untmur's lips. "I was well paid for those beads, needed or not."

"Vigen, you lie." She almost touched the bead to the lamp, but hesitated to invoke Ormek's strength again. Even without contact, the talisman had its effect. Untmur bent over in agony, his hands pressed to his face. Her own fingers felt the burning, and she pulled them back.

Untmur could not speak. He clutched the edge of the workbench and stared at her with frightened eyes. "Look for yourself, if you don't believe me," he whispered at last. "I've no more of it."

"Then this was your prize for our contest? This meager bottle? No wonder you offered all you had." She was tempted to apply the lantern again. But she could not believe that Untmur would invite such suffering if he might prevent it. He had given her all he possessed. She brushed the powder back into the jar, pushed home the wooden stopper, and added it to Watnojat's box along with the pouch. *One vial.* For a moment she was lost in anguish. A handful of beads was all they might cast from Untmur's glass. Yet there was something more she must do here.

The Vigen stirred and tried to move away from her.

"I'm not finished with you," Kyala said. "Show me how you control the townsfolk."

"I will give you other pigments. Look. Anything I have here is yours. Take it all."

"Don't distract me. Must I use the talisman again?"

Untmur bowed his head and shuffled to the side of the room, then opened a door to a side chamber that reeked of burning oil. Three large-bellied lamps with double wicks and open flames cast their light from a low platform; ringed about them on broad folds of leather lay the beads of Vanikval. Blues, greens, grays. For each of his subjects, he had a talisman.

"Now you know," said Untmur. "I have power beyond that of any mere Vigen. I am the true master of glass."

Only for a moment did Kyala study the display on the floor. From the ceiling hung medallions like those she had seen in the square—disks of different sizes, but all of that same strange wine color. She gasped as the dizziness struck. *The disks!* They were fighting her own talisman, trying to bring it under Untmur's control along with the others. She took a step backward, hoping to weaken the effect.

"Pick them up—" Kyala pointed to the beads on the floor, but could not finish her command. Her head seemed detached from her body, rising slowly toward the ceiling while the rest remained below. She wanted him to give her the talismans, to pack them in a box so she could take them away. She wanted him to smash the disks.

But the walls began to lean, threatening to topple. She had hoped to save the townsfolk and now she was losing even herself. Untmur was coming to retrieve his bead; she saw his face looming. *The disks. What was their source of power?*

She lurched to the side. Untmur came after her, his motions slow but relentless. She fell to her knees, her head still separated by an impossible distance from her shoulders. He reached for her foot and caught her boot. *The power comes from light and heat, from misusing Ormek's gifts.* Lamplight had been her friend, but now ... Her hand moved for her like a hand reflected in water. Yet she made it do her will. She pulled at a fold of leather and heard the beads scatter to the stone floor like so many pebbles. She threw the edge of the hide over the flames and two lamps went out. Untmur fell down beside her, trying to catch her arms before she could extinguish the other. She twisted and slashed out with her boots to kick over the last of the lamps. Her boot tip rang against brass, but the light still burned. Untmur's arm was at her throat. She kicked once more, this time smashing the wick tubes; the room went dark. Her head found her body, and the walls turned upright again.

"Give me my talisman!" Untmur shouted. Her hands were empty. The bead had fallen to the floor and was lost amongst the others. He clawed at her jacket.

There was no time to search for the piece; in the dark she had no chance to find it. Her control of Untmur was gone. "Here," she said. "This is yours." She felt about the floor, then handed him the first bead she could pick up. In a moment, by his sense of touch, he would know it was wrong.

"My talisman!" he cried. She wrenched free and ran out, pushing the heavy panel closed behind her. *He doesn't know if I still have it,* she thought. *Will he search the floor or come after me?* She saw rings on the outside of the door and on the frame—but no bar. How could she lock him inside? If she could find the handle of a tool . . . but around her she saw only glass bottles. She thought of the knife in her boot, pulled it free, and slipped it through the rings. Untmur pounded on the door, and the blade quivered under his blows. It would not hold him long.

In the outer room Watnojat's box lay where it had been left. She picked up the chest and the small lantern she had carried from the bedchamber, then hurried back toward the room where her Vigen was confined. This small building had but one corridor. She pulled open the door and found the glassmaker grimy and bedraggled, with dried blood on his face. "Wake up, Uncle. We must leave now." She shook him gently and then not so gently.

"Kyala . . ." He staggered to his feet, his breathing heavy and his eyes half open. He held his hands out in front of him and staggered toward the doorway. "Untmur?" She gave no answer, but pulled him toward the washhouse, to the one exit she had seen.

The corridor was empty, and the side door swung open at her push. They came out near the stable. There were no lights, but the half-moon cast faint illumination across the yard. Under the roof all was in darkness. Had Untmur brought back their rig as well as the chest? Kyala heard the quiet breathing of animals. She rushed to the sound and brushed her fingers over familiar muzzles. She knew the colors of their coats by touch. "I've found our grays!" she called, feeling the collars still in place about their necks. Beside them she saw the faint outlines of a wagon.

Watnojat made his way after her. "Can we hitch them in the dark? Maybe we should just ride the ponies out of here."

"I don't think I can find saddles." She wondered how much time they had before Untmur's men came after them. Should she leave the wagon? "We cannot ride bareback and carry your box," she said. "But I can hitch them, Uncle. They're nearly harnessed already."

Under her touch the first pair backed into the traces. She buckled the fastenings as well as she could, hoping they would hold for just a short while. Then she hitched the second pair while Watnojat brought the chest up onto the wagon.

They pulled out of the stable. She clucked to the grays, and the animals started to trot. A door banged somewhere behind, and she heard shouts. Untmur was already after them!

She begged the grays for speed. Just one road ran down the hill; there were no turnings until it reached the bottom. But in the town itself were many streets. Their pursuers would need time to search them all. *Faster!* The ponies ignored her pleas. She saw their ears prick up and then, as they started to descend, she heard a noise rising from the town. "Uncle, do you hear?"

"I hear horses behind us."

Kyala glanced back and saw a rider's dark shape bearing down on them. His face caught the moonlight—a blood-smeared face. Untmur himself was pursuing them! And behind him rode Potil and others. How much faster could they fly?

"Listen to the noises from the town!" Below she caught a glimpse of torchlight in the streets. *The festival? Was it still going?* At the bottom of the hill a disorderly procession appeared. She recalled the brief rebellion in the square. Now the townsfolk again held their torches high and they ran, shouting.

"Uncle, you taught me that one must *hold* a bead to wield

its power. But Untmur uses disks to spread his influence from afar."

"What is that to us?"

"Look! I put out his lamps! His power is gone."

Surely Untmur had rushed after her without stopping to rekindle his flames. For the moment the people had regained their wills, and she and Watnojat would be caught between the two sides. The crowd came sweeping up. How could the wagon pass on the narrow road?

"Make way!" Kyala shouted. The grays tried to slow their flight as the mob came on undaunted. "Make way!" she called again. The torchbearers were already surging past them, scattering before the plunging wagon.

The ponies weaved back and forth, trying to keep the flames away from their faces. The wagon groaned under the strain. "Death to the Vigen!" shouted some in the crowd. "Stop the ponies!" shouted others.

"Untmur's behind us!" Kyala called, but some of the passersby must have thought she was carrying their Vigen to freedom. Brands were thrown, some falling just behind her seat. Then she heard something heavier hit. A townsman, his face bloated with rage, clung to the lip of the wagon as it rumbled through the throng.

"The Vigen dies!" he shouted.

Kyala could not drop the reins. She looked back and saw that he was pulling himself up, lifting a leg over the side. "Uncle, stop him!"

Watnojat was trying to reach the rear section. She glanced over once to see him clutching at the seat back. The next time she looked, he had picked up a fallen torch and was pushing it into the interloper's face. "We tried to help you!" the glassmaker cried. "Behind us is your real enemy."

"Kill all Vigens," answered the townsman. "All die this night."

They had reached the bottom of the hill. Kyala steered into the narrow streets of the town, trying to guess which way might lead to the eastern road. She heard a thud and looked back to see that Watnojat had fallen to the floor. The townsman, still clinging to the lip of the wagon, flung away the brand he had wrested from the glassmaker. He was trying again to climb inside.

An intersection lay just ahead. There was a chance to rid herself of the interloper. But if she misjudged the corner, the wheels would smash and the ride would be over. She pulled the reins sharply; the grays turned and one wheel scraped against the side of a building. *Just right,* she thought as the man howled with pain. Yet when she looked again he was still there, pulling himself toward Watnojat. dragging his legs across the wagon's floor. "Soso," she called to the ponies, then dropped the reins. They would have to look out for themselves.

"Untmur must die," said the townsman. He picked up another of the torches, still smoking, and raised it for a blow at Watnojat's head. Kyala leaped over the seat back and fell on top of the stranger. He was too strong for her, pulling the stave free of her grip. She rolled aside to dodge his blow, then pulled herself to the wagon's lip as he raised the brand again. *His hurt leg!* She reached for a tattered boot, twisted the foot, and heard the man's answering scream. He swung at her clumsily. The wagon was still moving. She braced her feet and dragged the man to the edge.

"Untmur is on his horse, you fool!" Her words had no effect. He grabbed her jacket and tried to pull her down. There was another brand smoldering; she reached for it as she fell, and drove the charred end against his neck. He cried out and his grip fell slack.

"Die . . ." said the man, but now his voice was barely audible. His head fell back and he lay still.

Kyala rushed forward to regain control of the grays and halted their aimless motion in the middle of a street. A few people were calling to each other from doorways, but the main body of marchers were well behind her. As for Untmur and his men, she could not say. The crowds would deal with them.

"There's a man hurt here," she called to a woman whose shawled head peered out onto the street. *Two men*, she thought, though the stranger had gotten the worst of it. She returned to the Vigen; Watnojat stared at her groggily. "Uncle, what happened to you?"

"Don't stop for my sake," he said. He sat up and rubbed the side of his head where he had fallen. Meanwhile a small group of the curious gathered about the wagon.

The townsman lay on his back. She gripped him under the arms and pulled him head-first toward the onlookers. "Take this one," said Kyala. "Untmur drove him mad." A man and a woman helped lower the man to the street, then stood staring at him as he lay motionless on the dirt.

"It's Repstor," said one. "Y' can't just leave him there."

Kyala felt for the small purse sewn into her jacket and extracted a few coppers. "Get him to a healer," she said to the woman who had spoken. She handed down the coins. The woman looked up, her mouth wide with astonishment. *A modest sum anywhere else*, thought Kyala. *But in Vanikval possibly a fortune*.

The woman's look changed to one of suspicion. "I know you, girl. You were in the square."

"She was in with Untmur," said another. Pointing to Watnojat, he added: "And *he's* the one supposed to be a demon."

"Wait. He's no demon. He made the ponies dance. He made Untmur a fool."

Kyala didn't wait for the argument to be settled. She rushed to the reins and had the ponies moving before the onlookers could decide if they were enemies or friends. "Uncle, are you all right back there?"

"I'll rest, Kyala. You get us to Fargladden."

She turned the wagon into another narrow street. Now she had the moon behind her and knew she was headed in the right direction. One of these streets must run through and continue eastward. If the people had been friendlier, she might have gotten directions. Now she would need luck.

The narrow street ended. She turned again and made her way through a long, twisting alley until she reached what seemed to be the town's main thoroughfare. Wasn't this the road they had come in on? Glancing up, she saw flames on the hilltop. From Untmur's roofs fires licked at the dark sky.

Quickly she turned eastward again. This time the street did not end, but turned into a straight track that crossed the fields. They were out of Vanikval, but she did not feel safe. Not yet. She drove until dawn, until the modest cottages of Fargladden closed in all around her. Only then did she feel that she had escaped Untmur's pale.

# Chapter 15

Watnojat was snoring softly in the back of the wagon when they rattled into the yard of Fargladden's inn. Kyala was weary enough to want to drop down beside him and sleep on the hard boards. She doubted that she would know the difference between the wagon and the innkeeper's beds.

"Early, aren't ya." The stableboy yawned as he came up to take charge of the grays. "Or maybe y'r late." Behind him stood a crude but sturdy-looking shed. The ponies turned toward the place where their comforts lay.

Kyala motioned for the boy to hold the grays steady. There was sufficient light now to see the extent of Untmur's thievery. She would make a brief check of their equipment before turning over the rig. She stepped past the sleeping glassmaker and began to poke at the disarray of hides and barrels and boxes.

"May demons chew his bowels!" she shouted. Nothing was left of the tools of Watnojat's trade. The bellows was gone. Perhaps that and the pair of tongs had been left by the kiln in the square. But surely the mixing board and the sand crock and the small tools had remained on the wagon when Untmur took it to his stable. They also had been carrying supplies and trade goods. Of these she found one upended barrel—empty. A half sack of barley meal remained of the food and nothing more. Weapons? Arod had sent them off with a fine spear, but that too was missing. And where was the axe? She lifted the other hides and found only a sack of spare clothing and a few sooty cooking pots. *May Ormek singe his black heart.*

There was nothing more to see. Even Watnojat's coin purse was absent from its place on his belt. She would not tell the Vigen at once of their losses, she decided. He should have a hot meal first, and some comforts after the hardships. She touched the small purse under her coat; its few coins were all they had left. *Enough for a day or two.*

She bent to the glassmaker and tried to rouse him. "Uncle, we're safe now. You can drink ale and sleep in a soft bed and forget Untmur." Watnojat did not wake at once, and when his eyes finally opened he stared at her without comprehension.

"Uncle, what's wrong?" The puffy flesh trembled beneath his watery eyes. His lips moved slightly, but not to make words. "I don't understand you. Uncle!"

His lips moved again, but then his face fell slack. Kyala touched his cheek; the skin felt cold. She stroked his forehead gently, and when he did not respond she bent to hug him, rubbing her face into his coat to wipe away her tears.

"Uncle! Uncle!" She tried several times, but could not rouse him again. She glanced about wildly, wondering how she could find aid. Surely there would be no good in stopping at the inn. She called to the boy. "Where can I find a healer?"

"Not here."

"Where, then?"

"Down the road. That way. Three white poles in front. Won't take very long." He yawned again.

Returning to her seat, she took up the reins, waved the

boy aside. The ponies made a broad turn to head in the direction he had shown. They reached the place quickly. The morning sun lit up the stakes that marked points of a triangle in front of a small stone cottage. She banged a fist at the door of bundled branches, producing only a muffled sound. Then she saw a small gong and hammer suspended from the eaves. She struck a piercing note, then repeated it three times more.

"Enough," said a thin voice. "I'm not deaf yet."

The door opened so quickly that Kyala nearly stumbled across the threshold. She looked in at the slender, beardless person who stood back from the light. The hair was long and unkempt; by the voice a man had spoken. "I was afraid you wouldn't come," said Kyala. "Are you the healer?"

"For some. Others call me a weasel."

*A fine beginning!* But where else could she turn? "I have a sick man in the wagon."

"Well, bring him inside."

"He can't walk. He can't do anything."

The healer grumbled, reached for a floppy straw hat that hung on a peg. "I'll want payment in copper," he said. "No eggs. I'm up to the roof in eggs."

Watnojat was heavy. Straining and panting, they brought him from the wagon into the dark cottage and carried him to a low pallet beside the fireplace. Another man lay on the narrow bed. The healer used Watnojat's body to push the other aside, so that an arm and a leg slid off to dangle on the floor. "That one won't know the difference," said the healer. "Now tell me what happened to y'r old guy."

"He . . . He was beaten, I think. And last night he fell down in the wagon in a fight. Hit his head on the side." She showed the lump from the blow.

"Beatin's bad for one his age." The healer squatted and put an ear to Watnojat's neck. "Loosen the coat," he told her. He pulled up the shirt and listened to the Vigen's chest. "Not so good."

"He wants to go home to Darst."

The man grinned. "He told ya he wants to go? Not likely. And where in Ormek's pocket is *Darst?*"

"West. By the sea. A way south of Asep River."

"I wouldn't know it."

"It was late winter when we left."

"Spring's nearly gone. You've a long way back, and *he* won't be goin' with ya."

"He will." Kyala dropped down beside the pallet. She bent to the pale skin of Watnojat's chest, listening as the healer had listened. The sparse hairs rubbed against her ear, but she heard no sounds from his heart. She closed her eyes. The night's work had caught up to her; she felt as if she were sinking into a bed of soft feathers, into the bed in her mother's house. But how could she drift off now? *Uncle! Uncle, are you gone?*

"I'll need his chest bare," the healer said, "if I'm gonna work on him. Can you get the coat and shirt off?"

The coat was already open. With some difficulty she pulled his arms through the sleeves. Then she gathered up the goatskin shirt and pulled that toward his head.

"Get the hands in first." The beardless one helped her pull Watnojat's arms free of the shirt, and finally the garment slipped off over his head. As she put aside the goatskins, she caught sight of the tethered bead, fallen to the side and dangling against his shoulder. It was Watnojat's own talisman, the blue-gray color of his eyes.

"What's that for?" The healer picked up the glass, scrutinized it, then dropped it suddenly as if it had caught fire in his hand. "Where'd you two come from?"

"Darst. I told you."

"By what route? Not through Vanikval."

"Yes. We escaped from Untmur. I think he's dead."

"Dead?" The healer looked warily at Watnojat. "How?"

"The people broke free of his control. I saw his roofs burning."

The healer jabbed a finger at Watnojat's chest, but did

not touch the bead again. "Only a Vigen would wear that thing. You'd better take y'r old guy out of here."

Kyala felt her face flush. "He saved Vanikval from Untmur, and now you want him to die outside in a wagon."

The healer put his face in his hands. "What do I know about Vigens? If one demon beats another, does that make the victor my friend?"

"He's not your enemy. Listen. Healers and Vigens can help each other. He helped cure a man in Wintersgate. The herb-healer needed time for the medicines to work. Uncle made a talisman."

"For what?"

"With a bead you can help the cure."

"Can you hex a man back to health?"

"Sometimes. It depends on the case. You can hold his life in him for a day or two. That may be all you need." She picked up the talisman and cradled it in her hand. Her voice fell. "One must use judgment, that is what he taught me." She felt the color of Watnojat's eyes in the bead. Did she dare try to help him as he had aided Lemp?

"Glass talismans? Pig squirts!"

"Let him stay awhile and you may learn something," she said. "And I can pay you." She tapped her purse, trying to make it jangle as if it were stuffed with coins.

"Learn something? Pah! For your coppers, I'll give you 'til noon."

"Then brew some medicines. Whatever will do him good."

The healer shook his head, but when she jangled her purse again he turned to the clay jars and bundles of herbs that lay at the edge of the hearth. Kyala worked the cord over the glassmaker's head, then took the bead into her mouth and pressed it against the inside of her cheek. *It needs heat, but I must not burn him,* she thought. *Talisman, grow warm!*

At last she removed the bead and squeezed it in her palm. "Uncle. Uncle, do you hear me?"

Nothing.

"We're free, Uncle. We're safe in Fargladden." *The voice ... Where was his inner voice?*

"Enough of your play!" the healer grumbled. "I'll be wasting my herbs if I cook something up for ya."

"But you believe that a Vigen can bend a man's will?"

"A *Vigen* can do it. Not to a corpse, though."

"He's no corpse yet!" But was she certain? Had Ormek already called him? She took the bead back into her hand, then slowly exposed the ball of her thumb. "I'll want a knife," she said hesitantly.

"I don't do cutting."

"For *me*."

"Pah!" He waved his hand in disgust, but at last brought her a narrow blade. As she held up her thumb, she tried not to look at the skull carved into the knife's bone handle. The hearthlight flickered on tarnished metal. For a moment she glanced back at her Vigen, recalling how he had saved Lemp this way. She clenched her teeth. *Now.* The blade bit. She squeezed the flesh between two fingers of the opposite hand. A droplet of red fell onto the bead. "Uncle, do you hear me? Uncle!"

Then she heard a rustling that came not from the room. Watnojat had tried to describe the sensation of hearing the inner voice, but only now did she understand.

"Kyala." Was that what she heard? The whisper came through her ear, but not from its usual source. It was as if the ear possessed a twin, the second hearing sounds from a world she did not know. The Vigen's lips were still; yet his other voice grew louder until she could make out every word. "Kyala, you should not ... have called me. I ... am past a cure."

"How can you know that, Uncle? We haven't even tried."

"I am weak. I pushed myself too far. Now you will finish what I began."

"No, Uncle. We'll finish this journey together."

"Kyala, my oak tree is waiting. I need nothing but a good fire under me and then I'll join Ormek."

"Not yet, Uncle."

"Bring me . . . Bring me to Darst so I can burn . . . with my chosen tree. That is my one wish."

"You'll have your wish, Uncle. I'll cut your oak myself, when the time comes. But you won't last to Darst unless you take medicines."

"I cannot."

"Then your pyre will be in Fargladden. And I've seen no oaks here. Even the doors are made of sticks."

"Kyala, don't . . . deceive me."

"There is nothing else to burn. I'll build you a mound of the finest twigs. And maybe add some straw. They say straw makes a bright blaze."

"You jest about dying, Balin's daughter. Shame."

"You should tell my mother. But you'll need to swallow something if you want to see her again."

"Never mind that. Head north to Asep River. Take passage for us downriver on a barge. I'll sleep, and when I wake we'll be in Darst."

The beardless one grumbled. "You're talkin' to a dead man," he said.

"He's answering, but you can't hear. If you'll help me raise his head—"

"For what?"

"So I can show you how a dead man eats."

The healer sighed. "See if he'll take some breakfast. But if he doesn't, I'll have no more to do with you." From the hearth he brought a bowl of thin gruel. Then he lifted Watnojat, and she propped a folded blanket behind his head

"Uncle, open your mouth."

"I am comfortable, Kyala. Why do you trouble me?"

She squeezed another drop of blood onto the bead. "You taught me this. Now I command you to eat."

"You . . . command? You are my apprentice." The voice fell silent briefly. "You are my apprentice, but I sense something more in you. Something of Ormek."

"Uncle, you must eat! I need you to explain what happened to me in Untmur's workshop. Stay with me for that reason if no other." She squeezed the bead in her palm. Then for a moment she felt again the enveloping fire that had sprung from Untmur's lamp. The flames were gentler this time, but nonetheless startling. It was as if she carried Ormek's warmth within her, a power far greater than that of blood or flame. Was it possible? She saw the Vigen's lips part. They were moving, opening. She tilted the bowl and pushed a bit of the watery mixture into his mouth. "Swallow, Uncle."

"I did not know," the voice said. "I did not know what I was doing to the sick ones. I should have left them alone." But the muscles of his throat answered her command.

The healer began to mutter. "Sorcery. Dark arts."

"Arts you don't understand," retorted Kyala. But her voice quavered, for she was not certain what had happened. "I can feed him some medicines now. If you have anything that might help him, bring it here."

The healer shook his head in dismay, but he returned to the hearth. "I'll brew something for ya. If you can get it down him, it might do some good."

Kyala slept at last, fitfully, waking often to check on Watnojat. Several times more she used the bead to force him to swallow. Was there any benefit from this treatment? The healer admitted only to a slight improvement in his condition.

One time she woke to find the glassmaker alone on the pallet that he had formerly shared. The healer was stirring something in a pot over the coals, singing to himself.

> Nightfoot and grasshat
> webroot and clay
> heartwood and frogjewels
> mint and ratay ...

"Where's the other?" She pointed to the empty place by the Vigen's side. The healer had ignored the second man for the entire time he had worked on the Vigen.

"Ah, him. Nobody's sorry *he's* gone."

"For a healer, you have a strange attitude."

"They bring me all the hopeless ones. If I mourned each one I lost, I'd have a raw throat and a black face." He dipped a finger into cold ashes and smudged each of his cheeks. "Should I look like this every day?"

She had no answer. How could he care what happened to her Vigen, to a stranger? If his medicines did some good, it would be enough.

"Your old guy's better," the healer added. "He ate some by himself this time. He asked for you, but I thought you needed rest. You'll be sittin' up with him while I sleep."

"Kyala." Watnojat's voice was a hoarse whisper. She turned to see his lips barely moving, his eyes still closed. "Kyala, we must . . . leave for Asep River," he said slowly, as if each word required a separate effort. "Have you forgotten?"

"Uncle, you must rest before we can go. You're not ready to travel."

"Soon," he said. "Soon we leave for Darst."

Night came, and the healer began to yawn. He shared a simple meal with her of bread and roots, then bedded down in an alcove to the rear of the cottage. It was Kyala's task to remain awake and provide the Vigen with water and gruel and medicine whenever he woke.

The night seemed far longer than any she recalled. She found her head drooping, and several times dozed. At last she lay down beside the Vigen so that whenever he stirred he would wake her. Each time she fed him, he seemed improved. She began to hope that he would see Darst once again.

By the time the healer rose, Watnojat was sitting up and sipping tea that Kyala had brewed. "We must go at once," the Vigen said. Kyala looked to the healer for an opinion, and the man merely shrugged. Perhaps Watnojat could travel soon. But there were arrangements to be made, supplies to be replaced.

The Vigen continued to show progress throughout the morning. He chatted; he ate a bit of solid food. By midday she decided she could leave him and drive to the center of the town.

She needed so many things. Flint and ironstone. Lanterns and oil. Food. A journey of many weeks lay ahead of them, and all their supplies had been lost. The coins in her own purse could not pay for a tenth part of what she must obtain. Despite her promises, she was not sure she could even pay the healer.

Fargladden, she found, was barely half the size of Vanikval. Its streets were uncluttered. Even in the town's center, there were yards running between the buildings; she glimpsed goats and chickens behind the houses. She rode up and down, studying the signs of the craft shops. Here was a weaver, there a potter. At the sign of the wheel she halted.

A brick stable and a shop stood together. In this place she would find a wainwright, and perhaps a blacksmith as well. The shop door was open and from within came the sound of hammering, of iron striking iron. A bulky man in dirty boots was coming out. "Lookin' for Mekoril?" he called to her. She eased the grays up to the railing and stepped down.

"Is he the proprietor?"

"It's his place."

"Then yes."

The man pointed over his shoulder. "If ya want somethin' fixed, it'll be tomorrow. He's got his hands full."

Kyala tied up the ponies, then entered the shop. The wainwright was bare chested, short and slender, but heavily muscled in his arms. He was rimming a wagon wheel, driving in spikes to hold an iron strake to the wood. The iron glowed dimly with heat. The apprentice steadied the wheel in the shoeing hole. When Mekoril was done hammering, the boy spun the wheel, quenching the metal in the water-filled hole.

"Not today," said the wainwright, without looking up from the steaming water.

"I need a cart. A two-pony rig. Do you have one?"

"Might. Payin' coin?"

Kyala hesitated. "I've got a four-rig I don't need."

"Swap a four for a two?" Mekoril turned from his work, his shaggy blond brows raised in interest.

"And supplies. I need dried meat, weapons, torches—"

"Enough! Do I look like a peddler?"

"Do peddlers swap wagons?"

Mekoril wiped his brow on his bare arm. "I can see I'll get no work done until I'm rid of ya." He brushed past her, leaving the boy holding the half-finished wheel, and strode outside to examine her rig. He crawled beneath it and spent some time scrutinizing the running gear. When he came out, the knees of his breeches were muddy and one hand was smeared with grease. He wiped the stain against his apron. "Y'll have two spare ponies if ya trade. Have ya thought of that?" He turned to peer at the grays, then ran his large hands up and down the forelegs of the closest. "They're not from these parts," he said with a tone of respect. He stepped back to view their haunches.

"I'll keep the grays. I just want to trade the wagon."

"Extra ponies'll just get in y'r way," he said. But when she didn't reply he headed toward the stable, looking back once at the animals before turning into the wide doorway. "Here's what you need," he said, leading her to an old rig in a corner. He picked up a tattered hide and began to beat some of the dust away. Kyala sneezed and retreated. "It goes like a bird. Just needs a little cleanin'."

The stable was lit through chinks in the mortar and through holes where a few bricks had been knocked away. As her eyes grew accustomed to the dark, she saw other carts lined up along a wall. She headed for one that appeared new; she could smell the scent of fresh pine.

"I just finished that one," Mekoril said quickly. "Had to pay a fistful of coppers for the planks alone."

"It's small," said Kyala. She tried to picture how she might arrange things. A pallet behind the seat for Watnojat. All the goods piled high in barrels. Without the kiln stones and the other Vigen tools they had carried earlier, she might be able to cram everything on.

"I won't swap you a fresh rig for your worn-out wagon," Mekoril said. "You can have this one. I'll grease 'er up for ya."

"If an axle breaks on the road, I won't have you there to fix it. I want this one."

Mekoril slapped the hide against the old rig, then came toward her. "Can't be done. For the wagon *and* the ponies we might work something out."

"Those grays are old friends."

"Then keep them. Keep it all." The wright tossed the hide down and headed for the door. When Kyala emerged from the gloomy stable, she blinked at the bright sunlight that flooded the yard. When she could see again, she noticed a short woman in a sheepskin cloak standing by the ponies. The woman was not much older than herself and quite pretty, her tawny hair fluttering in the breeze that swept the yard; she was talking to Mekoril and he was frowning.

Kyala walked slowly to her rig. The woman turned to one gray and stroked its muzzle, then spoke again to Mekoril. When Kyala reached the wainwright, he waved the woman away, then beckoned the Vigen's apprentice to follow him back into the shop. "Let me hear your peddler's list again," he said testily.

"I won't see my grays hitched to a plow."

"Plow? You silly girl. My wife wants them to pull her cart through the town. She's probably feeding them carrots already."

"Then tell me how much the barge will cost," asked Kyala. "I must take your two-rig down the Asep River with myself and my Uncle."

Mekoril groaned.

"I was going to take the extra ponies to the dock and swap them for passage."

"You want supplies *and* your passage? If it weren't for my wife, I'd toss you into a ditch. Why don't you hold a blade to my throat and make this an honest robbery?"

# Chapter 16

The healer seemed relieved when Kyala made ready to depart. Despite his ministrations to the Vigen, his uneasiness had continued throughout their stay. So he made no complaint when it was time to help Watnojat up into the cart. The beardless man did not even count the coppers that Kyala handed him.

The glassmaker lay down on a pallet in the narrow space between driver's bench and baggage. Kyala draped one of Mekoril's blankets over him, and then she took up the reins. Behind her she heard the clanging of the healer's gong. She turned to see him standing in the doorway, grinning as he hammered his farewell. "Keep y'r old guy comfortable," he called after her. "You *might* get 'im home. You just might do it."

"We'll both see Darst," she called back. "And with thanks to you for helping us." The grays pulled out of the yard, their strong necks bobbing.

The road led north from Fargladden and then began to curve slightly to the west. They were heading to the swamp towns that had been recommended days earlier by the woman at the washhouse. It might have been better, Kyala thought ruefully, to have heeded the woman's advice when first offered. Ah, but now it was done.

The little two-rig proved speedy. By late afternoon Kyala caught her first smell of the marshes. She thought of the harsh odors of stables and middens and latrines. The ground to the side of the road was dark and sodden, often covered with swampgrass or stink cabbage. The small village where she stopped did not even have a name.

"Uncle, can you walk?"

Watnojat stirred and rubbed his eyes. "Have we reached the river?"

"We've just started on our journey there, Uncle. Should I call for someone to carry you?"

He shook his head. "I am weak, Kyala, but not helpless." He pushed himself up, and she helped him get his legs over the side. Then, with some assistance, he made his way into the moss-covered inn.

That night she brought soup and bread to the Vigen as he sat propped against the stone wall behind his pallet. His appetite was improving, she noted, but she held little hope for a full recovery. If she could bring him back to Darst, it would be enough. If she could let him see again the town he'd served...

Tattered blankets hung between the beds. While Watnojat ate, Kyala heard snoring from other guests.

"The healer's place was quieter," the Vigen observed. "But no matter. I seem able to sleep anywhere."

"We've had worse accommodations, Uncle. Do you recall those winter nights on the wagon?"

"I remember. I thought you might leave me then, ride back to Darst in a peddler's cart."

"I might have done that. Only there were no peddlers foolhardy enough to be traveling those roads!"

Watnojat laughed weakly. "I was wrong to take you so quickly into that winter journey. Now, what have we to show for it? A tiny vial of astablak."

"Don't be too harsh on yourself, Uncle. We did all we could. And remember how we helped Vanikval. Future Vigens will thank us for that service."

"Thank us, yes. Untmur said we are the last of our kind, but I know he was wrong. You must carry on, Kyala, and surely there will be others."

She did not speak at once. "I will carry on, Uncle. But we must continue our lessons. There's so much I still must learn from you."

Watnojat sighed. "It is late to be thinking of lessons."

"Uncle, there's one thing that troubles me most. You've not explained what happened when I touched Untmur's bead to the lamp."

The Vigen shook his head. "On that matter I can't help you. I've never before heard of what you described."

"But Uncle, I felt power. The lamplight alone wasn't strong enough, yet the bead did its work."

The glassmaker smiled faintly. "What can it be? Perhaps Ormek has granted you a special favor. But don't look to *me* for an explanation. You must trust in the Bright One to bring you the understanding that you lack."

*Understanding?* She searched within herself for the fires she had felt at Untmur's shop, and later at the healer's cottage, but now found no trace of them. Watnojat's words troubled her. Why should Ormek confer a special gift? It was enough that she had the color talents, that she could practice the Vigens' art. Perhaps there was nothing more. If her mentor had no ready explanation, then perhaps her vision of the enveloping flame had come from her imagination. "But you will complete my training, Uncle."

"Ah, Kyala," the Vigen said sadly. "I fear there will be no more training."

The next day they continued, winding their way to Southbog. From Southbog they reached Middlebog, and Kyala counted her coins and wondered if there would be enough. She haggled over the price of the inn, arguing that she and

Watnojat should be charged for but one meal between them. "Should I have a boy sit and tally what you eat?" retorted the proprietor. She was obliged to pay the full amount.

The swamp towns came one after the other. They traveled six days more, finally crossing into Northbog on a marshy, rutted road. A few hours of daylight remained, and Asep River lay at the far end of the town. "We may find a barge docking for the night," Kyala said. "Perhaps I can arrange our passage." So she did not stop at the inn called Fishhead but continued on the track to the dock. A few carts and wagons rattled past, and then she saw the path's end. The bank sloped gently here. A sagging rope, strung between two poles, separated land from water.

The river was narrow, but the flow in the middle was swift. The green water looked cold. She was not eager to leave solid ground, yet she knew the route would cut many days from the journey home. *If* they could find passage. She glanced about and saw only a boy waiting, sitting with his bare feet in the shallows. "Will there be a barge?" she called down. He turned and swatted at a fly that was buzzing about his ear.

"Had one yesterday," he said. "Maybe one tomorrow." He slapped at the fly again, then wiped the dead insect from his face.

*Maybe tomorrow?* Every day was precious. She resolved to stay until dark. The thirsty grays stretched their necks over the rope and drank river water. When they were through, she brought them hay from a bundle tied atop the cart. Then, while they ate, she leaned out over the rope to peer upstream.

She had only seen barges from a great distance. From the hill she called Uncle's Seat she had watched dots float down to the sea. She had also seen the remains of barges after they had been broken up for firewood, but she could not guess how large they had been when afloat. *Even if one comes, it may be too small to hold the rig.* And without the rig, how would she get Watnojat home through the forest that lay between Darst and the river?

She did not trust water travel. At some point they might have trouble and be forced to continue the journey by road. No, she resolved, she would not abandon the cart.

Sunset approached. The boy began to throw pebbles into the water. "Why do you stay here?" asked Kyala.

"To watch."

"For the barges? You said one wouldn't come."

"Can't tell. Today. Tomorrow. When he comes I run down to the shop there." The lad pointed to the first of the brick buildings at the edge of the town, then returned his attention to the river. He leaned forward in sudden excitement. "Maybe he comes today after all. See? Signs in the water."

"I see ripples from your stones."

The boy didn't answer, for he was already gone. Behind her she heard the patter of his bare feet against the dirt. *Barge? Where?* Then she saw a long platform of logs bouncing on the stream. "Uncle!" she called. "It is here!"

On the barge a man stood with a pole, his face red with the last of the daylight; another man squatted in the rear. Between them, barrels and crates were stacked high. *So full!* Even without the cargo, she thought the craft might be too small to hold the cart and ponies.

The poleman lifted a ram's horn to his lips and gave three blasts. Behind her, from the shop, came an immediate answering blast. Evidently the boy had done only part of his job, for he came bounding back to catch the rope thrown by the poleman. He pulled it through an iron ring set into the ground, then tossed the end back to the barge as it neared the shore.

The poleman wore an armless shirt of goatskin, and knee-length breeches. He secured the rope end, then hopped ashore carrying another lashing to thread through a second ring. The other man wore only a tabard that reached to his thighs. He tossed a ramp of rough boards to the bank and pulled up one of the poles that roped off the end of the dock. Then, with the first man's help, he began to roll barrels from the barge.

The poleman sang loudly as he stepped ashore: "Goods f'r Renistok, f'r Wakkal, f'r Teeg." He looked at Kyala. "You one of 'em?"

"No. I . . . I need passage. For the rig also. If it isn't too big."

"Rig, huh? Have to look at it." He finished inspecting his unloaded cargo, then dropped to his haunches to view the underside of the cart. The craft rose and fell on the current, its bindings creaking and its kegs knocking against each other. "Where goin'?" asked the poleman.

"Darst."

"Darst?" He turned to the other. "Ecker. Over here. What say?"

The other man approached. "We not goin' down to Darst," replied Ecker. "Goin' to Halfriver. Long way to get back from Darst. Hey, Bettmano?" He slapped the poleman's shoulder. "Long way to get back."

"I can pay," said Kyala. She named a sum less than the wainwright had used in his figuring.

Bettmano began to laugh. Ecker scratched his head and smiled. "We not goin' to Darst."

"I'll pay more. Tell me if the rig can fit." Kyala offered the total in her purse.

The poleman grinned at her new offer, but shook his head. "Can fit. Can fit," he said. "But what else got ya? Somethin' in your cart to trade?"

She named the contents. Food for the journey. A few tools. Hay. Lanterns. Torches. The man only shrugged.

"Bettmano! They comin'." Ecker slapped at his companion. Kyala heard the clatter of hooves and turned to see several wagons rolling up behind her cart.

The first of the newly arrived drivers waved a whip at her. "Load up and get on!" he shouted. "Clear the dock." When she didn't move, the irate man left his rig and approached the poleman. The driver showed a seal-ring, and in response Bettmano began to roll a barrel toward the wagon.

"Better ya pull out of here," the poleman said to Kyala as he passed.

She was not ready to abandon the dock. She climbed back into the cart. "Uncle," she said softly. "We must trade one of your beads. That's all we have left."

Watnojat was asleep, his breathing slow and regular. It was best not to wake him; she would have to make the decision herself and hope that the bargemen knew the value of talismans. She opened the trunk and took out the pouch she had retrieved from Untmur. The light was growing dim, and it was more by touch than by sight that she studied the contents. One by one she considered the beads; each might have a special meaning to the Vigen. At last there was only the fox eye of her own making.

She closed up the box and climbed down to find Ecker shoving the ramp back onto the barge. *They were leaving already!* "Will you ride the river by night?" she asked.

"With a bright moon, why not?" Bettmano answered.

She opened her fist. "I'll make your journey pay. Do you know the value of this?"

Ecker was impatient and turned away from her to prepare for casting off. Bettmano picked up the bead of glass and squinted at it in the failing light. "Hunter's hex piece," he said. "Worth a couple skins."

"Worth an *armload* of skins," she said. *And to me much more than that.*

Bettmano scratched at his ear, as if recalling something. Slowly a smile grew on his face. "Ecker!" The poleman used his free hand to pull his companion away from the ropes. "Goin' to Darst," he said. "For this and the coins, goin' to Darst."

"For what?"

Bettmano showed him the talisman and whispered in his ear. Kyala heard only the word *hunter* repeated several times.

"If you lie, I push it up your nose," said Ecker aloud. He kicked at the ground with his bare heel, splashing some river water on Bettmano. The poleman just stood there with his arms crossed, and finally his companion settled back to work. Ecker tightened the lashings and brought back his ramp. The two men pitched into the task of shifting cargo on the raft, soon bringing half to rest at the side of the dock. "First get the ponies away," said Bettmano.

Kyala released the traces and led the two grays clear of the work area; Ecker began to pull on the cart's tongue while Bettmano stepped behind to push the rig toward the barge.

"Heavy," complained the poleman.

*Heavier than you think.* She did not want to tell them about Watnojat. If he climbed off, the load would be lighter, but when they saw him they might up their fee. "Let me help," she said. She joined Bettmano as he grunted at the rear. The wheels were stuck; they would go forward slightly, then fall back into their ruts. "Together," said Bettmano. "Hey—hey—ho." At "ho" they strained and pushed forward, turning the wheels a bit more, but again the wagon fell back into place. "Will go," said Bettmano, wiping his forehead with the back of his hand. "I say will go. Now hey—" Kyala heaved all her weight against the cart. This time the wheels began to turn and did not stop.

There was a downward grade to the river; once started, the rig quickly gained speed. Too much speed. "Hold. Hold!" shouted Ecker. The two in back tried to dig their heels into the slick dirt. Kyala's boots slid along the ground as the wagon careened forward. *Into the river,* she thought. *Watnojat drowned!* She could not hold back the heavy rig. It hit the ramp, then bounced onto the log deck of the barge. The craft dipped, and she thought that all would sink. Water splashed at her feet as she was dragged to the river's edge. The wagon bounced up again and finally halted, its rear wheels on the ramp, its front in the barge.

She followed the poleman forward to see what had happened to Ecker. She heard splashing; he was in the water, stroking fitfully against the current. Bettmano calmly picked up the barge pole and held it to his companion. Laughing, he pulled Ecker to shore.

And what of the Vigen? She climbed up and found him half awake. "Uncle, make no sound," she whispered. "We are almost onto the barge." She climbed down quickly.

"Need one more push," said Bettmano. Ecker, now back on land, shook himself like a dog and brushed the wet hair from his eyes. Then he returned to his place at the tongue.

"Almost there," said Bettmano. "Hey—hey—ho." They pushed once more, and the rear wheels rolled down the ramp.

As soon as the cart was positioned. the men began to slide barrels and crates between its wheels and under its belly. With some coaxing and tugging, they brought the ponies aboard. The animals too had crates shoved under them.

Dusk found the men still at the loading. "Some space left in the cart," said Bettmano, poking his head up to look behind the seat. "Hey? Should be lots of room."

"Not there!" shouted Kyala as he caught sight of the Vigen.

"What got here? A stowaway!"

"He's with me."

"Didn't tell us about another." Bettmano scratched his head.

"He might as well be a corpse," Kyala confided in a low tone. "Will you charge for a corpse? I can pay you in barley."

"Barley?" Bettmano looked for Ecker, but the other man was busy behind the cargo.

"Barley and old cooking pots."

"No time to argue." In the gloom they could scarcely see the remaining crates on the dock. "Give me a light, will ya?" he called to Ecker. While the other fumbled with strikers, Bettmano began to lift smaller boxes onto the seat of the cart. Ecker got a torch going and held it high. Now Kyala could see how low they rode in the water; the least wave would spill over the lip of the craft.

"Got to pile 'em higher," said Ecker, glancing at the shaky tower of barrels that stood between ponies and cart. Bettmano climbed onto a crate so he could reach to the top of the pile. He added a few more kegs. "One left," he said. Kyala was squeezed against the cart's front wheel. When Bettmano brought the last barrel aboard he dropped it in front of her, blocking her view as well as closing off any room for movement. She heard him splashing about, grunting as he made his final preparations. Then she felt a lurch as the barge moved out into the current.

The craft swayed; she grabbed the wheel for support as water sloshed across the deck. She closed her eyes, but that made her discomfort worse. When her eyes were open, she could see only barrels. If she could watch where they were going, follow the progress along the river, then perhaps she would not be so frightened. Behind her Kyala found a small stretch of the cart's edge that she could sit on. She pulled herself up and perched with her back against a crate and her legs dangling.

From the height the swaying was magnified. Now she could see the tower of kegs shift with each motion of the craft. She clutched at her seat, fearing that at any moment she might fall to the watery deck, the barrels toppling down to bury her. "Uncle!" she called. "Uncle, this is the way you chose to ride to Darst. I would have taken the roads."

"It is not so bad, Kyala." He rubbed his eyes and sat up slowly. "You've never sailed in the Footprint. We hit a storm one night that cleaned the deck—"

"Don't tell me about it." She held tighter to the wagon, swearing to herself that she would never again set forth on water. But the Vigen watched for a while, speaking quietly of the river towns he had seen in his journeys.

The moon rose, and Bettmano showed no sign of tiring. The moon's reflection shimmered before them in the water, keeping its distance constant as they rode. What might have been a pleasant sight from the shore was here only a distraction from her misery.

After Watnojat dozed off again, she tried to interest herself in the poleman's work. Sometimes great branches of the shore trees dipped down to the river; Bettmano was ever alert, lest his cargo be swept off by an overhanging limb. Once he sang out a warning, and there was a deep grinding as a submerged log struck the craft. More water poured onto the deck, but for that the bargemen showed no concern. They gleefully tossed chunks of bread and cheese to each other. Kyala could not think of eating.

And sleep? The space for Watnojat's pallet was narrow, but at last she squeezed in beside him. She nodded off briefly, but the pitching made her queasy. After several tries at sleep, she abandoned the idea and lay with her eyes open looking up at the sky. With the moon so bright, the stars were dim, so she could not even enjoy Ormek's dreams.

At some point she heard the bargemen tie up at shore. The water was calmer here. She closed her eyes and found that the gentler rocking lulled her. How long she slept she could not know, but when she looked again they were already underway, drifting under a sky that showed the first hints of morning.

They reached a town called Thornsen, and Bettmano used his horn to rouse the people from their beds. The bargemen cursed and grumbled, carrying many loads to the dock before the cargo was properly sorted out. When they were finished there was more room on deck. Kyala, though her legs were shaky, was able to stretch her arm to the ponies and feed them small bundles of hay.

As Bettmano's pole carried them back into the current, Watnojat sat up again. Kyala, perched on the cart's lip, at first viewed the Vigen's action with alarm. "What is wrong, Uncle?"

The breeze ruffled the white hairs of his beard. "Nothing is wrong, Kyala. I like the smell of the river in the morning." He took a deep breath, then looked out with interest at the houses on the bank. "I know this place, Thornsen. I once dug iron pigments from their bogs."

"You must be better, Uncle." She had not seen him so attentive to his surroundings since the start of his illness. "Will you eat something?"

"If you join me."

Kyala shook her head.

"Then I'll wait," he said. She propped up his head, and for the rest of the morning he gazed at the muddy banks and the occasional towns that flanked the river.

They stopped first at Hornbend, then at Clayrek, later at Pelpokin. For every crate the bargemen took on, they would leave two others behind. So, as the days passed, the load gradually diminished. Kyala found that she did not grow accustomed to the pitching of the craft. She could hold down no food and subsisted on sips of water. But Watnojat grew stronger; she saw him thriving on the river air. Kyala became the invalid, watching from the pallet through half-closed lids as the Vigen ate. What an appetite he had developed! He cut himself a strip of cured ham and began to chew on it. Kyala couldn't watch. Would she ever eat again? Surely not on that river.

When they docked at Singford, Watnojat told her he was going ashore. He climbed down from the rig, and she heard him speak to the bargemen as he left. Kyala managed to lift her head and look about, first noting how the river ran wide and shallow at the ford, then watching the Vigen set off toward the brick shops of the town. Her attention lingered on the dock, where boxes, kegs, and several live pigs waited beside the barge. The poleman was conferring with Singford merchants, and there was a great deal of argument, hands waving in the air and shouts she couldn't understand. She lay back on the pallet, content merely to listen. She felt the barge lurch each time a new weight was added to the load. Later she heard grunts as the pigs were driven aboard. Company for the ponies, she thought. *We're a floating farmyard now.*

At last the talking ceased, and she heard no more scraping

of crates. When she looked out again, the dock was empty. Bettmano had finished his work and stood impatiently kicking at a piling. The glassmaker, holding something in his hand, was making his slow way toward them. She lay back once more, only mildly curious about the Vigen's errand.

The barge began pitching again, so she knew that they had moved back into the current. The cart creaked as Watnojat climbed up and then stepped over her. His face looked troubled, the recent improvements in his disposition seemingly masked by some new concern. Perhaps he feared for Kyala's well-being. "I have something for you," he said. She heard utensils rattling. Then he leaned over her, holding a small cup. She turned her face away, but he lifted her head and brought the tin vessel to her mouth. The odor of the contents was of things long dead. "Drink this," he insisted. "The herb-healer promised a cure."

*Herb-healer!* She recalled the one in Fargladden and turned away again. But Watnojat was persistent. He pried open her lips with the edge of the cup. Some of the bitter drink got onto her tongue, and she could not help but swallow it. The potion spread out like a warm covering inside her stomach. "No more, Uncle," she cried.

He let her rest awhile, but then was back with another dose. Again she protested to no avail. She noticed, however, that the pitching of the boat seemed to bother her less now. Had they reached a stretch of calmer water? She lifted her head to peer out; the river appeared unchanged.

By nightfall he had forced two more doses of the medicine into her mouth. By then the discomfort had eased enough that she sat up to watch for the moonrise. The Vigen brought her water and put a piece of bread in her hand. From the smell, it was newly baked. A Singford loaf? For days she had possessed no appetite, but suddenly she was hungry. She bit off an end, and her stomach did not rebel. Slowly she chewed while she watched Bettmano work, his only light coming from two torches that overhung the stream.

"Uncle, has the ride grown smoother?" The bread tasted even better than it smelled. "Or has the healer's brew truly made a cure?"

He smiled and answered: "Singford is another town I know from my journeys. The healer who mixed the herbs is a man I trust, one who owed me a favor." But when his smile passed, the same troubled look returned to his face. Something besides her health was worrying him.

"I owe much to your healer," she said cautiously. She finished the bread and looked about for more.

"Eat a little at a time, Kyala. Too much at once will be bad."

She nodded. "Uncle, there's something else. Since you came back from Singford you've been fretting."

Watnojat sighed. He glanced over his shoulder at the bargemen, then leaned to whisper in Kyala's ear. "There is troubling news from downriver."

"Uncle?" A sudden chill shook her, though the breeze was warm.

He nodded his head. "It is true. As I had feared, but far sooner. Lame Ones."

"Attacking again?"

He put his finger to her lips. "I thought they would wait until winter," he said fiercely. "But already they have been seen at Jannford."

"Jannford. So close to home." Kyala tried to recall the place. Only once had she visited the small river town that lay beyond Darst's hardwood forest. "Then they must be the ones—"

"Who killed Torged. Surely the same. Now that they've lost their fear of men, who can say what will stop them?"

He turned to the chest and slowly undid the belts. Then he took out Untmur's bottle, pulled the stopper, and stared in at the dark contents. "We've enough for three beads, maybe four," he said. "We may need those talismans sooner than I'd hoped." He returned the vial to its box, then slumped down beside her and closed his eyes.

\* \* \*

In the next days Kyala noticed signs of uneasiness among the bargemen. When they docked, they would often linger to chat with the townsmen long after their business affairs were done. Surely they were discussing the reports of trouble downstream. At times Kyala saw the two arguing together on the bank, Ecker splashing angrily at the water while Bettmano tried to shove his friend back to the raft.

A dozen stops later, the men finished unloading at Halfriver, leaving their deck empty but for the belongings of the two travelers. Bettmano and Ecker began another of their arguments, but this time Bettmano squatted down by the water and did not try to bully his partner. At last the poleman came to Kyala and sheepishly held out to her a handful of coins. "We're not goin' down to Darst," he said with a shrug and a grin. "Not safe down that way. You drive inland. Get home by road."

"Uncle?" Since Singford, she had been expecting this outcome. She did not know how Watnojat would react.

"I don't blame him," said the Vigen solemnly. "But we'll take the river road home." He shaded his eyes and peered along the bank as if he could see all the way to Jannford; his brow furrowed and he licked his dry lips. "Come. It is not so far. Let's get the ponies off the barge."

# Chapter 17

Kyala was not unhappy to have ground beneath her legs again. She harnessed the grays, took a last look at the bargemen, who were already negotiating the sale of their craft, then climbed up beside Watnojat to drive. "You supplied us well in Fargladden," the Vigen told her. "We have only one matter of business in this town. We'll need a potter who can lend us the use of his kiln."

Kyala nodded, then clucked to the grays. The animals were sluggish from lack of exercise. Slowly they headed into Halfriver's central street, a wide dirt track flanked by shops built of broad wooden planks. Here the people were busy with their usual errands. Kyala's mouth watered at smells from a bakery. She glanced at two women carrying long loaves in their baskets. "It's as if nothing has happened," she said as they continued along the way.

"Jannford is still far from here," Watnojat answered. "At Halfriver they have nothing to fear."

"For now," replied Kyala. But when the Lame Ones finished their pillaging downriver, how far might they travel?

No town in the region would be safe. She put that worry aside as she scanned the signboards that hung out over the street. "Look, Uncle." She brought them to a halt beneath a small urn hanging from a painted board. She noticed a stout brick chimney projecting above the roof to the rear of the shop.

"No smoke this morning," said the Vigen. "We may be in luck."

They climbed down and stepped into the sunlit doorway. A young girl was laying out glazed water jugs on the floor. She glanced once at Watnojat, cried "mama," and ran into a curtained passageway at the rear of the room. Kyala was surprised at the girl's fright. She'd grown used to the Vigen's appearance, but when she looked at him she noticed his grimy coat and torn trousers and the sooty tangle of his beard. His lined face showed the strains of the journey; she was certain that her own appearance was equally unsettling.

A woman whose head was covered by a lacy white cap pushed the gray curtain aside. Behind her Kyala glimpsed a large workroom with benches and a wheel. The woman stared uneasily at the newcomers. "Pick out what you want," she said in a cautious voice. "Copper's best for payment, but I do some swapping. Pick out what you like, and then we'll talk."

"We're not here for your goods," said the Vigen.

The woman retreated in alarm. She shouted to the girl behind her, and suddenly a series of growls and barks sounded from the rear of the workroom.

"Hold off your dog," said Watnojat. "Do you take us for robbers? Here." He held out his hand to Kyala for the purse holding the coins returned by the bargemen. He tossed the purse at the woman's feet. "We need one thing from you only. Lend us the use of your kiln for half a day. You'll find more profit in that than in the pots you'd be firing."

The woman did not take her eyes from the glassmaker. She took a step forward, then used the back of her heel to kick the purse behind her. "Count it," she said to her daughter.

When the girl answered, the woman's tense expression softened only slightly. "So you've pots of your own to fire? You'll be setting up a stall in the square and selling them at half my price."

"We have no pots," the Vigen said with sigh. "Only small bits of glass that must be fused."

"Glass!"

"Don't bother to hide your eyes," said Kyala as the woman pulled the cap down over her brow. "We've seen the color already. We're bound by our craft's honor not to use it against you."

"Honor! You? Vigen?" The woman could scarcely get out her words.

"We need to make talismans against . . . forest creatures," said Kyala. "Your kiln will serve a good cause."

The woman patted her cap and rubbed perspiration from her face with the heel of her hand. "Ah, what a day for me," she said. "Two robbers turn into Vigens and choose my shop for it." She turned briefly and made a signal to her daughter. "You'll have what you want from me anyway," she said in a tone of defeat. She looked past them at the wagon outside her door. "If you're honest folks, bring your rig up to the back so you don't spook my customers."

Kyala wasted no time in complying. She tied up the grays in the narrow, bare yard, then carried the chest of vials through the rear door of the shop. Just inside she nearly dropped her precious package when the shopkeeper's guard dog lunged at the bars of its wooden cage. The cage walls, of sticks tied together with heavy twine, twisted ominously. "Uncle," she said, trying to keep her voice from breaking. "I'd like to hold one of your dog eyes, if you don't mind."

The shopkeeper glared as Watnojat plucked a talisman from his pouch. "Quiet!" he said to the growling creature. It slunk back from the bars and fell silent. Kyala, relieved by the quick obedience, took the bead and tucked it into a pocket. Then she turned to look at the potter's kiln, a wide, squat affair of sooty brick.

"We'll need a heap of wood to heat that," said the Vigen. Kyala had seen the woodpile outside. She set down the box and scurried to ready the fire.

When the kiln began heating, she turned to find Watnojat finishing an improvised mold, a broken earthenware platter from which he had gouged out three pits with an iron spike. He blew the last loose fragments away. Then Kyala opened Untmur's tiny bottle and poured out grains of astablak glass into each of the pits. "Did he leave me my copper strips?" asked the glassmaker as he picked up the mold and brought it to the shop's greasy window.

"I've seen them somewhere." Kyala began to take the vials out of the chest, pushing aside the cushioning straw. About halfway through, she found the container that held the thin strips that were used to tether talismans. "I have them, Uncle." She brought three strands to Watnojat's mold. He was still staring at the powdered glass, squinting as he watched the sunlight on the dark fragments.

"Study the sheen," he said, lowering the mold to her eye level. "I was concerned before, but now I am certain. The glass is not as pure as it should be."

Kyala examined the red glow that tinged the surfaces of the grains. "I thought it had the right appearance."

"Close. But the glow could be deeper in shade. Untmur was careless with this batch. We won't know for certain how well off we are until we see the finished pieces."

"Untmur!" Kyala shook her head. She did not want to think any more about him. Carefully she took the mold and slid it into the kiln.

The shopkeeper's girl, who had watched the proceedings silently, remained in her place by the wall. Kyala began to pull on the overhead handle, which connected by a pivoted beam to the leaf of the bellows. The girl followed her motions with her eyes while twisting her stained smock around her hand. "We'll need more heat than you're used to," Kyala said to the girl. The dog stirred in its cage, and Kyala noticed that its long snout now poked out into the room. She began to pump faster, eager to be done with the work.

The pumping went on well into the morning. The room grew warm, and Balin's daughter was constantly wiping her face on a rag. The little girl did nothing but stare, with her mouth half open, at Kyala's exertions. "Makin' pots is easier," was all she said.

"The glass is fused," Kyala announced at last. She opened the kiln slightly and stepped away to escape from the emerging heat. From the outer room came sounds of customers. Pots scraped against each other. A townswoman haggled with the shopkeeper over the price of a bowl. Watnojat was sitting on a stool, slumped against the shop wall, seemingly asleep.

She must cool the astablak beads carefully, lest the sheen be lost. Of all Vigen lore, that rule was familiar even to children. Everyone knew how Kolpern's bead had miraculously achieved its fire despite the hasty cooling. But Kyala expected no legendary wonders here. She opened the kiln a crack at a time, giving the glass the time it needed. Again and again she returned to push the bricks slightly farther apart. Occasionally she would step outside for a sip of water from the pump. By the time the beads were finished, the Sun was well past noon.

"Uncle, we are done," she said at last, shaking his shoulder gently. Slowly the glassmaker opened his eyes. "Look at the beads and tell me what you think," she said, holding the mold before him.

He rose with a grunt from his stool and waved for her to follow him into the yard. There in the light she saw tiny flames dancing over the surface of each dark talisman. "You have done well," Watnojat said. "The best that could be done with what Untmur gave us."

"They could be better?"

The Vigen hesitated. "The color of the sheen is a bit

pale. If a beast is strong willed, then these may not hold it."

*Untmur the demon!* She did not say what she was thinking. Let Watnojat have hope. "Perhaps, Uncle, perhaps we'll meet no Lame Ones at all. We may not need the beads."

"*You* need not meet any." He looked up from the glass and pointed along the alley. "There's a road that runs inland. You can take the safe way home. I'll trade a bead and get you a pony."

"Uncle!"

"It would be best."

"I'll not leave you, Uncle. Don't talk about such ideas. Now let's pack up before we have trouble in this place."

Watnojat handed her the talismans. "These will serve against Lame Ones," he said thoughtfully. "Our wills must be stronger than theirs. That is what matters in the end."

They drove along the river road, reaching the outskirts of another town before dusk. They camped in a small grove of birches, slept on the wagon, then rose at dawn. With the days long and the roads lightly traveled, they made good time.

As they drove toward Jannford, they found the settlements ever more widely separated. They passed wild sections of river where they could ride half a morning without sighting a dwelling. The hardwood forests, thick on both banks, rose to leafy hills.

Each night when they camped, they set an astablak talisman beside a lantern that burned until daybreak. They each kept an astablak bead tied about the wrist. It was impossible to know how far the Lame Ones had wandered.

One morning they were obliged to pull aside so that a peddler's cart could pass on the narrow track. The wagon was piled with crates and barrels of odd shapes. From the lashing poles, ribbons of faded red and yellow cloth fluttered in the breeze.

"Where goin'?" asked the plump, broad-faced driver with

a scowl. He halted as he came abreast of the Vigen's rig. "No business down that way. Better turn."

"What news from Jannford?" asked Watnojat.

The peddler shook his head. "Nothin'. But I wouldn't go within two days' ride of the place."

"Have you seen signs of Lame Ones?"

The driver screwed up his face and reached for a disk of Ormek that hung above his seat. "None, thank the 'Giver," he said, clutching the carved image of the Sun. "By the time you *see* 'em, it's too late anyway."

"Then we thank you," said Watnojat. "And good journey."

"But ain't you gonna *turn?* I tell ya there's no business down that way. There's nothin' at all."

"We have reasons," said the glassmaker.

The peddler studied the back of the Vigen's rig, thought for a moment, and licked his lips. "Wanna lighten your load, maybe? I could use a few things, if y'r price is fair."

"We've nothing to trade." The Vigen fell silent.

Kyala shuffled her feet, waiting for the wagon to drive on. "You think we'll be dead soon!" she shouted suddenly. "You think we won't need anything then, so why not let you take it."

The fat man hunched his shoulders and looked at his boots. "Nothin' of the sort," he mumbled. "Just bein' friendly." Then he clucked to his team and pulled away.

After that they passed no other travelers. Kyala made little effort to keep track of their progress. She guessed they had been riding ten days from Halfriver when Watnojat pointed to a great oak that spread its branches over the road. "Jannford is up ahead," he told her.

"Then we can reach Darst by tonight, Uncle," she said with a glance at the sky. "We can be home." There was no hope in her voice.

"I wish we could go home tonight."

They saw the first cottage, a roofless structure overgrown by vines. Then the trees thinned and they glimpsed the rest of the village, a cluster of wood buildings set back a short distance from the water. The houses were built on stone foundations, each with two or three steps to climb before reaching the door. "Sometimes in the spring, the river runs over its banks here," Watnojat said by way of explanation.

"I think the people have all been swept away," Kyala replied. Nothing moved through the streets; shutters covered every window.

The road forked, and they took the branch that ran straight toward the bank. Where the track vanished, poles in the water marked the way across the ford. Kyala stopped short of the bank and turned into the closest street of shops and houses. The dirt way was deserted, the buildings silent. The noise of the ponies and cart seemed unnaturally loud in the emptiness.

*Were Lame Ones even now prowling here?* she wondered. The beasts weren't fond of daylight, but who could be certain? She glanced at her wrist to check that the talisman still hung there. She still had her protection. No creatures of any variety showed themselves.

Perhaps the peddler had been right, and the place was fully abandoned. She scrutinized doorways for any sign of motion, but found none. But then she noticed a faint scent and began to sniff the air. "Soup cooking," she said suddenly. She glanced up at the chimneys and saw light smoke rising from one.

"Then they aren't all gone. We'll find someone to tell us what's happened."

They tied up the wagon and walked out onto the deserted street. "Try this house," said Kyala, pointing to the one that had shown smoke. The Vigen climbed the steps and rapped the wooden ring against the door. "We are travelers passing through!" he shouted. "We ask for news, nothing more."

Kyala remained at street level, squinting up at the shuttered windows for a sign of the occupants.

Watnojat stamped his boots with annoyance when his call

was ignored. He reached again for the chained ring and hammered until the planks of the door seemed ready to cave in. "Tell us about the Lame Ones," he called. "We have protection. With some help, we can go after them."

Then Kyala heard a high-pitched, muffled voice. "Don't smash my door. They'll come in. They'll come in." The tone rose in panic. A small opening appeared in a shutter as a slat was pulled back. Only half a face showed, a woman's eyes and cheeks.

"When did you see them?" asked the Vigen.

"Go away. I can't help you," the woman answered. "Talk to Lebbon. Oh, go bother Lebbon." The slat closed with a snap.

"How do I find this Lebbon?" he demanded. He pounded again with the ring when there was no immediate reply.

"The big house at the corner," the woman answered, the slat open again just enough to show her mouth.

"That way?" The Vigen pointed. When she gave a grudging assent, he turned and walked stiffly down to the street. Kyala ran ahead of him to the two-chimneyed structure that stood at the junction with the ford road. She thought she saw wisps of smoke from the closest of the two stacks.

Watnojat was still making his slow way; Kyala could not wait for him. She bounded up the steps and swung the knocker at the iron plate that was bolted to the center of the door. The crash was loud enough to echo from the opposite house. "If you're in there, you heard that," she called to the covered windows.

The signboard over the broad entrance showed the place to be a trading shop. Here, she imagined, trappers and miners used to stop for supplies before crossing to Asep's far bank. Now they would be avoiding the village, trekking upstream to a safer crossing despite the extra travel. "Open your door, shopkeeper!" she cried. "Open it, if you have dreams of seeing customers again."

From above she heard slats opening; someone was watching her. The Vigen arrived, trudged up the steps, and leaned against the door. Then she heard the scraping of heavy bars within.

Watnojat stepped back as the door was pulled open. A small, wiry man stood well inside, his graying beard trimmed close, his head covered by a beaverskin cap. In his hand he carried a short spear. "Got furs to trade?" he asked cautiously. "Got any meat?"

"We're not here for trading," said Watnojat. "We need to talk to Lebbon."

The proprietor eyed him suspiciously, glancing down at the Vigen's soiled boots and bedraggled clothing. *Surely,* thought Kyala, *we look no worse than his usual customers.* "Talk's worth nothin'," the man said. "I'm Lebbon. What d'you want from me?"

"News about Lame Ones," said Watnojat. "Are you the Magistrate here?"

"Mag-istrate?" A momentary hint of amusement showed on Lebbon's face. "I guess you might call me that." Suddenly he poked his head outside to peer up and down the street.

"No beasts prowling yet," said Kyala. "Do you want us to stand here 'til they come?"

With a quick motion, the trader waved them to follow him inside. He slid two heavy bars down to secure the door behind them. The interior of the shop was large and gloomy, lit only by a few beams of light that came through cracks in the shutters. The air held odors of old furs and spices. Kyala could see the outlines of piles of goods on shelves and tables. Her hand brushed against coarse grain sacks that lay to the side of the door.

"This way," said Lebbon. They followed him through a narrow hallway into a modest room furnished with hewn-log benches and a table. Light filtered in from small openings high on the walls. "Sit," said the trader, pointing to a bench by the cold hearth. A sack stuffed with straw served as their cushion. Lebbon remained on his feet, still wary, but he leaned the spear against the wall.

"Do you know what this is?" asked the Vigen. He held up his wrist to show the tethered talisman. The man made no step closer.

"Hunter's bead? I've seen plenty of those."

"For Lame Ones," said Watnojat.

"F'r Lame Ones? Some good that'll do!"

"This is true astablak. Have you seen others like it?"

"How would I know 'blak from mudstone? I don't deal in such things. What I know is..."

"Yes?"

Lebbon turned away for a moment. His voice cracked as he began to talk. "The youngsters went after the critters. My boy and a couple more. It's a month they're gone and not a word."

"A month!" said the Vigen. "When did you last see the beasts?"

"They come and go as they please," he answered in a tired voice. "Yesterday they smashed at some doors down the street, then loped into the woods. All three shaggies still lookin' healthy. But no sign of our fellas."

"Your youngsters had a talisman?"

"Had *two*. What fools to trust a Vigen."

"Which Vigen?"

"Old whiskers. Res-Reslunin, I think they called 'im. Long ago he traded a couple to my uncle. I was a tyke then, but I remember him comin' to the shop. They told us t' hide behind the sacks, but I peeked."

Watnojat scowled and rubbed his cheek. "Reslunin's beads would be strong against the beasts. Maybe the trackers lost their courage and ran off. Maybe they never met the Lame Ones at all."

"You think they'd leave us here to be starved out?"

Watnojat shuffled his boots against the rough floor. "We must put an end to these creatures now," he said quietly.

"When they've finished here, they'll move elsewhere. No town will be safe."

"If they move, we'll be rid of 'em," said Lebbon. "That pack of demons—"

"They must be killed," said Watnojat. "I see you have weapons."

"Weapons?" The trader pointed at the spear next to the wall. "Plenty. But who'll use 'em? We lost our battlers. You thinkin' of sendin' women and old men into the woods?"

The Vigen sighed. "That may be all we have. I've seen women and old men put up a worthy fight."

"There's not a person left in Jannford who'll walk out on the street," said Lebbon.

"Then you're waiting to die here," Kyala retorted.

"We've sent for help. Sent a rider to the Mej for soldiers. It's *their* job."

"Soldiers?" Watnojat forced a laugh. "And when do you think they'll get here? They're more frightened than you are, and they've never even seen a Lame One."

The small man shook his head. "They'll come. We've got food stored, and some of the livestock's left. We can last a bit longer."

Watnojat stood. "I've no faith in the Mej." He pointed at the disk of Ormek that hung above the hearth. "Trust in the Bright One," he said. "Otherwise, we're all lost." He motioned for Kyala to follow him. They retreated through the passageway into the shop.

"Are y' goin' after them," the trader asked as they reached the door.

"I have a score to settle," said the glassmaker.

"Then take these." Lebbon reached up onto one of his high shelves and brought down a pair of stout hunting spears. "You'll need somethin' sturdy when you meet the shaggies. Take 'em. No charge." He thrust the shafts into the Vigen's hand, then opened the door quickly.

Kyala had no time to adjust to the brightness of full

daylight. Her eyes half closed against the glare, she stumbled down the steps into the street. The door shut behind them, followed by a hasty rumbling of the bars.

When she could see again, she headed toward the cart. "Won't anyone come with us?" she shouted up as she went. "Come out of your houses. Bring your weapons and fight." She picked small stones from the street and flung them against the shutters. "Come out here, you geese," she called.

In that manner she ran to the end of the row. Turning, she saw that Watnojat was already sitting on the wagon. There was no time to canvass the other houses but she continued her cries as she returned to the Vigen. Was anyone listening? The houses all seemed lifeless, but she was certain the villagers could hear her.

"Look!" said the glassmaker as she was climbing onto the cart. A door nearby swung open. A boy of about ten years rushed out with a broom in his hand.

"Yaaa, Lame Ones," he said, flinging the broom as if it were a weapon. Then a woman flew down the steps, picked up the boy, and dragged him back inside. The door shut and the street was empty again, but for the fallen "spear."

"That was their last hero," said Kyala. She snapped the reins angrily. The grays snorted and began to move.

# Chapter 18

As they left the village the road forked, the wider path following the riverbank. "This way leads to Darst," said Watnojat, pointing to the rough track that entered the forest. The ponies stopped of their own accord at the junction and bobbed their heads uneasily.

"We can get help from home," said Kyala. "Some towns-folk would fight with us."

Watnojat laughed. "Darst has fewer heroes than Jannford. And who would trust a talisman after what happened to Torged? No, Kyala. We are on our own."

"Tell that to the ponies." She pulled the reins to head them into the woods. Then she was obliged to tap their flanks with her switch to get them moving. The animals snorted and grudgingly advanced up the hill.

As they rose from the river the stands of ash and oak grew denser. A canopy of branches overhung the trail, filtering the light that fell onto the matted dead leaves of many seasons. "Uncle, we'll need a flame," Kyala said. "There's not enough light here for talismans."

The Vigen agreed to a halt. He picked up one of Lebbon's spears, a better weapon than the ones brought from Fargladden, and held it ready while Kyala struck sparks into a pile of chaff. She blew up a flame and lit a taper. Watnojat's hand shook so when he held out the lantern that she took it from him to fire the wick.

"How will we find them, Uncle?" she asked gloomily as she urged the grays to continue. "The forest is too big for us. There are logging roads everywhere that we might follow."

Watnojat sat with the lantern between his boots, the spear close to hand. "They'll find *us*, Balin's daughter. I do not think we can miss them."

The travelers continued, crossing the faces of the hills, then switching back to climb higher. Kyala studied the road for pawprints, but saw only wheel ruts in the dry dirt. Suddenly, at the end of a long rise, the ponies shied. They swerved sideways on the path and tried to turn back. "Spoor," said Watnojat, pointing at a dark pile on the ground. "From Lame Ones. And fresh by the smell." Kyala fought the grays, who twisted and whinnied as they tried to escape the Lame Ones' scent. At last she regained control and managed to bypass the place. The foul odor lingered, as if following them. She thought the woods must be filled with the creatures' droppings.

After that every shadow seemed to hide a shaggy foot. Every crack of a stick beneath the wheels sounded like a beast's approach. "Why don't they come?" said Kyala in despair. "They must hear us by now. If we're to die today, let it be over."

"Kyala, you too must keep your faith in Ormek. He protected you from the snow cat and from Untmur. Do you think He'll abandon you now that the task is nearly done?"

But Kyala's hands were trembling. She tried to focus on the small disks of Ormek that hung from the ponies' traces. Was it true that the Lifegiver had watched over her? She could think of no reason she should be singled out. Torged, as skilled in Ormek's arts as any Vigen, had fallen in this very forest. How could she hope for better?

"Uncle!" A great leg seemed to stir in the forest. She waited for the crashing as the beast charged, but the leg was only a dead stump.

"It is nothing, Kyala. Drive."

The attack did not come. She began to think they might reach Darst after all. If they continued without hindrance, they would reach the crest and begin the long descent. If the beasts stayed away, she wondered if Watnojat would insist on prowling the side roads. But the light was dimming. Dusk was at hand. "We'll need a torch, Uncle," she said in a quavering voice. "Can you light one from the lantern?"

The Vigen pulled a pitch-smeared brand from a barrel behind him, opened the lantern, and ignited the torch. Shakily he stood and placed it in a socket above the seat. The pale light barely showed on the path ahead.

Onward they climbed as the woods grew black. The foul scent seemed gone now. Had she merely grown used to it? The forest sounds were normal—the chirp of insects, the hoot of an owl. She watched the ponies, thinking that if danger came she would see the first signs in their frenzied straining.

"We are at the top," announced the Vigen. The road leveled out, curved, and then straightened again. The torchlight cast only a few steps beyond the noses of the grays, illuminating pebbles and fallen twigs. Kyala tried to keep her imagination in check, blinking and squinting whenever she thought her eyes were playing tricks. No, that is only a dropped piece of harness. And that—

Then a ferocious snapping sounded in the dark woods. Now there could be no mistake. The grays bucked wildly. "The spears!" shouted Watnojat. While Kyala fought the animals, she saw him throw the weapons to the ground, then roll over the side, taking the lantern with him. "Jump off!" he shouted. "You can't hold them. Jump."

Without the cart, how would she and Watnojat get home?

The ponies turned from the track and tried to run between the trees. Perhaps they would snag themselves, she thought. She dropped the reins and leaped to the side of the road. Watnojat was holding the lamp next to his wrist that bore the talisman. She picked up the other spear. "Where is it? Where's the beast?" she shouted.

The answering roar was so loud that she leaped back in fright. More branches snapped. "Stay where you are," said the Vigen toward the forest. The bead at his wrist glowed with a reddish light.

The noises ceased. Watnojat raised the lamp and peered into the darkness. Amid the tree trunks, Kyala could not pick out the beast's outline, but she heard its rasping breath. The Vigen took a step in the direction of the noise. All stayed quiet, and he advanced again.

Another roar. This time she saw something move, a great shaggy arm and then the bulk of the thing's body. "Stop!" cried Watnojat, shining his lamp on the talisman. But the creature continued to shift its limbs. "This one is strong willed," he said in a bitter voice. "We must kill it before it breaks free of what power we have."

The beast lurched, one huge leg stepping forward to crunch the sticks beneath its feet. Closer. Kyala felt stiff, her muscles rigid. *Lebbon's spear!* She had killed a snow cat—why not this shaggy creature? Suddenly she lunged with the weapon. The Lame One turned and deflected the blow with its shoulder. Before she could strike again, it fell to all fours, its tongue dragging in the dry leaves, its great teeth glistening.

In this position its vitals were protected. All around the creature the stout trees blocked an easy attack. Where could she strike? She raised the spear, aiming the point at its face. "Kyala, not the eyes!" Watnojat shouted. "Our power is gone without its eyes." He put down the lamp, stepped forward with his weapon, and jabbed at its flank, but the spear fell away without wounding. "Show us your belly!"

shouted Watnojat to the Lame One. But no light fell on the talisman; his words were useless.

Kyala circled the creature, seeking an opening. She saw that the beast was emerging from its spell; each motion was quicker than its last. Suddenly it roared and lifted its arms in fury. This was her chance. She rushed in, plunging the narrow point between the creature's ribs, driving into its chest. But not deep enough. Its rank breath surrounded her as she dodged its attack. She ducked the sweep of claws, and the weapon came free.

The creature, roused now from its lethargy, stood up and began to lumber after her. Watnojat staggered forward, but a swipe of the huge paw threw him aside. For a moment the beast's attention was on the fallen Vigen as he crawled toward his light. Kyala came up underneath again, pierced its belly with two quick thrusts, and darted away. It turned from Watnojat and howled.

The Vigen, clutching the lantern again, shouted, "Hold still! Hold, curse you!" But the beast was beyond hearing. It swung its arms frantically, its vital fluids spurting in all directions. The creature continued to stalk Kyala as she backed against a stocky oak. Its tongue slobbered, and its eyes were filled with madness. She tried to hold it off with feints to its neck, but the paws kept her weapon away. Watnojat came up behind the beast. He jabbed and struck until the pain made the creature turn. Then she made a thrust at the Lame One's throat, slitting the great artery and sending blood pouring down its chest.

A great gasp came from its mouth as it tumbled to the ground. The limbs flailed and twitched. Kyala, caught between tree and claws, squeezed past the dying Lame One and ran to Watnojat's side. "That one is finished, Uncle." She watched the limbs quiver in a final spasm. "And what about you? I saw you fall."

She got no answer. From behind them, another roar sounded—a second Lame One. She heard Watnojat's voice, hoarse from exhaustion. "Kyala! Prepare yourself." He tried the talisman, but the new beast did not halt at his command. It loped up the road with its huge tongue lolling. In desperation the Vigen touched the bead directly to the hot cover of the lamp. The creature howled and raised its paws to its eyes. It fell to the ground, thrashed briefly, then rose again.

Kyala circled the body, sidestepping the flailing limbs. The creature was fighting the power of the glass, its fury equal to the pain inflicted by the talisman. "This one . . . is even stronger," the Vigen said with a faltering voice. For a short while, however, the beast's attention was consumed by the conflict with the bead's power. It groaned and lurched forward again. If Kyala could get close . . . She thought she had only a moment before it regained full control. *The neck.* She darted in; her first thrust missed and bounced off the jawbone. *Again.* The great head turned. The creature stumbled and its long claws raked the ground. It tried to rise, and for a moment the underbelly was exposed. *In!* This time she cut deep and well. The beast clutched at its torn guts spilling out onto the rubble of the trail. There was nothing more she could do, no way to attack again as the shaggy creature writhed in the road.

"There were three," said the Vigen as Kyala felt her grip relax on the spear shaft. "Lebbon told us there were three."

"But where, Uncle?" The second beast was dying and would trouble them no more. She turned from it to peer into the surrounding darkness.

"The torch," said Watnojat. "We need more light."

"Torch?" Kyala had nearly forgotten the ponies. To the side of the road she saw where they'd caught the rig between two young oaks. Trembling, they leaned pitifully in the traces with no hope of escape. Kyala ran to recover the brand that still burned in its mounting, its light bathing the sweaty flanks of the animals.

"I can't let you go," she said to the miserable grays. "You'll be safe," she added, trying to keep her voice to a soothing tone. Then she lifted the torch and hurried back to the Vigen.

"I hear nothing from the third one," he said softly. "Come, let's walk a bit. It cannot be far from its brothers." He lifted the lantern. Using the spear handle as a crutch, he began to hobble along the path.

"Uncle, are you hurt? The Lame One—"

"Listen!" He cocked his ear toward a place where the forest thinned. She saw jagged outcroppings of rock and a tangle of bushes. A rustling sound, and then a snapping of wood came from beyond the rocks. Some smaller creature?

"I think it must be a deer," said Balin's daughter.

"Let us look." The glassmaker left the road and made his way slowly up toward the exposed stone. The torch showed only shadows. Eager to be done with this diversion, Kyala ran ahead of him, skirted several rough boulders, and reached the edge of a broad pit. She peered down briefly at the excavation and saw nothing stirring on the rubble-filled bottom. Some miner or Vigen had dug here once. But the source of the noise—

A deep growl came from just behind her. She whirled in time to see a monstrous paw batter Watnojat against the rocks. The lantern landed with shattering of glass and smashing of metal; the light went out. "Uncle!" she cried, but there was no time to see to the Vigen. The beast ignored the fallen one and turned its attention to Kyala. It raised its head and took a few steps toward her, swinging its long arms as it came. The giant figure was dark but for the shimmering of its eyes.

She retreated, stumbled, then lost her footing and began to slide down the steep side of the digging. *The torch!* Kyala held onto the brand as she tried to use her feet to slow the fall. Gravel and roots tore at her legs. She tasted earth and rotted leaves as chaff flew at her face.

Her breeches tore. Sharp gravel bit her knees and thighs until she screamed with pain. *Keep the torch!* She clutched it tighter, losing control of her fall as she finished the slide on her belly. The light still burned when she came to a stop on a pile of scree; she had saved her flame.

But her other hand was empty! She searched around in panic, raising the light to peer at the rough slope above. The weapon was gone, dropped somewhere and now out of sight. All that remained for protection was the talisman at her wrist and the flame of the torch. They would have to serve.

The beast crouched and lowered its huge legs over the side of the pit. She raised the bead to the flame. "Stop!" she shouted. "Hold your place." If she could keep it bound until she found her weapon, she might have a chance. But the Lame One merely grunted as it dropped closer. She saw its eyes clearly now, holding the same black depths she carried in her talisman, with flames like those that flickered across the bead's surface. The match was not perfect; the beast's fires were a deeper red. She understood how Untmur's impure astablak had weakened the bead's power.

"Halt," she said again as she warmed the talisman in the flame. The creature hesitated, but only for a moment. The bead had some strength, but not enough for control. For a true effect she knew she must touch the talisman to the fire. She grasped the tethered bead between her fingers and brought it closer, feeling the searing heat on her fingers. The creature groaned and pawed at its eyes. Ignoring her own pain, she held the bead steady. But the creature shook off the effect of the talisman and began to shuffle toward her, snarling and salivating. As it came into the torchlight she saw a mass of boils and facial protrusions covered by wiry hairs. She had never before seen clearly a Lame One's features.

"Halt!" Kyala screamed as she pressed her back against the rising slope, reaching frantically behind her for a handhold that wasn't there. She scraped her heels against the scree but succeeded only in loosening the pile. The creature was nearly on her. *I am lost*, she thought. Watnojat had told her to trust in Ormek, but in the end He had abandoned her to Torged's fate.

Already she felt the Lame One's claws in her flesh, its teeth piercing her bowels. What good were her Vigen talents now? She should have stayed home and mothered Jelor's brood, learned to sew and cook and clean. Some other instinct had driven her, an instinct that she had trusted, and now she would never learn its reason.

"No!" shouted Kyala. She was thinking only of herself, not of Ormek. He had come to her before. When she'd struggled with Untmur, she had felt His power. How could she have doubted that? She recalled with certainty how the lamp's flame had engulfed her, how the flash had knocked Untmur to the floor. "Ormek!" she cried, as she struggled to picture the Sun's face, to let His image blot out the Lame One's widening jaws. "Ormek, You are with me." Then she pushed the talisman again into the fire.

Suddenly the blaze flared up. Flames roared around her as if she were inside a huge kiln, with all the forest for fuel and the wind itself for bellows. The heat was terrible in its fury. *I am a bead in the fire*, she thought. *I am a talisman forming under the Master's hand.* The blaze streamed through her veins, scorched her skin, consumed her hair. She was changing, melting, flowing into the shape that had been chosen. Yet she was still Kyala, preserved through Ormek's power.

But outside her, what terrors had been wrought? "Enough!" she cried, lest the whole world be crisped for her sake. She could see nothing beyond the inferno. "Enough! It is more than I can bear." Then the brightness faded, and she found the forest intact above her and the wall of the digging at her back. The great fire had been no illusion, she was certain, but it had burned in some other place. Perhaps she had seen directly into Ormek's heart and witnessed His full glory.

And the Lame One? The beast now writhed at the pit's bottom, its paws scrabbling at its eyes as it strove to tear out the source of its suffering. Charged by her new source of power, the bead had overcome the creature. But her fingers were burnt; she could hold the talisman to the torch no longer. On impulse she rushed toward the beast and thrust the torch at the shaggy hairs of its head. They caught quickly. The fire spread, and she knew it was the Bright One's fire, covering the beast with a swiftness that startled her. The Lame One beat at the flames to no avail. The smoke rose dark and vile, but the creature was not yet dead. It rose to its feet, stumbled, and rose again.

Pulling at roots and rocks, Kyala scrambled up the slope. By the fallen Vigen she found his spear. The creature below was groaning, and she thought she heard more than just animal sounds emerging from its mouth. "Dyelo..." it seemed to say, as if calling on its god of old.

"You are finished, hunter of men," she replied, as she descended the opposite, gentler side of the pit. She lifted her weapon. The beast sagged against the slope, its head lolling. "Dyelo will do you no good." She leaned through the smoke and plunged the spear into the Lame One's mouth, piercing through to the brain. The beast thrashed once more, dropped, and lay still.

Kyala did not stop to catch her breath. In moments she was scaling the rise again, making her way back to Watnojat. "They are dead, Uncle!" she cried as she leaned over him. "All three of them, surely the last of the Lame Ones in these parts." The Vigen did not answer. "Now we can go home, Uncle."

The light from the beast's burning was almost gone. Through the opening in the trees, faint moonlight fell on the Vigen's face, his slack features, his dirty beard. When she touched the side of his head, her fingers came away sticky. Did he live? Yes, for a time. She could faintly hear his shallow breathing. "Uncle!" she cried again, but with no response. He was in worse condition than he'd been at Fargladden.

She needed light if she was to do anything for the glassmaker. Below in the pit a few tongues of flame still danced. She felt around her for anything that might burn—leaves, twigs, branches. Averting her eyes from the charred body, she climbed down to build her fire. The dry wood caught, giving enough light so that she could gather more fuel. A sickening smell of burnt meat and hair rose from the pit, but she did not stop throwing down branches until a huge fire roared there.

Now the Vigen's face was bathed in orange light. She reached into his shirt, eased out his talisman, and turned it to catch the glow. She must speak with him, if only through the bead. Perhaps he could be saved. She had brought him back once, why not again?

She heated the talisman in her palm, then tried to call him. "Uncle, we're going home," she whispered. "Will you ride with me to Darst and claim your victory?"

He gave no response. She tried warming the bead in her mouth, but still he would not answer. She hesitated, knowing there was but one way to call him now. At last she reached for the small knife he carried in his belt, sliced into her thumb, and let the blood spill onto the glass.

"Uncle," she called. "Uncle, I can bring you to a healer in Darst. But I don't know the way. You must get me home through the forest." Still he gave no reply.

She smeared the talisman again. "Uncle!" she cried softly. "Must you die here? Answer me."

At last she heard a voice, nearly as quiet as the hissing of the fire.

"Ormek . . . Ormek is bright, Kyala. You . . . you do not know His glory."

"Uncle, I think I do . . . I felt His power . . ."

The voice waxed and waned in strength, so that she missed some words and heard others clearly. "You . . . know but . . . smallest piece of it, Balin's daughter. Yet you have more . . . Lifegiver in you than I did. More than any Vigen . . . has had."

"Get better, Uncle. Then you can teach me what it means."

"Too late, Kyala. I can teach . . . nothing more. But He . . . has chosen you. For that be glad. Treasure . . . gifts you have and learn what . . . must do with them."

"But you must help. I can bring you to a healer."

"Kyala, no. Do not take me from my proper end," his voice whispered. "I-I see His glowing face. Do not call me back. Vigen . . . You . . . are Vigen now."

"How can I be Vigen? I know nothing."

"You know much. And . . . teach yourself the rest. With Ormek's help. Now go home. Go . . . Your mother waits."

"But how do I find the way?"

The voice grew fainter again. "Way . . . Way . . . It is not far now. Go straight. Cairn . . . marks the junction. Turn right . . . yes, and from there on take . . . all downhill turnings."

Kyala threw herself down on Watnojat's chest. She thought about her experience at the healer's place in Fargladden. Ormek's power had come to her then, and she'd brought the Vigen back despite his protests. But now . . . now it was not the same. His inner voice had changed—it was fragile and distant and carried an undertone of joy that she had not heard from the Vigen's lips. Knowing this, her tears flowed onto the tatters of his coat. "Then it is over, Uncle," she said at last. "Once you told me I must use my judgment. I will not force life on you."

She let the talisman fall back against the glassmaker's shirt. Then she took a brand from the fire and used it to light her path back to the grays. The creatures' panic had ended; they stood limp in the traces, still caught between trees. "We must go to him," she said softly, pushing them gently to back them out onto the road. The ponies turned slowly aside. One sapling split as the cart was pulled free, a sound that startled her in the new quiet of the woods. She led the grays along the path to the edge of the pit. Watnojat did not stir.

"I must drag you to the cart, Uncle. This is not dignified, but I've no other way." She bent down and began to pull.

Her eyes filled again with tears, and she did not have to look at his battered head as she moved him slowly down the small rise. By the time she had wrestled him up onto the cart and laid him out on the pallet, he was dead, his eyes shut, his face peaceful at last. For a long while she lay beside him, mourning with her parched throat. *Uncle, you are gone. But Darst will not forget you.*

At last she stirred. At Fargladden she had made Watnojat a pledge—to cut his oak and to build his pyre. Now she would fulfill that promise. At his burning she would tell the people of Darst all that had happened. Those who had scorned the Vigen in his time of need would be shamed, and those who had helped him would share his victory.

After that she must begin her work—open the shop, fire the kiln, begin the making of glass. And above all, she must seek the answer that Watnojat could not provide. Ormek had gifted her in a special way. She must learn the purpose she was destined to serve.

"I'm taking you back, Uncle," she said. "I told you I'd bring you home." She rose, climbed up onto the driver's bench, and took the reins. The ponies snorted. At her order they pranced forward eagerly. The cairn that marked the turning lay just ahead. The Vigens of Darst were going home.

# By the year 2000, 2 out of 3 Americans could be illiterate.

It's true.

Today, 75 million adults… about one American in three, can't read adequately. And by the year 2000, U.S. News & World Report envisions an America with a literacy rate of only 30%.

Before that America comes to be, you can stop it… by joining the fight against illiteracy today.

Call the Coalition for Literacy at toll-free **1-800-228-8813** and volunteer.

## Volunteer Against Illiteracy. The only degree you need is a degree of caring.

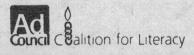

Ad Council    Coalition for Literacy

Warner Books is proud to be an active supporter of the Coalition for Literacy.